THE INVITATION

"I still want to know w
Volkers interjected. "I
dier, a mathematician,
best team to handle t
would be better equipp

Lamb looked at her. "As we told you—the message
from Ayers Rock consisted of three parts. . . . It is because of the third part that you are here."

Lamb flicked a button and words showed on the
screen. "This is the third part of the message when transcribed from the digital code."

HAWKINSROBERTVOLKERSFRANCINEBATSONDONALDLEVYDEBRA

"It took us a little while to recognize the names
among the letters, as they were all just strung together."
Lamb hit the forward and the message appeared, this
time broken down.

HAWKINS ROBERT

VOLKERS FRANCINE

BATSON DONALD

LEVY DEBRA

"The message repeats your four names six times and
then the entire message starts over again."

"Why us?" Volkers asked the question they all had.

Lamb turned off the screen. "I was hoping one of
you could tell me that."

THE
ROCK

ROBERT DOHERTY

A DELL BOOK

Published by
Dell Publishing
a division of
Bantam Doubleday Dell Publishing Group, Inc.
1540 Broadway
New York, New York 10036

ISBN: 0-440-22072-6

Printed in the United States of America

Published simultaneously in Canada

January 1996

10 9 8 7 6 5 4

OPM

To the imagination
and all those
who try to make their part of the world
a better place to live.

Thanks to Debbie Ivandick for helping get this started in the right direction one afternoon.

CONTENTS

Prologue

THE CHAMBER CONTAINED ENOUGH ENERGY TO DESTROY the planet five times over. More than two kilometers in diameter, one kilometer from floor to ceiling, and three times that depth under the planet's surface, it echoed with the crackle of directed power beams, all focused on a black sphere dancing in the center, just above the metal floor. The sphere was fifty meters in diameter and did not appear to be made of any solid substance, but rather contracted and expanded in a rhythmic pattern.

Halfway up the far wall, a half kilometer from the sphere, a recessed window slid open, revealing a control room lined with consoles. Three figures dressed in long black flowing robes stood. Wires flowed from the back of the hoods to the glowing screen in front of them on which the thoughts each wished to express were displayed in a manner all could understand.

"It is time for run four-five," the figure on the left communicated.

"Proceed," the one in the center ordered.

The power beams shifted across the color spectrum as the levels were increased. The sphere slowly began to change its own shade, the pitch-black gradually changing to gray then fading away until an image appeared, incongruous among the technology and power of the cave: an aircraft hangar, the edges abruptly cut off where they met the edge of the power of the sphere. Inside the hangar an old man in a military style uniform waited patiently.

"WHAT IS THE LOCATION?" THE FIGURE IN THE CENTER asked.

"Coordinates two-three-five-eight dash four-eight-three-four. A town called Leesburg, in the state of Virginia, in the country called United States."

"Local date, time group?"

"Nineteen ninety-one. The twenty-second day of the sixth month. Two forty-seven local time."

"Continue tracking."

A MILITARY TRUCK SUDDENLY APPEARED IN THE SPHERE, bumper first, the entire vehicle filling out as it entered the power frame. A man jumped off the truck, wearing unmarked black fatigues and carrying a weapon. He greeted the general with a handshake. "It's good to be back, sir."

The general slapped him on the shoulder. "Good to have you back, Captain Hawkins. I've got the transcript of your in-flight debriefing and the President is very satisfied with the results of your mission."

The man nodded wearily and watched as his three men threw their rucksacks onto the floor of the hangar and secured their weapons with the unit armorer. "I'd like to give the men some time off, sir."

The general nodded. "Take a week and then give me a call. I'll put Richman's team on standby alert."

"Thanks, sir."

"Damn good job, man." With a slap on the back the general was gone, walking out of the range the sphere could see. The captain gave his men the good news and the figures dispersed one by one until only he was left standing there. He finally moved out himself, heading toward the hangar door that glimmered in the light of the sphere.

THE FIGURE ON THE RIGHT GAVE THE FACTS. *"HAWKINS, ROBert D. An officer in the military. Commander of a special-operations team. Program seven-one-three-two. Probability seven-six. Terminal impact projected six-three."*

"He's the object. Track him," the figure in the center ordered. Around the hub of the chamber the machinery hastened to follow the command in an intricately organized dance of power and technology.

THE SPHERE FLICKERED SLIGHTLY, THE IMAGE GOING OUT OF focus, then Hawkins reappeared in the parking lot outside the hangar, walking toward a pickup truck, a young woman leaning against the front bumper. A smile blossomed across her face as she spotted Hawkins and she ran to him, throwing herself into his arms.

"I'm so glad you're back!"

Hawkins held the woman in his arms for almost thirty seconds. Finally he stepped back and looked at her. "I missed you, Mary."

"Well, you're back and you don't have to miss me for a while," she replied, sliding her arm through his and pulling him toward the pickup. "Let's go home. I've got something special planned for you."

"TIME LINE?" THE CENTER FIGURE INQUIRED.

"Three minutes, thirteen seconds," the figure on the right answered.

"Keep us on line."

WITH HAWKINS AT THE WHEEL THE PICKUP TRUCK ROLLED OUT of the parking lot.

"KEEP TRACKING!"

The power being fed to the sphere surged as the automated machinery struggled to maintain pace with the truck. The vehicle appeared to be stationary, caught in the center of the sphere, the two-lane road sliding beneath its wheels, the countryside suddenly appearing at one end of the sphere and flickering by to disappear at the other end.

THE ENTIRE CHAMBER SHUDDERED, EVER SO SLIGHTLY. THE center figure's hood twitched upward toward the metal-reinforced ceiling. *"Report?"*

There was a slight pause and then the figure on the left spoke. *"A strike on the fourth perimeter. Magnitude three point three. Security is holding at level eight. Risk factor up to one-three. We are secure."*

Attention returned to the sphere. Every few seconds the image would fade and then regain its sharpness as the technicians struggled to keep track of the vehicle.

"Time line?"

"One minute, ten seconds."

"Maintain."

THE PICKUP TRUCK TURNED ONTO A TWO-LANE HIGHWAY. Mary Hawkins leaned across the front seat and nuzzled up to her husband's right side. White teeth flashed as she nipped his earlobe.

"Hey, that's not fair." Hawkins laughed.

"THIRTY SECONDS."

HAWKINS LET GO OF THE STICK SHIFT AND WRAPPED HIS right arm around his wife, pulling her tight against his body.

"TEN SECONDS." THE PICKUP TRUCK WAS ROUNDING A curve in the sphere, the road appearing to the watchers as it did to the man behind the wheel.

HAWKINS REACTED, SLAMMING HIS FOOT ON THE BRAKE and twisting the steering wheel with his left hand. The right front end of the pickup truck smashed into the rear of the stalled tractor-trailer rig with an explosion of glass and metal. Hawkins was thrown forward against the seat belt and just as abruptly slammed back against the seat in recoil. Mary Hawkins was ripped out of the desperate grip of her husband's right hand and her head thrust into the windshield, forming a flower of cracked glass as her chest crumbled against the unyielding plastic of the dashboard.

"Call an ambulance!" Hawkins screamed as he slowly pulled Mary back and laid her down on the seat. She was unconscious, her breathing coming in labored gasps. Hawkins gently slipped his hand around her head and cringed as he felt the blood slowly flowing out. He carefully pressed his hand up against the wound and held her head still.

THE TABLEAU APPEARED FROZEN IN THE SPHERE. THE FIGURE in the center finally spoke. *"End four-five. Proceed with four-six."*

The image of Hawkins holding his wife in his arms faded as the sphere turned black and the power shifted.

INITIATION

Vredefort Dome, South Africa
17 DECEMBER 1995, 0315 LOCAL
17 DECEMBER 1995, 0115 ZULU

WITH EACH MILE TRAVERSED TOMMY MEDUBA FELT THE death force rise up in him. Lona leaned over and crooned his name and whispered of warriors and revenge as the sweat slowly dripped down his body, splashing unseen onto the floor of the truck. Blood pounded in his temples, the sound of the truck's engine faint in his ears.

Lona had searched him out and found him in the gutter yesterday, covered with dirt, sweat, and blood. His brother was dead and there was no family left to him, so he'd bought eight cartons of Bantu beer and tried to obliterate reality. Lona and Nabaktu had offered him another way—a warrior's way that would strike back at the killers of his brother.

The drugs she'd given him had done something to

1

his body. He'd never felt like this before. He could barely feel the bumps as the truck negotiated the dirt road leading to the back entrance to the mine, but he could acutely feel Lona's hand on his arm. He wanted to avoid her dark eyes staring intently at him and not hear the words she mouthed. He ran his eyes around the enclosed interior, taking in the large crate squatting in the center, but again his eyes flickered back up to hers and his ears listened as if he had no control.

"Soon you will be the greatest warrior. Your name will be spoken of across the land with the deepest respect. You are a man—not an animal. You must die a man's death, not lie in the street like a dog. You must avenge your brother."

A small part of Tommy's brain wanted to think, but it would require too much energy. The truck came to a halt with a squeal of brakes. The tarp covering the tailgate was thrown back and a large figure dressed in traditional robes appeared, silhouetted against the night sky. "It is time to go." Lona leaned over and placed something in front of Tommy's face. He snorted reflexively and felt the power kick in.

Tommy looked from Lona to Nabaktu. Their eyes were locked on him, willing for him to move. He stood and stepped out of the truck.

Security was oriented inward at the entrance and that was logical. The powers-that-be were concerned with what could be taken out of the mine, not with what could be taken in. The long line of dust-covered workers emerging like moles from their twelve-hour shift below the surface was subjected to strip searches by guards with cold hands and blank eyes. At random a few men were having their bodily cavities invaded by gloved fingers, probing and searching. Behind the initial row of security personnel looking for the gold were other guards watching the searchers. And above the second rank were video cameras, overseeing the watchers. And all that redundancy was logical, too, as this toothless opening less than eighty miles southwest of Johannesburg led to great coiled intestines of gold- and uranium-laced rock.

Tommy had been working here for eight years, six days a week, in twelve-hour shifts—long enough that any other existence before the mine was forgotten. He smothered his hatred and tried to avoid looking at the guards as he went past. That most of them were black also didn't matter. Some of these same guards had beaten his brother to death two days ago after finding a piece of rock in his pant cuff. No matter that it could have gotten there by accident. No matter that it contained no gold. The rule was that nothing came out that hadn't come in. When done they'd thrown his brother's body into the putrid shaft of an abandoned mine where all the other bodies had been dumped over the years. That the guards who had beaten his brother to death were Xhosa did matter very much to Tommy—they were the favorite of the ANC and the change in power had brought little change to the mines—and the Sothos, of which Tommy was a member, migrant workers from Lesotho, still suffered at the hands of the overseers.

Night or day mattered naught in the black holes of

the mines. The caged electric lights strung along the rock roof cast a dingy glow on the dark, perspiring bodies below as the line of arrivals trudged forward. Their shift started at three, but they weren't paid for the time spent getting there—only the toil of their hands started the clock.

Tommy Meduba was pouring sweat also as he drove the small electric cart at a walking pace down the right side of the double set of rails. He was on the ground level leading to the massive elevator that would carry the cart and forty workers down into the depths. Tommy was sweating not so much from the thick air and scorching heat, though: Large beads of perspiration beaded his skin, forming rivers that gravity dragged down his body, because this was to be his last night alive and he hadn't assimilated that concept.

No guard spared him or his cart more than a glance as he rumbled onto the wrought-iron floor of the elevator. With a slight start, and then a steady stuttering, the platform descended. Dank rock walls on four sides guided them straight down. For twenty-four minutes, at a steady pace of more than four hundred and seventy feet per minute, they went down. They had to switch elevators twice and use horizontal tunnels that pushed them more to the southwest. More than two and a quarter miles into the earth. Straight to the heart of the richest vein of gold and uranium in the world: the Red Streak, a treasure trove that angles under the mystifying geological feature known as Vredefort Dome, so many kilometers directly above.

Never before had a mine been dug so deep and so directly under the Dome itself. But the upper regions had been plundered for more than a hundred years, forcing the engineers to probe and invade the earth farther down into the dark nether regions in search of their mineral gods. The Red Streak had been touched less than three years previously and had already produced two thousand tons of gold bullion and a classified amount of uranium.

Gold and uranium were the fuel that ran the South African economy, and Tommy was the cutting edge of a plan bent on stopping that engine and gaining the notice of the ruling ANC. He glanced over his shoulder with deadened eyes at the bulky metal container perched on the small flatbed. The casing was stenciled with English, Bantu, and Afrikaaner words indicating: DRILLING EQUIPMENT.

It was so easy that even Tommy's drug-infused brain felt a certain euphoria at having gotten in. Nabaktu had said it would be easy. Dear, sweet Lona had whispered it in his ear as she took his body and mind. And they had been right.

As the platform came to a final halt, Tommy fought the hysterical urge to laugh at the dulled men on either side of him as he slipped the cart's stick shift into drive and slowly rolled off the platform. A rock foyer beckoned with three dark openings less than twenty meters away. Wealth that would make most Third World nations weep with envy slithered back out of those holes and up the cables to the surface every day.

Tommy stopped the cart as the other workers disappeared into the various tunnels. He walked around to the rear of the vehicle and flipped open a panel. Nabaktu had made it as simple as possible, but still Tommy hesitated. A worm of fear pierced the core of his being as his hand hovered over the red button. Through the drugs and the scent of sex a part of his mind rebelled.

TWELVE MILES AWAY, ON THE SLOPE LEADING TO THE EDGE of the Witwatersrand Basin, Kamil Nabaktu swiveled his pitch-black irises from the fluorescent dial of a cheap Mickey Mouse wristwatch to Lona. "He's down by now."

The two were crouched in a thicket of scraggly, stunted trees that had never known enough water, just as Nabaktu's people had never known enough freedom since April 1652, when the first white men had set foot to stay on the southern end of the Dark Continent. They had hoped it would change in April and May of 1994, when the whites had amazingly given up power, but from their perspective, huddled in the shacks among the other tribal minorities, little had changed. In reality, the fact that the face now in charge in Pretoria was black made it all so much more galling.

"He is a weak man," Lona said. "You should have let me take it."

"No women in the mines," Nabaktu replied patiently. They'd had the argument hundreds of times. He checked his watch again. At the very least he hoped Tommy had gone down. If not, things were going to get very ugly, very soon.

Twenty men had died sneaking gold out to pay for the bomb—Tommy's brother one of them. It had taken them a year to accumulate enough. This was the end result of that blood.

"Thirty seconds."

TOMMY LOOKED BACK TO THE ELEVATOR, HIS MIND SCURRYing through various options. He took his hand away from the red button and breathed a sigh of desperate relief. He shook his head, trying to clear the fog demons that were scampering about, dulling his brain. His eyeballs felt as if they were going to pop out of his head as he considered his position. He knew he was dead regardless. He couldn't go up. The guards would want to know why he wasn't on his shift. He couldn't go into one of the tunnels and take his normal place, because sooner or later someone would wonder what was on board the abandoned vehicle, and when they looked, there would be hell to pay.

A soft click caught his attention and Tommy glanced down. His eyes widened even more as he watched the red button slide down of its own accord into the metal plate.

Tommy never saw the plastic reach the bottom as he became a small patch of molecules vaporized by the nuclear blast that flashed into the rock around, which in turn dissolved and flowed.

* * *

THE EARTH BURPED. NABAKTU LOOKED AT LONA AND THEN
out into the dark night again. He'd expected more.
Still, it was more than two miles down.

"Let's go." He grabbed Lona's arm and they
sprinted back the way they had come so many hours
earlier. To the truck where the two waiting men threw
questions at them. Could that small earthquake have
been it? That's all? Where was the cloud?

Nabaktu ordered them silent and they sped away,
down toward Soweto Township to hide among the
hundreds of thousands huddled there in the cheap
shacks.

AND BELOW THE DOME, TWO MILES DOWN, THE ROCKS
took hours to cool and congeal; microscopic bits of
foreign matter that had once been men joining the
minerals and stone.

Deep Space Communication Center, Site 14
Vicinity Alice Springs, Australia
17 DECEMBER 1995, 1330 LOCAL
17 DECEMBER 1995, 0400 ZULU

THE SUN BAKES THE SANDY SURFACE AROUND ALICE
Springs, the intense heat causing the light to waver
and bend. The only humans native to the Australian
Outback—the Aborigines—did so through hundreds
of generations of adaptation to their harsh environment. Life for them was finding water and food.

Australia is the oldest, flattest, and driest continent, equal in size to the continental United States.
The Aborigines are estimated to have been there for
more than thirty thousand years. For all those years
they were completely isolated from the rest of the
world. The ancient Egyptian empires, Rome, the
Dark Ages, the Renaissance, the Industrial Age—all
came and went and the Aborigines remained the
same until the coming of the white man.

When the first Aborigines arrived in Australia, the
center of the continent was fertile, containing lush
jungles and swamps. The present Red Center was
born approximately ten to twenty thousand years earlier when the world's climate changed and the land
dried up. As many plant and animal species died and
were blown away by the harsh weather and terrain,
the Aborigines adapted and survived.

The white man was an extreme latecomer to Australia when Captain Cook landed at Botany Bay in
1770. It took another hundred years before the first
white men managed to cross the Red Center, going
from Adelaide in the south to Darwin in the north. In
the process of accomplishing this, many white men
lost their lives, wandering through the deserts in desperate search of water and relief from the brutal sun.

The overland telegraph line was built in the late
nineteenth century from Darwin to Adelaide, and
midway across the continent the town of Alice Springs
was born to serve as a telegraph station on that line. A
thousand miles from the seacoast and five hundred
miles from the nearest town, Alice Springs is perhaps

the most isolated town in the world. Because of that isolation, in the late 1950s, the United States, in cooperation with the Australian government, established Deep Space Communication Center (DSCC 14) sixty miles outside Alice Springs. The lack of interference from other radio emitters common in the civilized world made it an ideal spot to place the large receivers.

This afternoon in 1995 eight large dishes pointing in various attitudes were spaced evenly across the sand, the sun reflecting off the metal struts and webs of steel that reached up to the sky. Thick loops of cable ran from the base of each to a junction box set in the lee of a large, modern three-story building. In that building all the incoming data that the dishes picked up were fed into a bank of computer screens, one for each dish.

Inside the air-conditioned comfort of the DSCC control building, Major Mark Spurlock, U.S. Air Force, watched his monitors with the bored gaze of one who'd been here much too long. Spurlock's primary task was receiving classified data from the network of spy satellites that the U.S. had blanketing the planet as they passed overhead, encoding and passing on the data to the National Security Agency at Fort Meade, Maryland, on the other side of the world.

The job had been exciting the first two months he'd been here—handling top-secret data and working with the codes—but the novelty had quickly been scrubbed away by the heat and stark living conditions. Spurlock was from a small town in Oklahoma, but even that place was lively compared to Alice Springs. He'd started his "short-timers" calendar last month, checking the day off each evening as he got off shift. Booze—readily available at the commissary—was the common cure at the base for the loneliness and isolation, but Spurlock had avoided that trap. He focused on his job, practicing his skill at encoding and decoding, trying to break some of the simpler codes used in the computer. He could often be found late at night, scrunched in front of his terminal, his fingers tentatively tapping out solutions.

He was in the process of realigning one of the dishes to pick up an INTELSAT that was just coming into range over the western horizon when his computer screen went crazy. A jumbled mass of letters and numbers filled the entire display. His attempts to clear were fruitless. He scooted his seat over to an empty console nearby and booted that computer up. Everything worked fine until he accessed Dish 4, the one he had been realigning.

"What's the matter?" Colonel Seymour, the station commander appeared over his shoulder. "Trouble?"

Spurlock worked the keyboard. "I don't know, sir. Could be the main drive. I get the same garbage on both screens when I access dish four."

Seymour checked the clock. "INTELSAT 3A is going to transmit in two minutes."

An abnormality—Spurlock was ready to see Seymour's head start spinning in circles. The Air Force didn't assign people to DSCC because they were highly adaptable to a rapidly changing environment. They were assigned because they could do routine and do it well.

As he watched, the figures on the screen began shifting in a hypnotic fashion, the numbers and the letters realigning, drifting from one place to another. He'd never seen anything like it.

"What the hell is going on?" Seymour demanded.

"I don't know, sir."

"Get that damn thing back on line. I'm going to have to file a report if we miss the burst from 3A."

Spurlock frowned as he watched the screen. "I don't think it's the computer, sir." He checked the status board. "Dish two's free for a half hour. I'm going to use it on 3A." He gave the proper commands and dish two powered up and turned, lowering toward the western horizon to catch the satellite.

"Shit," Spurlock muttered as the screen dissolved into the same shifting pattern. "Something's transmitting on very high power to the west. It's overpowering everything else."

"Air or ground transmitter?"

Spurlock played with the controls, moving the dish ever so slightly. "I think it's on the ground and stationary. I go a few degrees up and we lose it. Southwest of here." He checked the status board. "Are there any military operations going on out in the Gibson Desert? Maybe somebody failed to file their freqs with Control and they don't know they're screwing up our receiving."

Seymour shook his head. "As far as I know we've

got nothing out there, and the Aussies haven't told us anything."

"Well, sir, there's a very high-power transmitter out there and until we get it off the air, we're not going to pick up anything in a twelve-degree arc from the horizon."

Seymour ran a hand through his thinning gray hair. "I'll get a helicopter up. If it's that strong they ought to pick it up pretty quickly and get it shut down. Contact Goddard and inform them of the situation." Seymour left the room.

Spurlock cleared the computer and accessed the direct satellite modem link to the Goddard Space Flight Center in Greenbelt, Maryland.

>GSFC, THIS IS DSCC 14. WE'VE GOT COMPLETE SYSTEMS OVERLOAD HERE FROM A TRANSMISSION AT 223 DEGREES AND AN ARC OF PLUS 12 FROM ZERO ON THAT AZIMUTH. WE'RE LOSING OUR DATA AND REQUEST THE OTHER STATIONS PICK UP THE DOWN LINK.

There was a long pause—much too long. Spurlock grew worried and repeated his message. The reply was not what he had expected.

<DSCC 14, THIS IS GSFC. WHAT ARE YOU PEOPLE DOING?

Before he could react, a new message from Maryland appeared.

<DSCC 14, THIS IS GSFC. REPEAT. WHAT ARE YOU DOING? WE'VE GOT REPORTS FROM ALL STATIONS OF HIGH-FREQUENCY TRANSMISSIONS ORIGINAT-ING FROM AN UP LINK FROM YOUR AREA.

Spurlock reflexively checked his screens.

>THIS IS DSCC 14. WE ARE NOT TRANSMITTING. RE-PEAT. WE ARE NOT TRANSMITTING. ALL OUR RE-CEIVERS ARE ALSO OVERWHELMED BY THIS WHEN THEY ALIGN IN THE INDICATED DIRECTION.

<WHO IS SENDING, THEN? WE'VE GOT IT COMING DOWN OFF METEOR BURSTS ALL OVER THE PLANET AIMED AT SPECIFIC LOCATIONS. ARE YOU GUYS PLAYING A GAME?

>NEGATIVE, GSFC. WE ARE NOT, REPEAT, NOT TRANSMITTING.

Spurlock paused and rechecked the other screens and the dish alignments. He tapped the keyboard.

>WE'RE RECEIVING FROM THE GROUND, NOT THE SKY.

A new message from Goddard Space Center.

<DSCC 14, THIS IS THE GSFC COMMANDER. I DON'T KNOW WHAT KIND OF GAME YOU PEOPLE ARE PLAY-

ING, BUT WE'RE GETTING IT ALL ON TAPE AND WE'RE
GOING TO FIND OUT WHAT IS HAPPENING.

Spurlock typed in another rebuttal with sweaty fingers.

>THIS IS DSCC 14. WE ARE NOT RESPONSIBLE FOR
THIS. IT IS HITTING US TOO. I WILL FORWARD OUR
TAPES AND COMPUTER PICKUPS FOR YOUR VERIFI-
CATION.

The person on the other end seemed slightly mollified but more confused.

<ROGER THAT, DSCC 14. WE'LL CHECK IT OUT. THAT
TRANSMISSION IS GOING ALL OVER THE PLACE IN
TIGHTLY CONTROLLED BEAMS. WE'VE GOT MULTIPLE
DOWN LINKS AND INTELSAT SAYS THE UP LINK IS
IN YOUR LOCATION OR CLOSE TO IT. IF YOU AREN'T
SENDING, THEN WHO IS?

Spurlock turned and looked out of the large plate-
glass windows at the eight dishes and then beyond
that to the beginnings of the Simpson Desert that
stretched westward for almost a thousand miles. As if
drawn by a string his eyes looked upward at the pollu-
tion-free air.

Something out there in the desert was sending a
message, but what? What had the capability to over-
whelm their receivers here at DSCC 14 on the ground
and at the same time bounce radio waves off the belt

of meteors out in space and back to Earth? Spurlock knew that meteor burst was a capability that only the military used—it was the same as bouncing a message off a satellite except the military anticipated few satellites to be up there in case of an all-out conflict. Therefore in the late seventies they'd begun using the belt of meteors farther out in space for the bounce points. As far as Spurlock knew the Australians did not have the capability to do multiple messages with such power.

Spurlock slowly typed in his answer.

>GSFC, WE HAVE NO IDEA WHO OR WHAT IS TRANS-
MITTING. WE HAVE A HELICOPTER INVESTIGATING.
WILL REPORT AS SOON AS WE FIND ANYTHING OUT.

Spurlock leaned back in his seat and stared at the screen. Whatever was transmitting this was powerful and very quick. No human hand could be sending those data without the aid of a computer. The figures danced in front of him, continuously changing. There was something about parts of the message that seemed tantalizingly familiar.

Spurlock went to work. He copied a portion and slowed it down, reading the figures, trying to make some sense. He attempted a few simple transfiguration codes. None worked.

Some of it looked almost like mathematical equations, but none that he'd ever seen. Another part had what appeared to be a rhythm. That last word stuck in Spurlock's mind and he tried something different. He fed a portion of the data into a different program on his computer. Turning the volume up he ran the program.

He almost dropped his coffee cup when classical music, played at an extremely rapid beat, piped out of his computer. Why was someone sending out classical music in digital form on a frequency reserved for space communication?

The music suddenly changed into a country-western beat played at breakneck speed. Then rock. Then back to classical. Then it turned to unintelligible garbage.

Suddenly a mechanical voice spoke. It was speaking so quickly, he could understand none of what it was saying. Spurlock reran the tape, this time slowing it down so it was intelligible. The machine-generated voice rasped out of the computer.

"Dos vadanya. An yong haseo. Ma-asalama. Hello. . . ."* Spurlock listened amazed as numerous languages, most of which he couldn't even identify, whispered greetings.

It struck him suddenly. He spun around and raced over to the bookcase on the far wall, his eyes flashing along the shelves until he found what he was looking for: the master data binder on *Voyager 2.* He ran his finger down the index and turned to the appropriate page.

There was no doubt about it—he was hearing the record that had been placed on *Voyager 2* being played back in digital form at high speed. But why was it coming from land to the west?

He had no more time to puzzle over the problem as an extremely perturbed Colonel Seymour burst in the door and stormed over to the radio in the room. Spurlock started to explain what he had found, but Seymour cut him off.

"Listen to this crazy sonofabitch!" the colonel exclaimed as he turned the set on. He picked up the mike and keyed it. "Rover Two, this is DSCC fourteen. Repeat your message, please. Over."

"DSCC, this is Rover Two. I say again. I have located the source of the interfering transmission. It is two hundred miles from your location directly along the azimuth you gave us. We are hovering directly above. Over."

Spurlock frowned. "Why haven't they shut it down?"

Seymour hissed at him to be quiet. "Tell me again where the source is located. Over."

"Ayers Rock. Over."

Spurlock frowned. Ayers Rock was the most spectacular of the three great tors of Central Australia, rising out of the desert floor as if some giant had accidentally dropped it there. Spurlock had visited it on a tour after he'd first arrived on station.

"You must mean someone on Ayers Rock. Over." Seymour shook his head at the idiocy of the helicopter pilot as he released the send button.

"Negative. I mean Ayers Rock. I've got my skids less than ten feet above the top of this damn thing and that signal is coming out of solid rock directly below me. The needle is off the gauge on my receiver. I don't know what is going on, but something inside the rock itself is sending you a message. Over."

THE PLAYERS

HAWKINS
Bogotá, Colombia
19 DECEMBER 1995, 0200 LOCAL
19 DECEMBER 1995, 0700 ZULU

THE NIGHT WAS DEATHLY STILL, THE SOUNDS OF CARS RUM-
bling along the highway a kilometer to the east barely
audible. The two-story mansion was set well away
from the other buildings on the winding road, a sign
of the money and power of the man who owned it. A
concrete wall with a locked gate surrounded the spa-
cious grounds. A light flickered in the doorway of the
building inside—the guard there lighting a cigarette.

Squatting just inside the wall, Hawkins scanned
the building carefully, listening to the muted hiss of
the radio in his ear as his team members reported in.

"Puma ready. Out."

"Tiger ready. Out."

"Leopard ready. Out."

Hawkins's mind was calculating. Jaguar had thirty seconds. Then he would give the go with or without that element's participation.

"Jaguar ready. Out."

Hawkins stood, his tall, rangy build clad in black fatigues covered by a combat harness bristling with killing devices. His face was obscured by a black balaclava and the stubby snout of AN/PVS7 night-vision goggles. The silenced MP5-SD submachine gun was intimately comfortable in his left hand. The stock of the weapon was collapsed and the thick metal tube of the suppressor followed in short arcs wherever his eyes went. He spoke into his boom mike as calmly as if he were reporting the weather. "Angel, this is Cheetah. Ready to roll. Over."

"Cheetah, this is Angel. You have final clearance. Go. Out."

Hawkins's face was expressionless beneath the cloth covering it. "Break. Mother, what is your status? Over."

The muted sound of helicopter blades sounded in the background of the transmission. "Holding at eight klicks. All clear. Ready. Over."

"Mother, start final approach. The party's starting. Break. All elements, this is Cheetah. Start in ten, on my count." Hawkins moved forward, the three other men of his cell moving in perfect coordination with his vector toward the front door. He was taking the most dangerous way in—it was the way the commander should go.

"Five," he whispered. In the green glow of his

night-vision goggles he could clearly see the muted glow of the door guard's cigarette as if it were a brightly lit flashlight. The man was turned sideways to their approach, ignorant of the coming storm.

"Three." He brought up his submachine gun. "Two. One."

His burst of 9mm subsonic bullets splattered the guard against the door, the gun giving off only the muted sound of the bolt working. One of his men leaned over the body and placed explosives just above the lock. They stepped back and ducked. The blast was brief and then they were sprinting in. The power went off as Hawkins charged through the door, and everything inside went dark. Through his night-vision goggles Hawkins could clearly see the confusion as the guards blindly reacted.

Hawkins fired a sustained burst at a group of men to his right, sending them tumbling. His three men fanned out as they proceeded to clear the first floor. He stayed off the radio, listening to the progress of his other teams. Puma had already secured the field in back for Mother. Tiger and Leopard were working the second floor from opposite ends, having rappeled from the roof into the hallway windows. Jaguar was watching for any outside interference, providing sniper support after having cut the power. He could see what his team—Cheetah—was doing.

"Tiger. Two down B-four." Hawkins knew that meant that Tiger element had killed two people in the room they had designated as B4. He heard the crump of explosions as more doors were blown in. No sound of firing yet. That was good—his men were all silenced, so that meant no return fire. They were three quarters of the way through the first floor when the deep-throated roar of automatic rifle fire split the silence—the first opposition.

A laconic voice came over the radio. "Ah, Jaguar, this is Leopard. We got us one in B-seven. We took the door down but he's stitching the wall here and I'm holding for a sec on going in. Do you have anything in there? Over."

"This is Leopard. Negative on NVG. Going thermal." There was a short pause. "Roger, Leopard, we got him. One hot." Hawkins tilted his head slightly as a deep shot sounded from outside the building. There was no way to silence the fifty-caliber sniper rifle—not if it was going to shoot through walls.

"Leopard, this is Jaguar. Room clear. Over."

"Roger. Going into B-seven."

Hawkins's assistant team leader came out of the last room on the first floor with a thumbs-up. All clear down here. Hawkins spoke into his radio for the first time. "Mother, this is Cheetah. Status? Over."

"This is Mother. On schedule. Two mikes out. Over."

Hawkins turned and ran for the stairs. Tiger was outside B11. Their target was inside that room. "Jaguar, this is Cheetah. What have you got on thermals in B-eleven? Over."

"Still just two hot. Looks like they're hiding near the bed. Over."

A new voice cut in. "This is Tiger. Going in. Over."

As Hawkins turned on the second-floor landing, he was momentarily blinded as the blast taking out the door to that room overloaded his goggles.

"We got him!" An exultant voice came over the radio.

Hawkins ran into B11. Two of his men had cuffed and blindfolded their target: a fat, naked, blubbering old man. Hawkins looked at the second occupant of the room—a young woman. She lay there on the bed, covers pulled up to her neck, her eyes fearfully dashing from one dark masked figure to another.

"Get him out of here!" Hawkins brusquely ordered. Two of his men lifted the man off his feet and hustled him out the doorway, heading for the pickup zone.

"All elements. This is Cheetah. Pull back. Pull back. Over."

Hawkins swung the boom mike away from his lips and took a deep breath. Tiger team leader hustled his men out of the room and then came over to Hawkins. He didn't ask the obvious. He looked from the woman to Hawkins and then back to the woman, who was slowly sliding toward the far side of the bed, away from the invaders. "I'll take care of it, boss."

Hawkins flicked the selector switch on his MP5 and answered Tiger team leader's suggestion with one round through the middle of the woman's forehead, spraying brain and blood over the headboard. Hawkins stepped forward and ripped aside the sheet, un-covering a small derringer in the woman's right hand.

Hawkins briefly looked at Tiger team leader and shook his head. The two turned and ran for the stairs and out the back door.

The MH-53 Pave Low helicopter settled onto the lawn exactly on schedule and the members of Orion loaded smoothly, throwing their bound target in first. The back ramp closed as the bird lifted and they were winging for the coast, an Air Force escort of Stealth fighters flying cover overhead. The helicopter pilot kept them down in the treetops, using his terrain-fol-lowing radar to keep off the Colombian Armed Forces radar screens. They would be back on board the carrier before anyone in the country even had an inkling of what had happened.

Hawkins walked to the center of the cargo bay where the old man lay, the red night-lights on the ceiling reflecting off the pale skin. He'd fouled him-self already, shitting all over his pudgy thighs. Haw-kins slid up his night-vision goggles and slowly pulled his black balaclava down, exposing chiseled features and slate-gray eyes. He knelt down next to the man and stared. He knew the professional interrogators were waiting on board the carrier and they would ex-tract everything from the man's memory, but he'd paid a high price to get this man and he'd been on the hunt now for two weeks. He wanted to know. His executive officer—Richman—who'd been Tiger team leader on the assault, knelt next to him.

"Did you buy one?"

The man looked at him in confusion. "What?" he replied in Spanish.

Hawkins shifted to that language and spoke just barely above the whine of the engines. "Did you buy one of the nuclear bombs?"

"What nuclear bombs?" The old man shook his head. "What are you talking about?"

Hawkins peered intently into the old man's eyes and felt a sinking sensation. His instincts told him the man was telling the truth. All this for nothing. He looked at Richman, who grimaced and shouted in his team leader's ears, "Another dry well."

Hawkins wearily nodded, the adrenaline of the mission rapidly dissipating.

Richman squeezed his arm. "Sorry about the girl. She was in bed with the man when we went in. I didn't see the gun."

Hawkins ran a hand across his brow. "It doesn't matter." He went forward in the cargo bay, away from the other members of his team. He slumped down on the cargo web seat against the side of the aircraft. He peeled off his thin black gloves and the glint of gold on his left hand caught his eye. With his right hand he twisted the ring, feeling it cut into the flesh beneath. His eyes remembered the fear in the woman's eyes in the room. He didn't know who she was or why she was there. He had spotted the derringer a second before he fired, but he had no way of knowing for sure if she had intended to use it. It had been reflex—the killing reflex that had been drummed into him for years.

Hawkins felt a black void open in his chest—a

void he'd felt often in the past four years. He squeezed his eyes shut, trying to block out all the memories, but failed. Unthinking, his right hand left the ring and stole down to his right hip and unsnapped the cover on his pistol holster. He pulled the Beretta 9mm out and instinctively flipped off the safety.

A tap on the shoulder startled him.

"Sir, we've got a message for you on SATCOM." A commo man stood there, holding out the headset for a satellite radio, looking curiously at the pistol in his commander's hand. Hawkins followed the man's gaze and blinked. He awkwardly put the gun back in its holster and took the headset. "Hawkins here."

"Hawk, this is General Lowry. We've got an F-14 waiting on board the carrier all fueled and waiting for you. As soon as you get on board you go to that bird."

Hawkins shook his head to clear it. "What about debrief?"

"Don't worry about debrief. Richman will handle it. Something's come up."

Hawkins felt the trepidation of another mission. "You have a line on the other nuke?"

"No." There was a slight pause. "You get on that Tomcat and you go wherever it takes you. That's all I've got."

"Can you give me an idea where it's taking me, sir?"

There was a long pause. "From what I understand, you're going to Australia."

"Australia? Why?"

"To tell you the truth, Hawk, I don't know what's going on. This is coming from the very top. Just do what you're ordered to. Out."

The radio went dead. Hawkins ripped the headset off and slammed it against the floor, ignoring the looks of his team members. He pressed his fists against his temples, trying to block out all the faces, and one face in particular—a woman still alive, at least physically, lying on another bed, covered with a white sheet up to her neck, her large eyes staring aimlessly straight ahead.

BATSON
Socorro, New Mexico
19 DECEMBER 1995, 0015 LOCAL
19 DECEMBER 1995, 0715 ZULU

THE FIVE MEN AT THE TABLE TO THE LEFT OF THE BAND'S STAGE have begun verbally grading the women going to the bathroom over thirty minutes before. Their scale ranged from negative ten to a seven for a miniskirted young girl. Don Batson had ignored their raucous laughter. In the drunken glow of seven beers he was much more interested in the woman seated next to him. Linda was one of his graduate assistants and their relationship had recently become much more than professional.

Don looked much younger than he actually was, an almost indistinguishable sprinkling of gray in his black hair a hint to his thirty-eight years. Black steel-rimmed glasses framed a remarkably unlined face and covered dark eyes that bleerily took in his surroundings. Only in the light of day could the redness in his nose and sprinkling of burst blood vessels in his cheeks be spotted. He kept his body in good shape at the university gym and sweated out the alcohol every day. Don Batson took everything life had to offer him with eager arms. At the present moment one of those arms was occupied with Nancy's thigh, squeezing the smooth flesh in anticipation of a night's pleasure.

Peter, one of Don's third-year undergraduate students at the New Mexico Institute of Mining and Technology, had just finished describing his experiences the previous summer during an internship with a mining consortium in Colorado. As the humorous story drew to a close, Don finished his mug of beer and then leaned forward.

"I've got a small problem that I want you to solve." The younger students groaned with mock horror while Nancy smiled, used to Don's favorite game —setting up problems that required innovative solutions. He looked at her. "I don't want you answering either—you've heard it before."

Sure he had their attention, he continued above the muted clatter of the bar. "You have a half-inch-diameter, two-foot-long steel tube welded onto a steel deck, the tube standing perpendicular. The top is open. You also have a hanger, a pair of pliers, a four-foot piece of string, and a piece of eight-and-a-half-by-eleven typing paper.

"A Ping-Pong ball is placed in the top of the tube and slowly settles to the bottom. The diameter of the tube is barely one eighth of an inch larger than the circumference of the Ping-Pong ball. Your job"—he grinned—"should you choose to accept it, is to get the Ping-Pong ball out of the steel tube given what's available to you. And the Ping-Pong ball must be intact— no using the hanger to puncture it and pull it out."

Don sat back and listened to several of the usual solutions, pointing out how each one wouldn't work. Finally, he took pity on his students. "All right. Listen up. There's a teaching point here, as always. You all have focused on the material I gave you and not on the problem. You have tunnel vision. Someone give characteristics of the object you wish to remove from the pipe."

"It's round," one student drunkenly declared.

"True," Don acknowledged. "What else?"

"It's white," another announced to laughter.

"What else?" Out of the corner of his eye Batson noted that the men near the bathroom had now written numbers on napkins and were holding them up as women walked past.

"It bounces."

"Good. You're on the right track. More physical characteristics. How would you describe a Ping-Pong ball to someone who's never seen one?"

"It's a hollow plastic sphere."

Don smiled. "All right. What does a hollow plastic sphere do?" Seeing the frowns, he tried explaining further. "You've already said it bounces. What else?"

"It floats."

"Exactly!" Don looked at the student who'd come up with that. "How can you use that to get the ball out of the tube?"

"Well, you pour water in and it will float to the top." The student shook his head. "But you didn't give us any water as part of the material we could use."

Don shook his head. "That just reinforces the teaching point. You have to examine the problem without constricting yourself by given or known parameters. What do you always have with you when you approach any problem?"

"Your mind?"

"Yes," Don replied. "And your body. Isn't your body capable of producing fluid sufficient to get the Ping-Pong ball out of the tube?"

"Oh, gross," one of the students commented as he realized what Don was saying. "You mean take a leak in the pipe?"

"Exactly!"

With that, two men in three-piece suits slowly walked in the front door and gazed about, referring to a photo the lead man held in his hand. They looked out of place among the cowboy boots and hats.

"And speaking of that," Linda announced, "I have to take a little trip. Get me another beer, please," she whispered in Don's ear as she got to her feet.

Don's eyes followed her as she wove her way through the tables to the ladies' room. As she passed the rednecks, they held up their numbers. Don was pleased to note that she rated as high as the mini-skirted girl but dismayed when Linda stopped and tipped their pitcher of beer over, soaking half the men as it splattered across the table.

Don leapt to his feet and was halfway to the table as a fat drunken man with a large silver belt buckle jumped up, cursing Linda. "You fucking bitch! Who the hell do you think you are?"

"Screw you!" Linda yelled back. "I should be able to go to the bathroom without getting harassed."

"Hey! Let's chill out here," Don suggested, grabbing Linda's arm.

"She with you, asshole?" The fat man wasn't waiting for an answer, looming over Don's slight frame.

Don looked up and smiled weakly. "Come on. Let me buy you another pitcher." He fumbled for his wallet.

Another man from the table cast a tall shadow to his right. "Fuck you. We're gonna make you and your girlfriend here lick our table off."

A large callused hand grabbed the back of Batson's shirt and he tried to remember some of the karate he'd taken in one of his inspired moments several years previously. Unfortunately, nothing of use came to mind. "Listen, guys, there's no need to—"

The hand pressed him forward, lowering his head toward the wet table. Linda was kicking and biting at the man trying to hold on to her, his hands roaming toward intimate parts of her body.

A voice cut through the room. "Freeze! Breathe

and you're dead." The cowboys became statues, their eyes mesmerized by whoever had yelled to Don's rear.

The hand on his back let go and Don slowly stood up and turned. The two men in suits were standing there, one holding a mini-Uzi on the group, the other a large, wicked-looking pistol. The man with the pistol looked at Don. "You Professor Batson?"

Don nodded.

"Come with us, please."

The *please* sounded incongruous, considering the firepower. "Let's go, Linda," he said, tucking his shirt back in.

They made their way to the door—the two men covering their retreat—and went out into the parking lot.

"Who are you guys?"

The man put his pistol away and flipped his ID card out. "National Security Agency. We need you to accompany us."

"What for?" Don glanced at Linda, who was still shaking from the confrontation. She was eyeing him in a manner he couldn't quite figure out. He shook his head trying to clear it.

The man was leading him toward a black Bronco with tinted windows. "That will be answered when we get where we're going, sir. This action is authorized by your involvement with the Hermes Project."

Don halted, staggering slightly. "I'm not going anywhere until I know where we're going."

The man turned an impassive face to him. "Sir, we would very much like it if you cooperated. If you do not cooperate we are authorized to use force, and I'm sure none of us will like that very much. You agreed to participation in the Hermes Project. I can assure you that everything will be all right. All will be explained at your destination."

The other man stepped up close behind Batson, his manner calmly threatening.

"How long will we be gone?"

"I don't know, sir. A day at least."

"All right. I'll go along for the time being. Let's take Ms. Porter home first. We can drop her at my place while I get some stuff."

The man swung the truck door open. "We've already been by your house and have packed for you."

"How'd you get in?" Don protested.

The man looked slightly surprised, as if it were a stupid question. "We went in the door, Professor. Now please get in the truck. We have a plane waiting at the airport. Ms. Porter can take your car home. We have already notified the university that you will be on a leave of absence.

Don turned to Linda. "I'll give you a call as soon as I find out what is going on."

"Don't bother," she spat, grabbing the keys and walking over to his car.

LEVY

London, England
19 DECEMBER 1995, 0900 LOCAL
19 DECEMBER 1995, 0900 ZULU

THE LECTURE HALL WAS FILLED TO CAPACITY AND PEOPLE were even standing along the back wall. Debra Levy let the curtain slip back into place with a twitch of nervousness.

"I didn't know there would be so many!"

The coordinator from Oxford made clucking noises, presumably to soothe her. "Your reputation is unmatched. Your work is at the very cutting edge." He smiled. "In fact, you are beyond the cutting edge, as far as I am concerned. I am not sure I understood your last paper on the quantum theory of gravitation and the physics of the cosmos. Most especially the section on . . ."

Debra grasped her notes tighter in damp hands and pushed her glasses up on her nose, tuning out his words. That all these people should be here to listen to a twenty-three-year-old Jewish girl from Brooklyn! It was all so strange to her. Having lived her life, she didn't understand that others found her amazing. After graduating from high school at nine, she'd completed her doctorate in physics at MIT at fifteen. Since then she'd added several other degrees, but still kept her concentration in the world of physics.

It never seemed to occur to those around her that as much as they didn't quite comprehend her, she didn't quite comprehend everyone outside of herself.

To her it was quite natural to have progressed the way she did and unnatural that people her own age were still struggling in the graduate program she'd completed almost a decade ago. The egocentrism of the average human mind never ceased to confound her.

"Two minutes," the coordinator whispered to her, his body unnecessarily close.

He irritated her. She knew she was far from pretty but she also knew she wasn't ugly. Five and a half feet tall, the one hundred and ten pounds sparingly applied to her frame gave her an acceptable body, as far as present societal standards went, where it was always better to be on the lesser side of the weight scale than the greater. Debra couldn't have cared less, but her brain acknowledged that it sometimes mattered to others, most particularly men. Her face, devoid of makeup, was very pale and smooth. Her eyes were hidden behind functional thick glasses that were hopelessly out of style. Her dark hair was drawn back severely in a bun with a small ribbon and had never known the graces of a stylist's scissors.

"One minute."

Two figures appeared near the door to the stage wing, one of the professors trying to stop their entry. They pushed past him as if he didn't exist. The taller of the two men walked up to Debra.

"Miss Debra Levy?"

She nodded as the coordinator and several others hovered worriedly about, asking questions that went unanswered.

"I'm Agent Stone from the Defense Intelligence

Agency." He pushed a very official-looking ID card under her nose. "We have reason to believe that your life might be in danger and have orders to take you under protective custody."

Debra blinked in confusion. "What?"

They didn't even stop to explain. One on either side, they hustled her out of the lecture hall through a back door, ignoring the howls of indignation from the Oxford people. She was in a dark car and speeding away from the curb before the reality of what had happened caught up with her.

FRAN
New York, New York
19 DECEMBER 1995, 0442 LOCAL
19 DECEMBER 1995, 0942 ZULU

THE COMPUTER SCREEN CAST AN EERIE GLOW ACROSS THE hardwood floors of the large den. Francine Volkers was facing the screen but her eyes were unfocused— she didn't need to see the numbers portrayed, because she'd created them and they were indelibly etched in her mind. She took another sip of her coffee and sighed as a light went on in the guest bedroom. Her husband padded out, his bathrobe half thrown on.

"Are you going to get any sleep?"

Francine shook her head. For the past forty-eight hours she'd had to face her own numbers and she didn't like them one bit. She'd transmitted them as required on the secure modem as soon as the calculations were complete. Now she could do nothing but look at them.

"No."

Her husband cursed under his breath. Their marriage had been one of convenience for many years now and she was currently an irritant—upsetting the unspoken truce. "Jesus Christ, Fran! You've been sitting in front of that damn computer since I got home. The glow is coming right in my door."

"Then shut your door." She was surprised he'd noticed how long it had been. He worked on Wall Street, crunching his own set of numbers and all he truly cared about was that they turned out in the black, and in at least six digits a month. The numbers had brought them together fifteen years earlier in college, but had subsequently taken them in radically different directions. His had ended on Wall Street. Hers had taken her to Columbia University, where she had helped pioneer the field of statistical projection. She took facts and figures, collated them into numbers a computer could read, and then tried to project out what the possibilities of various future events would be. Right now they read very poorly.

A few years ago a group that had kept what they called a Doomsday Clock had moved the minute hand back from two minutes before midnight to almost fifteen minutes prior to midnight. The breakup of the Soviet Union and the worldwide cutback in military spending had been the impetus. Fran had disagreed with that move, but kept it to herself. Her own calculations would have edged the minute hand a shade closer to the dark hour. The loss of the relative stability of the Soviet Union and the formation of numerous splinter countries all armed with nuclear weapons certainly did not bode well for mankind in her mind or in her calculations. Nor did the world economic condition. The haves were teetering and the have-nots were getting angrier.

She didn't even bother to look at her husband. "Go to bed, George. You need your rest so you can make money tomorrow, or should I say later today."

A year before he would have retorted angrily to the dig, pointing out that his money paid for their exclusive Central Park West apartment. It was a sign of how low things had sunk between them that he simply turned and stalked back into the bedroom, slamming his door behind him. Fran was in her mid-thirties; a tall, slender woman whose dark hair was now streaked with gray—a sign of premature aging she refused to color. As a result of that and the creases around her eyes and mouth, she looked almost ten years older than she really was. It wasn't something to concern her. Such trivial matters bothered her little when weighed against what her numbers told her day in and day out.

She was not overly surprised when the building intercom buzzed. She got out of her chair for the first time in hours and walked on stiff legs to the voice box near the door.

"Yes?"

"Mrs. Volker, this is Ed, downstairs. There are two men here to see you. They say they're from the government. They do have IDs."

"Send them up, Ed. It's all right." She unlocked the apartment door and swung it open. Then she headed for her own bedroom and started packing. It took the men a few minutes to appear.

"Mrs. Volker?"

She nodded as she pulled clothes out of the closet. "Yes."

"Ma'am, we're here to escort you. This is sanctioned under the Hermes Project."

"I know. I've been waiting for you."

The two looked relieved that she was cooperating.

"Are we going to Washington or to the center in West Virginia?" she asked as she sat on the edge of her bed and pulled on a pair of boots. The numbers had gone to D.C., but they usually met in the bunker burrowed under the hills of West Virginia.

The agents' faces were impassive. "Neither, ma'am."

That was the first surprise for Fran. She stood and looked at them. "Can you tell me where we are going, then?"

The two exchanged looks. Finally one replied. "Australia, ma'am."

"Australia? Why are we going there?"

The one who had answered, shrugged. "We don't know. Our job is to get you there. We have military transport waiting at LaGuardia."

Fran considered what she knew about Australia—

factoring in that it was summer in the southern hemi-sphere—and placed some T-shirts and shorts in her bag.

She threw a bag over her shoulder while one of the agents grabbed the other. "Can I tell my husband I'm leaving?"

"Yes, ma'am, but not your destination."

"Oh, hell," she said. "I'll just leave him a note on the fridge."

FIRST BRIEFING

===

Deep Space Communication Complex 14.
Outside of Alice Springs, Australia
21 DECEMBER 1995, 0830 LOCAL
20 DECEMBER 1995, 2300 ZULU

HAWKINS CHECKED HIS WATCH FOR THE TWENTIETH TIME IN
the past hour. He paced back and forth in the tiny
cubicle they'd assigned him and then went back to the
military issue desk. He snapped open the file folder
he'd been given on arrival and studied the documents
inside for the hundreth time.

The flight in the backseat of the F-14 Tomcat had
left him none the worse for wear. He'd had nothing to
do stuffed back where the flight officer normally sat,
so he'd slept, the roar of jet engines a comforting and
familiar sound. He'd awoken from a troubled sleep
several times, usually when they'd slowed down to
rendezvous high above the Pacific with a lumbering
KC-135 tanker for refueling.

He'd arrived here six hours before, been given this folder, and told to wait until the meeting. He'd bristled at the lack of information, but it seemed as if no one else around here knew anything more than he did. Having been in the Army fourteen years, Hawkins was used to "hurry-up-and-wait."

There was a lot of military activity going on—Hawkins's professional judgment estimated at least a battalion-sized Marine Landing Force was staging out of the immediate area of the tracking station. He glanced out a thick window as a CH-47 Chinook helicopter lifted in a cloud of sand and winged to the southwest carrying troops and cargo. It flew over the eight large dishes that were pointing at various attitudes into the early morning sky. Hawkins peered beyond the dishes toward the desert sands. There was something out there that was attracting a whole lot of attention, and Hawkins hoped this upcoming meeting would tell him what it was.

The file folder certainly didn't do that. The papers inside were brief biographies on personnel that a cover letter said would be attending the briefing. Hawkins couldn't figure out what someone would need this strange assortment of people for. Besides himself there were three civilians—two women and a man—along with an Air Force major assigned to the base here and the Marine full colonel who commanded the soldiers outside.

He scanned the picture of the older woman—Dr. Francine Volkers—implanting it in his memory. A professor at Columbia University in New York. Field of expertise: statistical projection, whatever the hell that was. Hawkins shook his head as he flipped the page.

The second woman looked much too young to Hawkins to be on any sort of classified operation—even if it just involved thinking. Debra Levy. A physicist, specializing in quantum physics and a whole bunch of other things that Hawkins had no idea what they meant. Hawkins had to smile grimly to himself. So far he was 0 for 2 in understanding exactly what these people did.

He could figure out what the third civilian, Don Batson, did for a living, although why the man was here was as much a mystery to Hawkins as why he himself was here. Batson did consultant work for various mining corporations around the world. His specialty was geology, and in addition to the consulting work he was employed as adjunct faculty at the New Mexico Institute of Mining and Technology with a secondary specialty of operations research.

The Marine colonel was next and Hawkins read his military data with a quick scan. Colonel Tolliver. Commander of Battalion Landing Team 2 out of Okinawa. Hawkins's mind snapped to professional considerations. What did they need a BLT out here for? And how were the Australians reacting to that many U.S. troops on their soil? Tolliver was here simply because he was the commander of the closest American forces.

The Air Force major—Spurlock—was a screen watcher from this station. Hawkins shook his head.

He had an inherent antipathy toward someone in uniform, the same rank as himself, who normally got paid the same amount of money each month, but the most dangerous thing they did was use the stapler.

So what had they seen on the screens here that was so important? Hawkins wondered as he glanced outside again at the large dishes.

A Marine lieutenant tapped on the door. It was time. Hawkins stuffed his green beret in a side pants pocket and strode out of the room, the file folder under his arm. Stoic-faced marines with slung automatic weapons were spaced along the hallway and Major Hawkins responded to their snap to attention with a curt nod.

Hawkins showed his ID card to the guard at the door and entered the briefing room. He noted the other people seated at the table as he made his way to the seat that had an index card with his name on it, matching the photos and data in the folder with the actual people. They eyed him with equal curiosity.

Volkers appeared to be on edge, her fingers tapping on the desktop, her eyes flickering about the room. Levy sat perfectly still, her eyes only briefly sliding over to take in Hawkins, then returning to a point in front of her on the tabletop. Batson looked terrible—hung over and worn out. A stubble of beard didn't help his appearance.

The door opened and a man in an expensive three-piece suit walked in. The newcomer was in his mid-forties, a slight puffiness in both the face and body showing the effects of a current lifestyle seated behind a desk. His hair was pure white and thick, combed straight back, a contrast to the slightly red face. The left side of the man's face was slightly concave on the cheekbone—an unsettling abnormality that Hawkins knew was the result of that bone having been smashed in and improperly cared for.

Hawkins had immediately recognized him as Steven Lamb—the President's principal adviser in intelligence matters. Despite the suit and slack body Hawkins respected Lamb. He knew something that few others in the world of covert operations knew— Lamb had spent four years in the CIA running missions out of North Turkey into the former Soviet Union and had been compromised on one of the missions and spent six years in a Soviet prison under horrible conditions before he was quietly exchanged back after the end of the Cold War. The broken cheekbone had occurred sometime during the first year and been allowed to heal on its own. Hawkins knew this because he had been tapped to plan a rescue mission into the prison—one of many potential missions his team—code named Orion—planned for but never executed because, as Hawkins's executive officer Richman liked to say, there was "a lack of intestinal fortitude on the part of the one who has to make the decision to go."

To many not in the know Lamb was simply the President's hatchet man. The one who took the hard jobs and got them done. Of course, he got them done by using other people to do the dirty work and that sometimes caused resentment in the covert community, but as far as Hawkins knew, Lamb had never shirked responsibility for anything he ordered, even when it had turned bad. That was rare in the world of government, from what Hawkins had seen over the past several years.

Lamb and Hawkins had worked together several times during the course of the past four years while Hawkins had been commanding Orion. Lamb more often than not had been the one giving Hawkins the missions for Orion. He'd been the one who'd supplied the questionable intelligence placing one of the bombs in Colombia and, using his call sign Angel, had given the final go.

Lamb moved directly to the front of the room and looked at each person for a few seconds, gaining eye contact before moving on the next, as if he were judging their capabilities with that look.

"Ladies and gentlemen, my name is Steven Lamb. I'm executive director of the President's National Command Crisis Team. Some of you know me from your work on the Hermes Project." He glanced at Hawkins. "Some from other operations.

"All of you had or have been given interim top-secret Q clearances, so we can speak freely in this room. I am glad each of you was able to make it here in time and—"

"I didn't exactly feel like I had much choice," Batson interrupted.

"I second that statement," Fran Volkers added. "I was told I was to be here because of Hermes Project, yet that doesn't seem to be the case." She pointed at the folder in front of her. Hawkins noticed for the first time that all the other people in the room had a folder similar to his. That meant they knew as much about him as he did about them, which bothered him.

Lamb dodged the question for the time being. "Dr. Volker and Mr. Batson are both members of a group called the Hermes Project and they were told that their presence here was because of that project. However, that is not quite true. The Hermes Project has over eighty members, but as you can see, there are only two of you here. I apologize for the slight subterfuge, but we felt it was the easiest way to get you to come here. This matter does fall under the scope of the contracts you signed with Hermes. I will explain in a little while why we had to bring you here, but let me start at the beginning."

Lamb gestured about him, taking in the room. "This installation is called Deep Space Communication Complex 14. Two days ago this station—and other tracking stations around the globe—picked up a high-frequency transmission that disrupted all normal communications for over three hours. Tapes were made of it at all affected stations and sent to Goddard Space Center in Maryland, which began the process of trying to determine several things: first, where the message originated from; secondly, where the message was being sent to; and third, what the message was. The answers to some of those questions were determined just eighteen hours ago and I will share them with you shortly, but bear with me as I stay in the order of events as they occurred.

"Initially, it was suspected that either a civilian or military radio was broadcasting somewhere to the southwest of this location. A helicopter was sent out to locate the emitter."

Lamb picked up a remote and clicked. The screen showed a massive red rock standing alone in the middle of what appeared to be a desert. "That is Ayers Rock. Located two hundred miles to the southwest of this station. The interfering radio waves were coming out of the rock."

"What do you mean, out of the rock?" Batson leaned forward. "You mean someone inside is transmitting?"

Lamb looked at Batson with a blank expression. "We don't know. Ayers Rock is the largest homogeneous rock in the world—there are caves along the face, but the rock itself has always been thought to be solid. It is 1,131 feet high, a mile and a half wide, and two miles across. Using sonar and magnetic resonance imaging equipment, we have narrowed down the source of the emitter to be center of mass, approximately six hundred feet in from the top."

Batson ran a slightly shaking hand through his hair. "No sign of a mine entrance or tunneling?"

"None. As far as we can determine from sonar readings, there is a chamber of presently indeterminate size in the center of the rock with no tunnels leading to it. We assume that is where the transmission originated."

Hawkins spoke for the first time. "What's it transmitting?"

Lamb pointed at the Air Force officer. "Major Spurlock was on duty when the radio waves were first received. I'll let him explain what happened and what he discovered."

Spurlock took a quick drink from a glass of water and then stood. "We picked up the transmission here only because of our proximity to the transmitter. It was picked up by other stations and satellites because the transmission was an up link to a meteor bounce. There were five directional down links.

"The transmission itself was digital—exactly the same mode used by some of our deep-space probes. Specifically, the same mode that *Voyager* uses. Despite that, at first I could not make any sense of it and thought it was just garbage. But then I ran it through the computer and saw that there was a repeating pattern. I isolated the core message from the repeats and discovered that the reason I couldn't decipher it initially was that the beginning of the message was musical."

He reached over and threw a switch on a tape recorder. The sound of classical music filled the air. He turned it off. "The music goes on for ninety minutes—a wide variety ranging from classical to rock and roll. At the end of the ninety minutes of music comes greetings in various languages. This part also threw me off until I had the computer analyze it. There are twenty-four languages represented."

Spurlock took another drink of water. "At that point it occurred to me that this message was very similar to something I knew about. I checked the data log for the *Voyager* space probe and found out that the ninety minutes of music and the greetings were the exact same as those appearing on a record built into the probe itself."

"Wait a second." Hawkins held up a hand. "You're saying that something in Ayers Rock is transmitting the same message that was placed on board *Voyager*?"

Lamb fielded the question. "Yes. On the off chance *Voyager* might run into another interstellar traveler on its journey among the stars, the designers had placed on board a plaque with engravings depicting humans and the location of the sun. Also, there was a long-playing record that contained spoken greetings in various languages, a selection of various sounds found on earth, and ninety minutes of music. In the grooves of the record there are also common mathematical and scientific codes."

"You said there were five down link sites? Where was the message sent to?" Hawkins asked.

In reply Lamb pressed a button on the remote and a black-and-white outline map of the world appeared with five red dots superimposed. "The message was sent from Ayers Rock via very high-power meteor burst to five locations—one in each continent outside of Australia and excluding Antarctica."

Hawkins studied the overlay. There was a red dot in the southwest United States. One in Europe—someplace in Germany. One in the middle of Russia. One in Argentina. And one in the southeast part of Africa. That last dot—Hawkins leaned forward. "Do you have exact locations where the transmission was sent to?"

"We've triangulated the ones in the U.S. and Africa to within a hundred-and-fifty kilometer circle," Lamb answered. "It's rather difficult because we could only interpolate a best guess off what other tracking stations caught of each down link. The one in South America we've located down to within two hundred kilometers. The one in Europe we're within two hundred kilometers also. The one in Asia is down to within a four-hundred-kilometer circle in Central Siberia, and Russia is not cooperating in giving us any data."

Hawkins pointed. "Can you show us in greater detail where that one in Africa is?"

Lamb graced him with a slight smile, as if he had hit the jackpot. "Major Spurlock, you can leave now."

Lamb waited until the Air Force officer had departed the room before pressing the button on the slide remote. A strange domelike rock structure filled the screen. Hawkins felt a surge of adrenaline as he recognized the object—so this was about the bombs after all!

Lamb spoke. "The circle includes Johannesburg and Pretoria, but the center of the estimate is Vredefort Dome. As some of you know, a nuclear bomb was set off in a mine underneath that structure by terrorists three days ago. This occurred approximately four hours prior to the radio transmission."

Hawkins glanced at the other occupants in the room. He could tell by the expressions on their faces that Tolliver and Volkers had known about the blast, but that Levy and Batson were hearing this for the first time, and their faces showed their surprise. Hawkins wondered why Volkers had been told—as far as he knew, the incident was being kept highly classified and the media had no hint.

"The blast effectively destroyed the most productive mine in South Africa—the Red Streak." He paused briefly as Batson whistled in surprise, then continued. "That mine had produced almost two thousand tons of gold and an unknown amount of uranium over the past three years. The bomb was believed to have been one stolen from a Russian depot two weeks ago and set off by a radical splinter group of the Xantha freedom party opposed to the ANC. How the bomb got from Russia to South Africa we do not yet know. Because the blast was underground, the South African government has been able to keep it out of public scrutiny, although how long they'll be able to maintain that veil of secrecy is unknown. Our sensing stations around the world picked the blast up clearly and easily pinpointed the epicenter."

"How did they get a bomb into the mines?" Batson asked. "I thought security was very tight there."

"The security is designed to keep the workers from bringing gold out," Lamb briefly explained. "From what we can piece together, it was relatively easy for them to bring a bomb *into* the mine and detonate it once it reached the proper level. That is not the issue here and now, though.

"We do not know the connection between Ayers

Rock, Vredefort Dome—if that is where the message in Africa went—and the other four locations. We also do not know if there is any connection between the bomb and the transmission. How *Voyager* fits into this is also a puzzle."

"*Voyager* gave them the means of communication with this station," Levy quietly remarked.

"Gave who?" Lamb asked.

Levy shrugged. "Whoever is sending the message."

"But how did they—whoever they are—get a hold of the information on *Voyager*?" Batson wanted to know.

Lamb held up a hand. "There are many unanswered questions. Let's not go jumping to conclusions. You will be given access to all the data we have, and hopefully we can start coming up with some answers."

"I still want to know why we were picked to be here," Volkers interjected. "I don't see why a physicist, a soldier, a mathematician, and a mining engineer make the best team to handle this. Surely you have people who would be better equipped to deal with it."

Lamb looked at her. "As we told you—the message from Ayers Rock consisted of three parts. The first was the music from *Voyager*. The second, the greetings also recorded on *Voyager*. It is because of the third part that you are here."

Lamb flicked the button and words showed on the

screen. "This is the third part of the message when transcribed from the digital code."

**HAWKINSROBERTVOLKERSFRANCINEBAT-
SONDONALDLEVYDEBRA**

"It took us a little while to recognize the names among the letters, as they were all just strung together." Lamb hit the forward and the message reappeared, this time broken down.

**HAWKINS ROBERT
VOLKERS FRANCINE
BATSON DONALD
LEVY DEBRA**

"The message repeats your four names six times and then the entire message starts over again with the music."

"Why us?" Volkers asked the question they all had.

Lamb turned off the screen. "I was hoping one of you could tell me that."

REACTION

DSCC 14, Australia
21 DECEMBER 1995, 0900 LOCAL
20 DECEMBER 1995, 2330 ZULU

THE ROOM WAS SILENT FOR A LONG MINUTE AFTER LAMB'S question. Debra Levy was the one to break the silence.

"Why don't we ask the Rock?"

"What?" Hawkins asked.

Levy seemed nervous to have everyone staring at her. "If you've broken down the code, then we can send messages into the Rock. We can use the code and the same frequency to transmit. Why don't we ask whoever, or whatever, is in there, why we were selected?"

"I think first we need to have a better idea what we're dealing with," Hawkins interjected.

Lamb seconded that. "It has been decided not to attempt any communication with the Rock quite yet.

56

That's if there is anything in there to communicate with," he added. "Despite the fact that something apparently transmitted out of there, we can't be sure that it can receive."

"Well, what *are* you doing?" Fran asked.

"Colonel Tolliver's people have secured the immediate area of Ayers Rock with the help of the Australians," Lamb answered. "By the way, the Australian government is aware that there was a transmission out of the Rock and that it is somehow tied in to the explosion at Vredefort Dome and the missing bombs, but they do not know we have decrypted the message."

Fran rolled her eyes. "Besides guarding the Rock and keeping the message secret, what *else* are you doing?"

"It's more a question of what *you're* going to do," Lamb replied. "We are setting up living areas on top of the Rock. We're also bringing in mining equipment in case we have to dig down to the chamber. The Australians will not be very keen about that, since the Rock is a national landmark and legally it is set aside as a place of worship for the Aborigines, but if this is connected with the bombs, we might have to do that and they'll play along."

Batson raised a hand. "Can you show us the slide with the locations that the first transmission went to again?"

Lamb backed up the projector. "The one in North America is centered in northeast Arizona. Near the town of Winslow. The one in South America is in

Argentina near a place called Campo del Cielo. The one in Europe is centered around Nuremberg, Augsburg, and Stuttgart in Germany. The one in Russia is in Central Siberia."

Don Batson was suddenly alert. "Do you have an atlas?"

Lamb pulled one off the table and handed it to Batson, who eagerly thumbed through. "Campo del Cielo is similar to Ayers Rock and Vredefort Dome in that there is a unique geological feature. I want to see what's in Germany and near Winslow."

He flipped open to Germany and looked. "I've been here—Nördlingen is right there in the center of a triangle formed by those three cities. There's a feature called Ries Basin there. And I know what's outside Winslow." He started turning pages, then stopped and looked up, his finger pointing down at the page. "Meteor Crater is only twenty miles outside of Winslow."

"I don't understand," Fran commented. "What does that have to do with the message?"

Batson was tapping his finger on the atlas. "Campo del Cielo and the Ries Basin are also suspected of having been formed a long time ago by meteor impact. As is the area around Vredefort Dome. I think it's very interesting that four of the five areas the transmissions were sent to are very close to suspected meteor strike spots."

"What about Siberia?" Hawkins asked.

"I don't know about that," Batson admitted. He thought for a few seconds and tapped the map, which was open to Arizona. "But there is someone who might."

"Who?" Lamb inquired.

"Dr. Susan Pencak. She lives by the crater in Arizona. She's the best-known authority on it in the world. If anyone can make a connection between those various sites, it would be her. She makes her living studying strange geological formations and teaching." Batson smiled wryly in remembrance. "But she's also a little bit flaky. She has some weird ways of looking at things."

"I'll bring her here," Lamb decided. "We need every piece of information we can possibly get our hands on."

"Right now"—Lamb pointed to three boxes full of documents stacked on a table—"you have access to all information concerning these events. There are also computers linked into our main data base for your use. If there is anything else you need, please contact me immediately. We'll be moving to the Rock in about twenty-four hours, once everything is set up out there."

Lamb made his way out of the room, followed by Tolliver and Spurlock. Fran glanced around at the other members of the "team." Hawkins was hiding any reaction he might have. Batson looked befuddled after his insight into the transmission reception sites. Levy looked mildly interested in what was probably to her an interesting intellectual problem.

"He's lying to us," Fran announced.

"What?" Batson blinked at her.

"They're going to drill into that Rock the minute they have the equipment there to do it," she replied. "They're scared, and when they're scared, they usually overreact and keep everything a secret."

She'd expected Hawkins to get upset by her comments but instead he nodded slightly. "That's true. I'm sure they will start or probably have already started drilling." He looked at Batson. "You're the mining engineer. How long will it take them?"

Batson shook his head. "I'd have to know what kind of rock it's made of. Where they're starting from. What kind of equipment. What diameter bore they're making. It's impossible to just—"

"Just a SWAG, Mister Batson," Hawkins interrupted. "A simple wild-ass guess. A day? Two days? A week? A month?"

Batson rubbed his chin. "He said center of mass of Ayers Rock. They'd go in from the top. Say five or six hundred feet of tunnel through solid rock." He looked up at the ceiling briefly. "Five days. Give or take two days either way. That's if they only drill and don't blast, and I don't think they'll be blasting here on a national landmark."

"That's all well and good," Fran commented. "So we have a week of sitting around with all these data and no earthly idea where to start and no idea where we're going with it."

Hawkins stood. "Listen up for a second. You all are the scientists. I'm just a dumb soldier, but whenever I get a mission tasking, the first thing I do is organize the information I am given. I do that before

I start making my plans." He pointed at the boxes. "I suggest we break down the stuff in there. Mr. Batson—"

"Don," Batson interrupted. "Call me Don. *Mister* makes me nervous."

"All right, Don." Hawkins nodded. "You can call me Hawkins—I'm used to that from the military and I probably wouldn't respond if you used my first name." He glanced at the other team members and they introduced themselves.

"Fran."

"Debra."

"All right. Don, since it's your area, you become the Rock expert. You find out everything there is to know about Ayers Rock and then brief us on it later today."

Don looked relieved to have something he could handle. "All right." He moved across the room and began digging through the books and folders in them.

Hawkins swung his gaze around. "Fran, I hate to show my ignorance, but what is statistical projection?"

Fran was used to the question and was impressed that Hawkins was admitting his ignorance up front. "I take information, collate it, and then make a computer program that gives probabilities on future trends."

"You predict the future, then?" Hawkins asked.

She graced him with a slight smile. "It's not that simple. Let's say I predict possible futures and give you the percentage chances of them occurring."

"How about the present?" Hawkins asked.

"What do you mean?"

"Could you try to make some sort of connection between the Rock, *Voyager,* the explosion at Vredefort, and the messages?"

Debra Levy spoke. "You're making a flawed assumption."

Hawkins didn't seem bothered by either the interruption or the negative comment. "In what way?"

"There are too many unknowns here to even begin to think all those events are interconnected," Levy said. "We know the message and *Voyager* are connected because of the use of the information from the record on board the probe. We don't know that the messages and the explosion at Vredefort Dome are connected. If they are, then the explosion occurred first and we know—or at least Mr. Lamb has told us—that was caused by radicals in South Africa. So I would say that it is very unlikely that those same radicals are causing the messages to be sent."

Hawkins considered that. "Then the explosion prompted the message."

"Maybe," Levy answered. "Why not do a time line of events, so we can see them more clearly? That's always the first step in trying to understand a problem."

"Sounds good," Hawkins concurred.

"I'm really not sure where my area of expertise enters into all of this," Debra commented. "I think I'll just look through what's accumulated in the computer so far and see if I find anything interesting."

"I have some things I have to check on," Hawkins said as he left the room.

21 DECEMBER 1995, 0930 LOCAL
20 DECEMBER 1995, 2400 ZULU

LAMB SAT IN THE SECURE COMMUNICATIONS CENTER AND waited impatiently while a technician finished making contact with the appropriate satellite and, through it, Washington.

"You're good to go, sir." The man scuttled out the door and locked the thick hatch behind him. The center was now impervious to external eavesdropping. The microphone was voice activated and the television screen in front of Lamb showed a large desk and chair. He fought the urge to stand as the President entered the field of vision of the camera and sat down at the desk.

The weight of three years in office showed in the lines on the President's face. "What do you have, Steve?"

Lamb looked at the camera looming a few feet in front of him, just above the screen. "The team is working on the data we've accumulated. Nothing very surprising so far. None of them has a clue as to why they were chosen—or let me say that none of them has indicated having any idea. Volkers and Batson have clearances from Hermes, so they should be all right. Levy worries me. We've given her an interim clearance but we know little about her. I've got my people checking on her in the States. The strange thing is that Levy's name was on the roster to be considered for addition to the Hermes Project in a couple of months."

He looked down at his notes. "We're bringing in another person. An expert on meteor craters from Arizona."

The President frowned, as if this detail was bothersome. "Meteor craters?"

"It looks like four of the five reception sites for the message have suspected meteor strike spots in the immediate area. It may be nothing, but it's worth checking out."

The President was reading a note someone had handed him from the side. He returned his attention to the camera, dismissing the meteor issue. "So, nothing on the people so far. What about the Russians?"

Lamb wanted to sigh but held it in. The term *Russians* now covered a score of various independent republics, all with their own agendas, their own set of severe economic problems, their own nuclear weapons, and worst of all, their own deep sense of historical paranoia. Lamb knew the Russians very well and like any other student of that country, he knew that they were almost impossible to second-guess because their mindset was so different from that of someone from the West. In the years since his release Lamb had tried to subdue his visceral emotions whenever he had to deal with anything about the country he had been a prisoner of—at certain times he did that more successfully than at others.

"They had to have picked up the transmission into Siberia. I'm sure they have a better idea than we do of where it was aimed. I'm checking on that. They definitely know about the explosion under Vredefort Dome—their sensors had to have picked it up just like ours did. I'd say they probably have a good line on Ayers Rock being the source of the transmission, because their space lab was overhead when the transmission occurred. They're going to want to know what's going on. We can't hide the equipment we're putting on top of the Rock. It's totally exposed to satellite imagery.

"The Seventh Fleet has picked up movement from Russian Pacific Fleet elements. They're moving a carrier task force south toward us."

"Are you sure it's connected to the transmission?"

Lamb glanced down at the satellite imagery of the fleet movement he'd been faxed less than an hour ago. "Yes, sir. They've got the research ship *Kosmonaut Yury Gagarin* as part of the element. That ship is their floating version of this station. It has two large steerable aerial dishes and two smaller ones built on top of the deck. Looks like they want to be in a better position to pick up any more transmissions. They've also got the *Krym,* one of their Primorye-class intelligence-gathering ships, among the flotilla."

"Christ," the President muttered. "They're going to push this, Steve. I've been on their case concerning the bombs, telling them they need to be more open.

Now we're holding something back from them. Do you think they might have something to do with all that's happened?"

"I don't know, sir," Lamb answered honestly. "But it seems to me that they are reacting just as much as we are."

"That could be part of a deception plan," the President noted.

"Yes, sir, it could. Until we find out what's in the Rock, we won't know. We may be holding what we know back from them, but at the present moment I see no reason we should share anything with them," Lamb said. "This doesn't concern them."

"What about the Aussies?"

"They're not happy, sir, but they're going along so far."

"All right. Keep me informed if anything comes up."

The screen went dead. After a short pause Lamb flicked a switch on the console. The door to the shelter opened immediately and Hawkins walked in, a bundle of file folders crammed under one arm.

"What's the latest on South Africa?" Lamb asked.

"This is the most current satellite imagery of the site." The words flowed across the small room and sank into the special acoustic tile that lined the walls and ceiling, as the analyst laid the photos on the desk.

Lamb flicked his gaze from the folder to the speaker. "I don't see anything."

"That's because there's nothing to be seen," Hawkins said. "As far as can be determined, the explosion occurred over two miles underground."

"Any fallout?"

"No. It was all contained."

Lamb swiveled his chair around to face the console. "Well, then, since the damage seems to be minimal, our main concern must be to find out who was behind this and where they got the bomb from. Which is what we've been trying to do now for a week. The question is, how did the bomb get to South Africa?"

Hawkins sat down in a chair on the far side of the desk and rubbed his left temple. "We don't know that. All we know is that the underground yield and signature are similar to the AG-35 Russian warhead. Our friends in the SVR are not being very cooperative, but as you know, they did give us enough information two weeks ago to confirm that two of those type warheads are unaccounted for in their arsenal holding area."

"So where's the other one?" Lamb demanded.

"It wasn't in Colombia," Hawkins snapped.

Lamb gazed across the table. "I'm sorry about that. Faulty intelligence."

"There's a little part of my mind," Hawkins said, "that wonders if maybe there wasn't any intelligence at all and you just used it as an excuse to take out that member of the Cartel."

Lamb's eyes didn't waver from Hawkins's. "If I had wanted your team to take that asshole down, I'd have simply ordered you to do it—I wouldn't have had to make up a cover story. I think the intelligence may well have been a setup by the source who fed it to us, but that's in the past and we have a whole big mess right here we have to deal with.

"We've got to get that other bomb tracked down. The President's talked to the Russian President to try and get some support from his people, but he's not having much luck. We were lucky with this one. The next one might end up in a city."

Hawkins tapped the folder. "While you were talking to D.C. I went through the latest analysis on the explosion and found out we *weren't* lucky on this one."

Lamb settled his eyes on Hawkins. "Go on."

Hawkins tapped the satellite photo. "The damage is only apparently minimal. That bomb obliterated the Red Streak series of mines. It is—was—the richest deposit of gold and uranium ever found. The loss of that mine will cripple the South African government economically."

Lamb already knew that. "So what?"

Hawkins opened a folder in front of him. "Your whiz people did a projection on the worldwide economic effect, and the results were extremely startling." Even as he said it, Hawkins wondered if Fran Volkers had had something to do with what he was looking at. Hawkins scanned the page that he himself had only just read. "There is a fifty-six-percent chance that the loss of that mine will trigger a global depression on the order of the crash of 1929—most likely worse, since it will come on top of the recession we've only just started to recover from."

"WHAT!" Lamb leaned forward. "How can that be?"

Hawkins slid a piece of paper across the table to his boss and tried to keep it as simple as possible. "I'm not an expert, but it's laid out pretty clearly there. As you can see, a large number of the world's countries still have a gold-based economy. Most of those nations are in the Third World. Over the past twenty years South Africa has been propping up many of those economies with gold that was not yet mined in exchange for various economic, military, and political concessions. Mandela hasn't changed that policy. Most of that gold is now lost inside what used to be the Red Streak mine.

"Without the gold to back up their currencies many of those countries will slide into economic chaos within a year. The ripple effect will take another year or so to reach us and the other industrialized nations."

Lamb quickly scanned the document, then looked up. "All right. If this projection is correct, what can we do to avoid the depression?"

Hawkins slowly closed the folder. "According to the last page of the report there's not much we can do. We are barely able to maintain our own economy —there's little we could do to help others."

Lamb flipped to the indicated page and read it. When he looked up, his eyes showed his despair. "If the projection on the first page is correct, this is like spitting in a fire. I'll get this thing reworked. I need some better suggestions before I go to the President

with it. He'll tear my head off if that's all I give him."
He stood, his body hunched over in weariness. "We've
got to get that other bomb."

Hawkins gestured around them, taking in the entire complex. "What about all this? Is there anything
you didn't tell us in the briefing?"

Lamb shook his head. "You know as much as I do.
We assume it's related to the first explosion because
of the down link to Vredefort Dome. We have no idea
if there is any connection to the second bomb, but it's
the only thing we've got."

"But in and of itself," Hawkins asked, "what do
you think we have here in the Rock?"

"I have no idea. I hope the other members of your
team can figure that out." He paused and then softened his voice. "I need your help with this, Hawk."

Hawkins shrugged. "I'm here. I'll do my best."

"I know you'll do your best. You always have."
Lamb looked down at his desk for a second. "I heard
what happened in Colombia. I was in the air on Looking Glass already heading here when I gave you the
go and I received the after-action report on the secure
line. Your men did a good surgical job."

"If you consider putting a nine-millimeter round
through the brain of a young woman a good surgical
job," Hawkins said, bitterly, "then I suppose it was."

"I heard about that too," Lamb said, his eyes fixed
on his subordinate. "I also heard you were acting
strangely in the exfiltration aircraft."

Hawkins stood. "I'm fine." He turned on his heels

and left the room, the door swinging securely shut behind him with a dull thud.

21 DECEMBER 1995, 1000 LOCAL
21 DECEMBER 1995, 0030 ZULU

"WHAT ARE YOU DOING?" HAWKINS ASKED, GAZING OVER Levy's shoulder at the screen of the computer she was working at.

"I'm looking at the original form of the message," Levy answered.

"Looking at it for what? Haven't they already decoded it?"

"They decoded it one-dimensionally," Levy said. "I'm checking to see if there might be another dimension to it."

Hawkins blinked. "You've lost me."

Levy removed her hands from the keyboard and swiveled her head to look at him. "This is an unknown communication. We don't know who or what sent it. Therefore we should not assume that simply because it has been deciphered one way, there might not be other ways to decipher it. There might be two dimensions to this message or even more."

She closed her eyes briefly in thought. "To give you a simple example, a stop sign has three dimensions: the shape of the sign, the color, and the actual word STOP itself. Any one of those by itself gives you a message if you know what you're looking for. In that case it's the same information—but you can also send different information on different dimensions of the same original message. In this case," she said, turning back to the computer and tapping the screen, "the actual physical arrangement of the characters might be informative in and of itself."

Hawkins looked at the arrangement of 0's and 1's. "Doesn't look like anything to me," he noted.

"I agree," Levy said, "but it was something I wanted to check."

Hawkins sat down and scooted his chair close to hers. "I looked at your record—as I'm sure you did mine, in the folder they gave you—and I'm quite impressed with your academic and intellectual achievements. If you were to speculate, what would you say we have here?"

Levy fixed Hawkins with an intense gaze. "You qualified your question quite interestingly, Major. Should I accept the inverse of what you said and assume that you are not impressed with me outside of my intellectual achievements?"

Hawkins returned her steady gaze. "Why should you assume something negative? I phrased it that way because I know nothing about you other than what was in the file and all that was in there was your academic and scientific record. So I assume nothing about you as a person."

Levy broke the eye contact. "I'm sorry. I've never really learned much social tact."

Hawkins softly laughed. "Hell, that's all right. They don't teach that stuff in school. I've been told I don't have too much tact either. My profession isn't noted for it." He paused. "Have you ever worked for the government before on a classified operation?"

She shook her head. "I've done quite a bit of consulting work on various research projects, but never anything like this."

Hawkins leaned back in his seat, feeling very uncomfortable. He was out of his element here. Even Levy's simple explanation of what she was doing had thrown him. He'd never considered a stop sign a three-dimensional message. Always before he'd used great innovation and expertise in his missions, but that was after someone else had given him the rules of engagement and the target. Here he had none. And not only that, but he had somehow automatically assumed the unofficial title of leader of the team. He wasn't sure if he had taken it, or if they others had handed it to him. But the other three all seemed to be immersed in something worthwhile—Batson looking at data on the Rock, Fran with her nose inches away from a computer screen, and Levy exploring the message. Hawkins felt somewhat useless.

His wife, Mary, would have laughed at his being so uneasy, Hawkins thought. She was the only person he had ever allowed to penetrate the hard shell his upbringing in the foster home in New York City and his time in Special Operations had wrapped about his emotions. And the great thing was, Hawkins would have laughed along with her. In their first two years of marriage she had started changing him. But all that had ended four years earlier, and if anything Hawkins was even harder than he had been. He savagely twisted his mind away from thoughts of Mary and focused on the young woman sitting next to him.

"So you have no idea why your name was on the list?"

"I have no idea why there was even a list," Levy answered.

"Fran and Don were on this Hermes project," Hawkins noted. "I work for the government. But you say you had no previous ties with the government." He shook his head. "It doesn't make sense."

"But the government didn't send the message," she noted.

"We can't be sure of that," Hawkins said. "We only have their information saying they didn't."

Levy regarded Hawkins for a few seconds, then a slight smile graced her pale lips. "Very good, Major. I like that. I was just looking at a specific aspect of the problem, trying to view it from a different angle, but you are looking at the entire situation in a different light."

Hawkins leaned forward. "Let's get back to the original question—what do you think we've got here in the Rock?"

"I think we have a touchstone," Levy said.

"A touchstone?"

"Did you ever see the movie *2001*?" Levy asked. Hawkins nodded.

"The stone they uncovered on the moon—that was a touchstone. It's a term used in scientific circles to describe an artifact planted by a more advanced race on a planet where there is a probability of intelligent life developing. To make sure it is activated at the proper time, it is located in such a place that a certain level of civilization is required in order to be able to uncover it."

"You think that's what we're uncovering?" Hawkins could see that this conversation had gained Fran's interest, and she moved her chair over to listen.

"It may be," Levy said. "However, it has always been assumed that a touchstone has to be physically uncovered. In this case the touchstone may have already been 'uncovered,' so to speak."

"What do you mean?" Fran asked.

"I mean that either the nuclear explosion under Vredefort Dome or the arrival of *Voyager* at a certain distance away from the sun might have activated the touchstone in the Rock and caused it to transmit—that's if my theory about it being a touchstone is correct."

"And if it is," Hawkins asked, "what should we do?"

"*We,*" Levy said, emphasizing the word, "might not be able to do anything. Unlike the story in *2001,* it is more likely that a touchstone is a warning for the more advanced race that set it up than a beacon for the less advanced one that sets it off."

"So we may have hit a trip wire," Hawkins said.

"Yes," Levy acknowledged. "And we have no idea who's heard it go off and what their reaction might be."

THE RUSSIAN I

Vicinity Chernobyl, Ukraine
21 DECEMBER 1995, 0600 LOCAL
21 DECEMBER 1995, 0100 ZULU

THE LAND WAS EMPTY OF ANIMAL LIFE. TREES STILL STRUG-
gled to grow, but it was obvious even they were losing
the war to live. Vast splotches of dead vegetation
pockmarked the area as far as the eye could see. Just
off the crumbling tar road, where the Zil-135 ten-ton
truck was parked, a large splatter of hastily poured
concrete lay barren of the blown snow that was whip-
ping through the area. There was nothing to indicate
that the concrete marked the resting place of eighteen
men.

In the distance the cooling towers the men had
given up their lives to cover stood under dozens of
feet of concrete—concrete that had been flown in underneath the men's helicopters while the radiation

had penetrated up through the thin skin of the air-craft and killed them with the slow death.

The Russian had spent eight days getting here. It was a detour he would never have allowed himself on an assigned mission, but this was different. This was personal.

He didn't consciously feel the cold wind whistling in from the Ural Mountains to the east. He was a hard man, his face leathery from years out in the weather. The mouth was set in lines that had known no laughter for many years.

His gray eyes pondered the concrete. They hadn't even put a marker up. Of course, the reasoning was, why put a marker up when no one could come here and see it anyway? The Russian knew he was the first person in years to stand here. And by doing so he had effectively condemned himself to the same slow death by radiation. That bothered him little—in fact, it gave him a feeling of connection with the men under the concrete, one of them in particular.

"For you, Gregori, I do this." His words were grabbed by the wind and spirited away among the sickly pine trees.

He saluted the grave and then turned to his truck. It was going to be a hard trip—about three days using back roads, he estimated—and he needed to start. As he clambered into the cab he glanced at the gauge on the instrument on the passenger seat. The rad count told him that he should survive and be reasonably functional for those three days. After that nothing would matter anyway.

Securely fastened in the cargo bay rode a large crate, the twin to the one that had exploded in South Africa. The Russian threw the truck into gear, and with a lurch it lumbered down the abandoned road, nose pointed southeast, away from Chernobyl.

METEOR CRATER

PENCAK
Meteor Crater, Arizona
20 DECEMBER 1995, 1600 LOCAL
21 DECEMBER 1995, 0100 ZULU

THE SUN HIGHLIGHTED THE DESERT TO THE WEST IN A PURPLISH haze. The old woman stood on the top of the rim, with the class gathered below her, their breath puffing out into the chill air. She was nothing more than a silhouette to them, but that was enough to display her deformities. Her right shoulder was hunched down as if she were permanently trying to squeeze her body through a narrow opening. That arm ended in a withered stalk instead of a hand. As she turned her gaze, the right side of her face absorbed the dying light across a series of slashes and wrinkles, as if the skin had been burned badly a long time ago and healed poorly. Where the right eye had been, there was simply the same scarred skin in the socket.

The class was looking up at her because she stood on the lip of the crater, the bowl before her, filling the horizon. Her voice was gravelly, as if her throat had also been afflicted by whatever disaster had befallen her. "Meteor Crater used to be called by several names, Coon Butte being the most popular. While it was known to the Indians of the area for generations, it first attracted the attention of the white man in the 1880s when it was thought there might be silver here. Although unfounded, the rumor interested A. E. Foote, a geologist from Philadelphia. He made the first scientific study of the crater in 1891."

She gestured with her dead hand as she spoke. "The far rim is twelve hundred meters away. It's roughly one hundred seventy-five meters from the surface level to the bottom, but, as you can see, the rim I am standing on adds another forty-five meters in height from the plain." The hand stabbed down and eighteen pairs of eyes followed. "There is no standing water in the bottom, but flat-lying sediments found there contain small shells, which indicates that a lake once filled the crater.

"The earliest studies of the crater initially speculated that it was formed by either a volcano or an underground steam explosion. However, the discovery of some iron fragments lying very close to the surface soon challenged that theory. In November 1891 two members of the U.S. Coast and Geological Survey examined the area intensely. They speculated that because the crater is round, a meteorite must have struck at a nearly perpendicular angle.

"They did a careful magnetic survey of the crater floor and discovered little evidence of buried metal. Using what I could best describe as the myopic-eyeball estimating technique, one of the men postulated that the amount of material on the rim would fill the crater completely." A snort indicated what the old woman thought of that. "Later, other more scientific studies clearly showed that the rim material is not sufficient to fill the crater.

"In 1895 at the symposium of the Geological Society of Washington, the geologist Grove Karl Gilbert made a presentation on Coon Butte. He presented the various hypotheses and the evidence supporting each one, ranging from volcanic origin, to steam explosion, to meteor impact. His conclusion was that one could make no definitive conclusion based on the evidence, but that the crater most likely had been formed by a steam explosion."

She was interrupted for the first time by a stocky figure sporting an Indiana Jones hat and a full beard. "Note how carefully Dr. Pencak describes Gilbert's presentation to the Geological Society. You will be required to read Gilbert's presentation before our next class meeting. It is a masterpiece of scientific inquiry."

Dr. Susan Pencak continued without missing a beat. "Your professor is quite correct about the substance of Gilbert's address. Let us hope you read it more carefully than it was received in 1895. The common feeling by those listening to Gilbert was that he was definitively stating the crater was formed by a steam explosion. For over a quarter of a century the theory that Coon Butte was formed by a steam explosion stood with no challenge—blindly accepted by all."

She turned and pointed behind her at the large boulders lying haphazardly on the rim. "It was not until many years later that the pattern of rock fragments scattered around the rim itself was examined. Large boulders, some weighing as much as five thousand tons, are found as far away as a mile from where I am standing. No steam explosion could have created that much force.

"Massive amounts of pulverized rock known as silica are found both in the rim and in the crater. It takes tremendous pressure and heat to make silica out of solid rock. Additionally, fused quartz sandstone found in the crater indicates that a temperature at least as high as three thousand nine hundred degrees Fahrenheit occurred here at one time."

Dr. Pencak paused and peered at the students, some of whom were diligently taking notes, others of whom seemed quite bored. She focused her single eye on a young man whose attention was wandering to the distant plain. "You there. Yes, you. Given all the evidence I have just presented and that which is laid out before your eyes, what do you think of the steam explosion theory?"

The student blinked and spoke slowly as he tried sorting out the data, desperately wishing he had done the required reading for this road trip. "Well, Doctor, I suppose that might be an adequate theory, but I don't think a steam explosion could have fused quartz sandstone. Some sort of thermal effect or explosion had to have occurred to produce temperatures that high—much higher than could be caused by steam."

"Ah!" she exclaimed. "A thermal explosion. Very good. Someone tell me what could cause such an explosion and leave a hole such as we have here."

A few students tentatively raised their hands. Pencak pointed her hand at one to reply.

"A meteorite would have a sufficient amount of kinetic energy that could be transformed into thermal energy upon impact." The student flipped a page in her textbook. "Gifford's table of energy in calories per gram of weight indicate that a meteor moving at ten miles per second would have almost thirty thousand calories of energy per gram."

Pencak's face lopsidedly twitched in what might have been a smile or a grimace. "True. Very true. And someone tell me the latest theory. How fast was the meteorite traveling that is supposed to have formed this crater?"

"Uh, twelve miles per second?"

"Are you answering me or asking me?" Pencak didn't wait. "Yes. Twelve miles per second, or seven hundred twenty miles per hour. And some number cruncher figured out that the meteor must have been about forty-one meters in diameter at strike and weighed some three hundred thousand tons. The blast would have been the equivalent of five hundred thousand tons of TNT. Quite impressive."

She paused and surveyed the group. They were

scribbling the numbers in their notebooks as if her word were law. "So, if a meteor actually had hit, what else should we find here besides a big hole, fused and pulverized rock, and big boulders thrown miles away?"

There was a long pause and then a hand went up. "Yes?"

"There should be some fragments of the meteor."

"Correct." She waved her hand around the crater. "And have they been found?"

"Not in any substantial amount," was the reply.

"So what happened to the material that made up the meteor? What happened to that three hundred thousand tons of nickel and iron? Where is it?"

Her questions were met with silence. The professor was fidgeting, uncomfortable with her questioning of the class. They were here for information, not intellectual challenge. These young minds were in pursuit of a grade, not knowledge.

She changed her angle of attack, trying to dredge up some sense of creative thought from the gray mass in front of her. "Can someone tell me what else could have caused this crater? Something that could make such a hole in the earth; fuse quartz sandstone; pulverize solid rock into powder; and not leave a trace fifty thousand years later?"

A quiet voice ventured something unheard at the back of the group.

"What was that?" Pencak tried to peer through the gathering dusk at the source of the voice.

A young man with a scraggly beard stepped forward. "I said a nuclear explosion."

"Yes. On the order of magnitude of five hundred megatons. Shoemaker in 1963 did something very interesting. I knew him then. Quite a man. He had this marvelous capacity to approach problems in reverse and oftentimes he came up with quite startling results. He studied a crater formed in Yucca Flat, Nevada, by a nuclear explosion and compared it to this crater here. Interestingly enough, he found numerous points of similarity. In fact, they were practically identical, although, of course, they were different in size because of the lower yield of the weapon used in Nevada."

"But as you said, this was formed approximately fifty thousand years ago," a confident voice from the front of the small crowd noted.

"Yes, I did," Pencak concurred.

The speaker grew bolder. "Then it could not have been a nuclear explosion."

"Why not?"

The speaker laughed. "Because nuclear weapons weren't invented until 1945."

"If you mean by man, you are quite correct." Doctor Pencak was about to continue when the professor quickly stepped forward.

"Thank you very much for a most fascinating day touring the crater, Dr. Pencak. I regret to say that we must be going now in order to make it back to the university on time." With a few muttered thanks from the students the group was gone, trudging over the rim where their bus waited, ready to whisk them back to the academic world where answers were as pat as those that were printed on the pages of the textbook.

Susan Pencak watched the taillights of the bus disappear into the growing darkness. The sun was almost completely down and the temperature had taken the quick dive it always does on a winter desert night. She could hear the noises of the night creatures coming alive out in the flatlands.

They always cut her off when she started challenging their reality. She found it quite discouraging. She was widely recognized among her colleagues as the foremost expert on the geological aspects of Meteor Crater, yet she infuriated them by not toeing the party line and blindly accepting that the crater had been formed as its name indicated.

She reached up with both arms toward the stars that were beginning to appear overhead. The five fingers on her good hand reached higher and higher, as if she were trying to touch the stars. The withered hand was inches below, forced down by the ruined shoulder. Slowly, she lowered her arms and turned her eye back to earth. With a slight limp she headed for the Jeep parked just off the rim road. Off in the distance she could hear the discordant thump of a helicopter headed in her direction and she paused and waited.

VOYAGER

The Edge of the Solar System
21 DECEMBER 1995, 0100 ZULU

OUTSIDE THE ORBIT OF THE FARTHEST PLANET IN THE SOLAR system, the effects of the sun are still present. A continuous stream of charged particles from the sun's magnetic field is swept by the solar wind and creates a huge bubblelike structure known as the heliosphere. From mankind's perspective it serves a most useful function by keeping the solar system relatively free of interstellar matter and slowing the entry of cosmic rays.

Voyager 2, intrepid visitor of four planets and fifty-seven moons during the past eighteen years, was only a third of the way to the edge of the heliosphere but well beyond the orbit of Pluto—a vast, empty hinterland where there is little for the probe's scanners to search out and examine. Indeed, most of the equipment on board the *Voyager* was turned off shortly after the probe passed Neptune in August of 1989. Since that time only the spectrometer—a device that detects ultraviolet radiation—has been kept active.

With its large dish oriented back into the plane of the planets and the high-gain antenna in the center centered on Earth, *Voyager* heads for the edge of the heliosphere, projected to reach it by the year 2000. The plutonium power on the probe is expected to run out in 2020. After that, it is estimated that it will take *Voyager* millions of years before it comes close to another star.

When *Voyager* was launched in 1977, there were people who believed shooting out into space what was essentially a guidebook back to Earth might not have been the most prudent idea. Those worries were overruled. After all, the scientists argued, the radio and television rays from Earth were much farther out already than *Voyager* would ever reach intact. Those rays not only pinpointed Earth's stellar location but also depicted life—and not a very flattering one, as a survey of the channels indicates—on Earth.

At precisely 0100, Greenwich mean time, the transmitter secreted away in the guts of the probe powered up and began pulsing out a binary code representing the readings from the spectrometer for the past twenty-four hours. The radio waves began their four-hour, ten-minute, twenty-three-second trip back to Earth to be gathered in at the deep-space communications center near Alice Springs, Australia, where a giant dish would grudgingly turn from higher priority missions to gather in *Voyager*'s data during its fifteen-minute daily allocation of dish time.

Seven minutes later—four and a half billion miles into its seventeen-year journey and midway through the transmission—*Voyager 2*'s journey ended abruptly.

DSCC 14, Australia
21 DECEMBER 1995, 1440 LOCAL
21 DECEMBER 1995, 0510 ZULU

HAWKINS FELT THE POUNDING OF A MASSIVE HEADACHE BE-hind his eyes. For the past several hours they had learned quite a bit about meteor-burst transmitting, Ayers Rock, digital encoding, and various other information, but it had added little to their understanding of the situation.

Mentally tuning out the headache, Hawkins slapped the end of his pointer on the surface of the easel. "All right, I know this seems rather simplistic, but bear with me. Basically we've got four items here."

NUCLEAR BLAST VREDEFORT DOME
↓
VOYAGER INFORMATION
↓
MESSAGE TO FIVE SITES (Including Vredefort Dome)
↓
OUR NAMES

"I don't think you should have those arrows. None of those items necessarily follows from the previous one." Levy's quiet voice filled the room. "I would admit that the *Voyager* information was the step prior to the message, since that information was used in making up the message. But how did our names come up?"

Hawkins shrugged. "We'll get to that later. I'm more concerned about the connection with the bombing. There's one more of those nuclear weapons out there missing. If whoever is behind these messages is involved with the bombs, we need to find that out."

Hawkins didn't think they should talk about the touchstone theory in front of Lamb. Levy's point had been valid, but if it was true, there wasn't too much they could do about it. Besides, there were still several other factors that didn't quite fit into that theory—at least not that he could see. It was those other factors that they were examining now.

"Look at those reception sites and add in the Rock." Levy was holding up a world map with the six red circles. "What does the spatial layout make you think?"

"One for each inhabited continent," Hawkins noted. Something had been bugging him for a while. "What if the others were diversions?"

"What?" Fran looked puzzled.

"What if the only true message was sent to South Africa, but the other ones were sent to throw us off track?" Hawkins warmed to the theme. It was something he might have done. "We're sitting here looking at where those beams terminated, but that doesn't necessarily mean there has to be anything there. We have no record of transmissions from those sites."

"Or there might have been something there once upon a time and it no longer exists," Levy commented. "But getting back to the layout of the six sites: Let's stop being egocentric and turn our gaze outward. Note that three are in the northern hemisphere and three are in the southern. Note that each set of three is laid out in a pattern that splits the world into three roughly equal parts."

Lamb had entered while Hawkins was showing the diagram, and he now spoke for the first time. "If you wanted to set up monitors to cover the whole world you might space them out like that. Maybe the Russians put together some sort of monitoring system in the past and the explosion at Vredefort damaged it?"

Levy was shaking her head thoughtfully. "No. That's not what I'm talking about. Think about where we're sitting right now. Why is this tracking station here in Australia?"

"So we can always have contact with our satellites and probes when they're on the far side of the globe from the United States," Fran answered.

"Right," Levy said, and waited.

Fran was the first to catch on. "Wait a minute! Are you saying that these six sites are the same thing? Monitoring or relay sites to space? But there's nothing there at the other sites!"

"There was nothing in Ayers Rock that we knew of until it sent out the message," Hawkins noted.

Levy pointed back at Hawkins's diagram. "We all seem to be ignoring the fact that the message relayed the data off *Voyager 2* with the addition of our names. Yet *Voyager* is almost out of the solar system. How could someone have gotten that information?"

"They don't necessarily have to have gotten it off the satellite itself," Batson replied. "That information is available in data bases here on Earth."

"So someone could have just used that *Voyager* information as a diversion," Lamb said.

Hawkins turned to Lamb. "When this crater woman gets here, we need to pump her for everything about Meteor Crater. I'm sure they've done sonar and electromagnetic resonance soundings in the crater. If not, we need to get some people out there. Maybe there's something in that area similar to what's in the Rock."

"Maybe." Lamb seemed bothered by Levy's quick dismissal of the Russian angle. "The Russians would have wanted to do something like that—set up sites around the world like we have. They could get access to the *Voyager* plate information—it's public information. Hell, maybe this thing in the Rock dates back to *Sputnik.*"

"What exactly do you think you have in the Rock?" Batson asked. He thumped a folder down on the table in front of him. "I've been going through the data picked up so far and it seems to me that all you know for sure is that there is an anomaly on your sonar and electromagnetic resonance mapping. Nothing on sound. Nothing on radio waves since the one broadcast. All your sonar and EMR tells you is that there is something other than solid rock down about five hundred feet. And the latest data indicate that it is approximately forty feet in diameter and fifteen in depth."

"True," Lamb acknowledged. "That is all we have."

Batson shook his head. "But for all we know that could have been in there forever. No one ever thought of doing any of those tests on the Rock prior to the messages. There is no sign of entryway or exit."

"We've got troops going over the exterior of the Rock and the surrounding area double-checking for that." Lamb replied. "We think it's possible the entry tunnel might be on the northwest side, which has been off limits for years to all but the Aborigines for religious purposes. Something might have been dug on that side and hidden."

"If you find no tunnel, how did it get in there?" Fran asked.

The question went unanswered.

"It gets back to the question of what 'it' is," Batson said. "It also has to be able to transmit through all that rock out into space with sufficient power to override your normal SATCOM traffic. I'm no expert on it, but I'd say we'd have a hell of a time rigging a transmitter to go through five hundred feet of solid rock."

"It's possible," Lamb answered. "We ran that problem through the computer. No one ever thought of doing it through rock before—no reason to—but if it was necessary, and you have a very strong power source, then you could transmit through rock on certain microwave frequencies."

"But where's the power source, then?" Fran asked. There were too many problems without answers here. She liked working with hard data—here there were no data, just pieces of a puzzle. Except the entire puzzle seemed to be a solid sheet of blackness that they were fumbling with in the dark, trying to connect each piece at a time to another one simply by feel.

"I think this could all be an elaborate setup," Lamb said.

"Setup?" Hawkins repeated. "For what purpose?"

"This is about the bombs," Lamb said. "It's got to be. I think someone is trying to divert our attention from the one still out there. Like Major Hawkins said, our primary concern must—"

He paused as an excited Major Spurlock threw open the door. "*Voyager 2* is off-line."

"What?" Lamb asked, confused.

"We just lost it in midtransmission." He went over to the computer and punched in. "Here, look." The team gathered around and peered over his shoulder. He explained as he typed. "In 1990 the *Voyager* Planetary Mission was completed and the name was changed to the *Voyager* Interstellar Mission (VIM) and its priority was lowered."

Digits on the screen transformed themselves into readable data—readable, that is, to someone with a doctorate in astrophysics and experience watching *Voyager* data play across the screen.

"We give fifteen minutes of down link time to *Voyager* every twenty-four-hour cycle," Spurlock continued. "We get it here, then burst it back into space to an INTELSAT V-F8 Communications Satellite in synchronous orbit above Australia. The satellite relays it to Vallejo Earth Station in California. The logical thing then would be for Vallejo to forward it directly to JPL—Jet Propulsion Labs, who's responsible for *Voyager*—just down the road, but that isn't what happens. Instead, Vallejo pulses the radio wave back into space to a CONTELASC ASC-1 communications satellite, which relays it to the Goddard Space Flight Center (GSFC) in Greenbelt, Maryland, which makes a copy of the transmission for their master data banks. Goddard then bounces the message to JPL in California using a GE AMERICOM SATCOM F2R satellite." Spurlock examined the screen. "Normally we don't even look at the data—just relay it. JPL called me just three minutes ago and told me that the data had ended early. I checked and this is what I found."

Data scrolled up and then abruptly ended. "I thought at first that the data had ended because the transmission was finished, but there was still eight minutes of dish time left when this break came and it always takes the full amount of time for all the data to get in."

"Could it be a computer malfunction?" Levy asked.

"I've checked that," Spurlock replied. "No."

"Maybe the damn thing's transmitter just broke," Lamb said.

"We can check on it," Spurlock said.

"How?" Hawkins asked.

Spurlock's fingers pounded the keys as his mind did the math.

>INITIATE WIDEBAND TRANSMISSION FOR BOUNCE BACK TO VOYAGER 2 DTG 21DEC0210 ZULU. WILL MONITOR FOR RETURN DTG 21DEC1030 ZULU.

"It will take over eight hours before the radio signal I just sent will hit *Voyager 2,* bounce off the high-gain antenna dish, and return to Earth—basically just like a radar wave would work. A successful bounce back means that *Voyager* is still out there and the problem lies inside the probe somewhere."

"And if you get no bounce back?" Lamb asked.

"Then *Voyager* is gone," Spurlock answered.

A long silence filled the room.

"Hell of a coincidence," Hawkins finally muttered.

Lamb shook his head. "You all know as much as I know. I need you to give me some answers. It was your names and not mine transmitted by the Rock." He looked at his watch. "I've got some other things I need to attend to."

Lamb made his way to the door and the door swung shut behind them, leaving the team to ponder this additional piece of information.

FIRST CONTACT

DSCC 14, Australia
21 DECEMBER 1995, 1200 LOCAL
21 DECEMBER 1995, 0230 ZULU

HAWKINS LOOKED AT THE TEAM MEMBERS. "ANYONE WANT
to get some chow?"

Fran stood up and stretched out her shoulders. "I
could use a little break."

Hawkins looked at Levy and Batson, but both indicated negatively. Together, Fran and he left the con-
ference room and made their way to the small mess
hall in the basement of the building.

"Sounds like you know Mr. Lamb from somewhere else," Fran commented.

"We've worked together before," Hawkins answered.

"You two go back a ways?"

"Five years," Hawkins acknowledged.

They entered the small cafeteria and Hawkins

97

held off on any further conversation until they had their food and were sitting in a booth.

"You saw my folder. Over four years ago I was picked to form a new special-operations unit. A team that would do the jobs that Delta or any of those other high-speed units wouldn't be able to for practical and political reasons. We were answerable only to the President.

"My military career was finished the minute I went on that team, as were those of the other nineteen men and four women who joined."

"You have women on your team?" Fran was surprised.

"Yes. They passed the requirements and it's very useful on certain ops to have a woman. Throws the bad guys for a second or two, and sometimes that's all you need." He smiled. "Besides, women think differently in certain circumstances and sometimes that different perspective can be very useful.

"Anyway—since we wanted to be totally dedicated to doing the job, we all recognized that we had to stop thinking about the military being our career. Our career was Orion—that's what we were called. So I got Lamb to approve a half a million dollars being deposited in a special bank account for each team member. Twelve million dollars is pretty cheap when you consider the cost of a jet fighter. That allowed each of us to concentrate on the job and not worry about whether we would have a retirement someday or whether those with families would have their people taken care of."

"Sounds kind of mercenary," Fran commented.

"I suppose," Hawkins agreed. "However, it's also realistic. We no longer existed. We weren't army anymore. We weren't in any records anywhere, so we didn't even have to bother to come up with a cover story like they do in Delta. We had no monthly paycheck. No promotion boards. Nothing." He pointed at his uniform. "This is the first time I've had this on in three years. My rank of major is permanent.

"Anyway—at first things went well. We ran four real-world operations our first year. All successful. No losses. Then came the new administration. I briefed the President on our team and our mission. However, it seem like the new administration had different ideas about what we were to be used for. The President appointed Lamb as our liaison and tried slipping in some questionable missions and I had to call him on it."

"What kind of questionable missions?"

Hawkins shrugged. "It doesn't matter. Suffice it to say they were based in the U.S. and involved eliminating certain persons. You've got to remember that everything we were doing was illegal—both in the United States and outside of it. It got kind of hard to see the lines sometimes, because there really weren't any lines. So we basically had to believe the information that Lamb was feeding us. He and I went round and round sometimes about how much my people needed to know. He believed in the minimum and I believed in the maximum. On top of that, I don't believe all the minimum information he gave us was legitimate. I couldn't exactly go check on all of it. That's not to say that whatever we did wasn't in the ultimate good interests of the United States. I believe it all was, but it's just that in the intelligence arena there's a lot of manipulation going on—getting people to do mission A for reasons that are actually connected to mission B—if that makes any sense.

"And that brings us to the present situation. I think we're getting the minimum information. And I'm not sure how much of the minimum is true. I'm not even sure if my name really was on the message or if the message is real."

Fran smiled. "Games within games, eh?"

Hawkins's face was dead serious. "That's the gray world you're in now. I've lived in it for many years. The number-one rule: Trust no one. Believe nothing you're told."

"Even what you tell me?" Fran asked.

"Yeah. Even what I tell you, if you're smart." Hawkins ran a hand through his hair. "The last thing my team was working on was trying to track down those two missing nuclear weapons. They disappeared from a Soviet stockpile in what is now Kazakhstan. We got that through a HUMINT—human intelligence—source sixteen days ago. Apparently the bombs have been missing for about three weeks now. We believe a former Russian general sold them to the highest bidder. Of course, the damn Russians, or whatever the hell you call them now, didn't bother announcing the news. How the bombs got out of the country and where they went we don't know. One of those bombs is now accounted for."

Fran nodded. "Vredefort Dome."

"Right. We thought we had a line on the other one in Colombia—a drug kingpin who certainly had the money to buy one and the smuggling capability to get it from Russia to South America."

"But why would he want a nuclear bomb?"

Hawkins shook his head. "I don't know. Lamb wouldn't tell me that. I had to guess. Why would anyone want a bomb? The ultimate power, I suppose. Blackmail. Whatever. Lots of people would like one. Turns out he didn't buy one, though. We went in and extracted him. He knew nothing about it." Hawkins shrugged. "At least we took him out of the drug network, although some other scumbag will take his place."

"Four years is a long time to be doing that sort of work," Fran commented.

Hawkins shrugged. "It's all I have."

Fran pointed at the ring on his left hand. "What about your wife? Do you have kids?" As soon as she said it, she could sense the shift in Hawkins. The hard planes of his face coalesced into a mask.

"We had no children and my wife doesn't need me much now."

Fran was confused. "Are you divorced?"

"No." There was a long, awkward silence.

Fran decided not to pursue that subject any further. "What do you think the connection with the bombs is?" This was getting very close to her computer printouts. They hadn't even told her about the other bomb still out there, just about the blast at Vredefort Dome. That other bomb on the loose would have made the results even worse—if it was possible to contemplate worse than what the numbers had shown.

"I don't know. As Debra said—the Vredefort explosion came before the transmission. I think the South African radicals got one bomb and used it in the best possible way they could. I don't think they could have afforded the other one. We just picked up some intel after I got here that Libya might have the other one. I don't know. My team is still on the trail. That's the only thing that makes me think that something very important is happening—they pulled me off my team to come here. And the fact that Lamb is here. He doesn't like wasting his time on wild goose chases."

Fran thought about what her computer had predicted. "I told you my job is statistical projection. Well, I did a run after the explosion at Vredefort Dome. Fed in all the economic and political data available—although they didn't tell me there was another bomb still out there. Not that it could have turned out much worse than it did."

"I know," Hawkins said. "I just looked at the projections."

Fran pushed the plate of food aside, uneaten. "The weird thing is that this whole incident with Ayers Rock is what I'd call a wild card. There's no way anyone could have predicted this. It really skews the data."

"Is that good or bad?" Hawkins asked, thinking about the spreadsheets and summaries he had just talked about with Lamb.

"I don't know. The original future courses and their probabilities were pretty grim, so any change may be for the better. There was a fifty-nine percent chance of—"

They both looked up in surprise as an agitated Debra Levy appeared at their table with Don Batson in tow and interrupted. "There's been another transmission!"

They followed Debra through the hallways to the main control room of the communications center. The room had been cleared except for members of the team, Major Spurlock, and Lamb. Spurlock was typing away at a computer keyboard, his attention focused on the screen in front of him.

"This one is different," he said. "It's on a shifting frequency, and the content that I can get isn't in the same format."

"Let me see," Levy said. Spurlock relinquished his chair and Levy sat down. Her fingers flew over the keyboard while the other members watched. After a few minutes she sat up in the chair. "He's right. It's different in more than one way." She stared intently at the screen, ignoring the rest of the people in the room.

"But we know it came from the Rock, right?" Lamb asked.

"Yes, sir." Spurlock pointed out the large windows at the dishes. "We've kept dish four dedicated at minimum attitude in the Rock's azimuth. It picked this message up."

"Was it directed up like the first one?" Hawkins asked.

Spurlock sat at another console, leaving the one he had been at to Levy, who was working again. "This one went out with a lot less power. If we hadn't been watching for it, we never would have caught it. This was more a broadband transmission at low power in all directions. I don't think it was specifically directed at any one spot."

"What about down links?" Lamb asked. "Was it trying to communicate with the other locations like the first one?"

"No, sir. Like I said, this one was just sort of put out there—we have no idea where it was directed to. It most certainly was not a meteor burst transmission like the first. In fact, it might not necessarily be a coherent transmission."

"What does that mean?" Fran asked.

"I mean it might just be a microwave burst of energy, not necessarily a message." Spurlock shook his head. "I don't know . . . I've never seen anything like this. If it was a transmission, I'm not sure what kind of transmission it was."

Lamb was exasperated. "You'd better start explaining this a hell of lot better than you are, mister, because right now you aren't making a damn bit of sense."

Levy's voice cut in. "I think I know what has happened. At 0246 hours Zulu, or Greenwich mean, dish four picked up a microwave transmission from the vicinity of the Rock. It was monitoring a wide band width centered on the frequency of the original transmission, but scooting up and down the frequencies on a fixed rotation every twenty seconds to make sure it didn't miss anything going out on those. The transmission it picked up was not directional. The transmission lasted a total of approximately twenty-three seconds, as best as can be estimated."

Lamb leaned forward. "What do you mean 'as best as can be estimated'?"

Levy was staring at the computer screen. "The transmission was picked up initially at fourteen twenty megahertz. The computer locked on and when the frequency started shifting, the computer shifted with it. The frequency started shifting up in the spectrum, then blanked out for two seconds, then was picked up at sixteen sixty-two megahertz, then again blanked out for two seconds on the way back down. The dish picked it up again, shifting back down the spectrum until it disappeared at fourteen twenty."

"Cut to the chase," Lamb said. "What was the content of the transmission?"

"I don't know right now," Levy said. "Part was in standard binary, but Major Spurlock's and my own analyses have currently detected no discernible code."

"Who sent it?" Lamb asked. "The same transmitter that sent the first one?"

"Most likely, but that can't be guaranteed," Levy said.

"I contacted Colonel Tolliver's people out with the advance party at the Rock," Spurlock said. "The marines assure me that no one out there transmitted. Their equipment did not pick it up because they're operating lower down in the band."

Spurlock removed his glasses and rubbed the bridge of his nose nervously. "This transmission is very strange—unlike anything I've ever seen or can find a record of. The latest military radios use frequency-skipping to maintain security. This message skipped around in frequency, but it also did something else, something quite unusual, during those times when it totally disappeared from the spectrum. I don't think the transmission stopped there—I think it skipped into a form that we could not monitor. We also don't know to whom the message was transmitted. The power level was not particularly high, but by skipping off the atmosphere it could be picked up by a receiver that was expecting it, pretty much anywhere in the world."

"If whatever is in the Rock wanted to communicate with us," Hawkins said, "it could have done that like it did with the first message—using the information off the *Voyager* plate. If this transmission was sent in a way that we wouldn't even have picked up if we weren't specifically listening, and in a format we can't decode, that makes me think we weren't the designated receiver for it. Someone or something else is the intended receiver, and they did get it. The question is, who and where?"

Lamb sat still for a few seconds, distilling the confusing information. "So basically what you're telling me is that we have something in the Rock transmitting an unknown message, using means we are not sure of, to a party we don't know the identity of. Is that correct?"

"Yes, sir."

"So about the only thing we do know is that someone was meant to pick this up—someone who *could* decipher it," Lamb said.

"Yes, sir," Spurlock said.

Lamb pointed at the computer. "We need that message broken. I've got to know what's going on. I want you to make that your number-one priority—is that clear?"

"Yes, sir, it's clear," Spurlock answered. Levy didn't even bother to turn her head. She was already on a different plane of reality, working on the problem.

Lamb left the control, closely followed by Hawkins.

21 DECEMBER 1995, 1400 LOCAL
21 DECEMBER 1995, 0430 ZULU

"WHAT HAVE YOU GOT ON LEVY?" HAWKINS ASKED LAMB IN the security of the message center.

Lamb smoothed out the computer printouts and ran his finger down the lines. "Debra Lynn Levy. Born 1972, Brooklyn, New York. Her father worked for the Transit Authority as a subway mechanic. Mother worked as a secretary. No history of exceptional mental aptitude in the family. Then she was born. She began speaking at age fourteen months. Reading at two years. She was in a Head Start day care program and they referred her to Professor Allen Steinwatz at New York University, who was quite well known for his work with child prodigies.

"Steinwatz convinced the parents to allow him to accelerate her education. She graduated high school at nine. She attended MIT and graduated with a doctorate in quantum physics at fifteen. For the next seven years she worked as a researcher in the physics department there. She started teaching at seventeen but apparently there was some problem with students eight to ten years older than her taking her seriously."

"What about her personal life?" Hawkins asked.

Lamb shook his head. "Nothing. She works, teaches, and goes home. We've still got people doing some checking, but we have no record of any boyfriend—or girlfriend, for that matter."

Lamb folded over a page. "There was something interesting, though. A year ago she had a breakdown and was committed to a mental institution for two months."

"What was the cause of the problem?" Hawkins asked.

"We're having trouble getting the hospital records.

It's a very elite place in upstate New York." He looked at Hawkins. "Why the interest in Levy?"

Hawkins shook his head. "I don't know. There's something about her that makes me feel uneasy. I can't put a finger on it. Let's just call it a gut feeling."

That was good enough for Lamb. "I'll get the records."

"Any problems other than the breakdown?"

Lamb looked at the security folder on her. "No. Only the fact that she's young and has never been exposed to this type of situation before."

"What about this crater person—Pencak?"

"She's on the way. We picked her up three hours ago. Should be here late tonight or early tomorrow."

"What about her background?" Hawkins asked.

Lamb frowned. "Not good. She's a class-one weirdo who also happens to do some brilliant work concerning strange geological formations." His face twisted, the muscles around his deformed cheek jumping. "We've got her listed in the computer as having made six trips to the former Soviet Union. First one in '59. Last one in '87."

Hawkins understood how Lamb felt about that. "What else?"

"Langley and the FBI had a folder on her. She had a Russian boyfriend for a while—they wrote back and forth quite a bit. A Felix Zigorski, an aerodynamics expert who was involved with their space program. It all seemed pretty innocent, but they wanted to keep an eye on her."

"Back up," Hawkins said. "Tell me about her from the start."

Lamb scanned the faxed printout. "Not much here. Born in Hutchinson, Kansas, in 1938. Her parents had a farm there. Both were killed in a car wreck when she was sixteen. She was banged up pretty bad and also severely burned. She was in the hospital for a while and then on her own—no known living relatives. Sold the farm and went to the University of New Mexico at Albuquerque. Undergraduate major was physics. Got a doctorate in geology. Then she went to Meteor Crater and has been there ever since. She teaches occasionally as adjunct faculty at various universities. Travels a bit. Writes articles for scientific journals."

"Personal life?"

"Nothing so far. Apparently she doesn't look too good. She lost an eye in the accident and was badly scarred."

Hawkins stretched out his back muscles. "I'm going to have to keep an eye on her."

"That you are." Lamb absently ran a hand over the reports on his desk. "How are you doing?"

"I'm fine."

"How's your wife?"

"The same," Hawkins answered succinctly, his tone indicating that issue was not to be discussed.

Lamb switched the subject quickly. "I had security go through the team members' personal baggage and they found several bottles stashed in Batson's small carryon bag. I had them confiscated—this isn't the time or the place to put up with that stuff."

Hawkins shook his head. "Sounds like we've got a winning team here. Anything else I should know about?"

Lamb pressed a button on his desk and the door opened. Colonel Tolliver who'd been waiting outside walked in, his fatigues drenched with sweat. "Colonel Tolliver just flew in from the Rock. What's the tactical situation?"

Tolliver pulled out a rag and wiped sand from his forehead. "The Rock is secure. We're a hundred and eighty feet in and the drilling is going well."

"Strategic SITREP?" Lamb continued.

Tolliver frowned. "The Russian Task Force is making the Australians very nervous. My Aussie counterpart says he's getting a lot of pressure from his higher-ups to find out what the hell is going on. That's besides the flak about the drilling."

"What's the location of the task force?"

"They're in the Coral Sea still heading south. Intelligence believes they will go around the east coast of Australia and position themselves to the south in the Great Australian Bight, a thousand miles to the south of here.

"One of the dish antennas on the *Gagarin* is oriented directly toward our location. The other tracks the sky above Australia in a sweep pattern. We're picking up a lot of secure SATCOM traffic between the Task Force flagship and Moscow."

"How long before they're in position?"

"Thirty-six hours."

"Think they picked up the second transmission?" Lamb asked.

Tolliver shrugged. "We were on top of the Rock and didn't pick it up because we weren't up in that band width. Depends if the Russians were—we have no way of knowing."

Something had been in the back of Hawkins's mind. "Is there any activity at the site in Siberia?"

Lamb reached behind him and pulled out some papers. "Yes. Our eye in the sky is picking up extensive military maneuvers being carried out there. They're looking for something."

"Their Rock," Hawkins mused out loud. "What else?"

"Langley is concerned that the Russians will try to infiltrate the project here."

Hawkins nodded. He knew that. He was worried about it, too, and having Levy here already and bringing in Pencak didn't thrill him. He looked at Tolliver. "Remind your men that we're looking for more than direct military action. It's more likely that any action that occurs will be covert. They're to check everyone and take nothing for granted. It's possible we've already been infiltrated."

"Yes, sir." Tolliver paused. "Of course, you know that the most likely source of a compromise is one of the outsiders that have been called in."

Lamb fixed the marine with a cold stare. "I know that."

He dismissed Tolliver and then looked back at

Hawkins. "Things are not going well in the big picture. There's already political instability in several Third World countries. The governments are keeping the loss of the gold reserves quiet, but some of those leaders are already scrambling to cover their own position—never mind worry about the welfare of their people. It looks like there will be at least four new governments before the end of the year."

He let out a deep breath and again changed the subject. "Anything from your people on the bomb search?"

"They're pursuing two possibilities," Hawkins replied. "One is Libya."

"He certainly had the money to buy a bomb," Lamb noted. "And it fits with some other intel I've been getting. Qaddafi's suddenly begun making noises again about his line of death in the Gulf of Sidra. The President is thinking about using the Sixth Fleet to push him on it. Intel believes that Qaddafi wants to draw the fleet in and then have a small boat—or more likely a submarine—with the bomb on board try to get near one of the carriers and detonate it."

Hawkins frowned. "Why is the President reacting, then?"

"That's his job. All I know is that a carrier task force is cruising the thirty-third parallel waiting on the President's word to cross." Lamb sounded frustrated. "I'm sort of out of the loop here, sitting on my ass in the middle of Australia." He shook his head. "What's Orion's status on Libya?"

"They've infiltrated two small recon teams. Nothing yet, according to the last transmission."

"What's the other lead?"

Hawkins picked a slim file folder marked TOP SECRET/Q CLEARANCE. "They picked up a smuggler who disclosed under questioning that he delivered something to an Arab. A check of his cargo hold picked up slight traces of radioactivity. That and the smuggler's description of the package makes it possible it was one of the bombs. He transported his cargo from a point on the northern shore of the Black Sea down to the Mediterranean and crossloaded offshore of Syria to the Arab."

"Do they have a line on the Arab?"

"Not yet, but they're pushing it hard."

"Could it have gone to Qaddafi?"

"Possible. Or it could be someone else—that is, if it was one of the bombs. It could even have been the South African bomb on its way down there."

Lamb rubbed his forehead wearily. It could be anyone in that cesspool known as the Middle East. The Syrians would love to use one on the Israelis. The Lebanese against each other. The Jordanians against just about anyone. "All right. Let me know right away if you break anything out on that second transmission."

Hawkins didn't move. "You've been deploying some of my people in Orion about, without consulting me."

"Yes, I have. We're *both* out of the loop here. We have to be prepared for some contingencies, and your people are the best ones trained for action if we need it.

Hawkins nodded and left the van, accepting the fact but intensely disliking that he had to accept it. He had a feeling they no longer were in control of much of anything—this whole business seemed to be an exercise in reaction, which was not a mode of operations that he preferred.

21 DECEMBER 1995, 1950 LOCAL
21 DECEMBER 1995, 1020 ZULU

When Hawkins got back to the control center, Fran and Don were gathered in front of the computer, peering over Spurlock's shoulders, awaiting the answer to their eight-hour question on *Voyager*. Levy did not appear to have moved from her position in front of the other computer. On Spurlock's screen the messages from the computer slowly scrolled up as the seconds went by.

<DISK ALIGNING V154P657 VOYAGER 2 VIM PROJECT.

<DISK ALIGNED V154P657 VOYAGER 2 VIM PROJECT.

<ALL SYSTEMS CHECK. AWAITING BOUNCE BACK TRANSMISSION.

Spurlock looked at the digital readout on the upper left-hand corner of the screen. It slowly clicked off the seconds, winding down. "Five seconds," he muttered unnecessarily.

The last digit flickered into a zero and then stopped. Spurlock blinked and looked at the screen.

<ALL SYSTEMS CHECK. AWAITING BOUNCE BACK TRANSMISSION.

He grabbed the keyboard and furiously typed out a message.

>CONFIRM NO BOUNCE BACK V154P657 VOYAGER 2 VIM PROJECT.

The reply was brief and to the point.

<CONFIRMED. NEGATIVE ON BOUNCE BACK V154P657 VOYAGER 2 VIM PROJECT.

His fingers slammed the keys again.

>CONFIRM BOUNCE BACK TRANSMITTED DTG 21DEC2010 ZULU.

<CONFIRMED WIDEBAND BOUNCE BACK TRANSMITTED DTG 21DEC2010 ZULU

Spurlock wasn't going to give up.

>CONFIRM DIRECTION OF BOUNCE BACK WAS
V154P657 VOYAGER 2 VIM PROJECT.

There was a ten-second pause during which Spurlock's fingers gouged the arms of his chair.

<CONFIRMED DIRECTION OF BOUNCE BACK
V154P657 VOYAGER 2 VIM PROJECT.

Spurlock let his fingers slide off the keyboard and turned to the others. *"Voyager 2* is gone."

"Gone?" Fran repeated.

"It's no longer out there."

"Maybe just the satellite's dish is damaged and that's why you didn't get a bounce back," Hawkins offered.

"Even without the dish we would have gotten some sort of signal off the body of the satellite itself— a radar image." He pointed at the screen. "There's nothing out there where *Voyager* should be."

Silence settled over the room as each person contemplated what that meant. After a minute Levy slid her chair back from the keyboard. She didn't even appear to have heard what had happened to *Voyager* as she turned to the other members of the team.

"I think I have some answers to the questions raised by the second transmission."

"Have you broken the code?" Hawkins asked.

"We don't have the entire message. Actually," she

said, "I think there are several messages, one of which was directed to us but the main part of which was directed elsewhere."

"Give us what you do have," Hawkins said.

Levy tapped the screen. "It's very strange. I think the part that slides up and down the microwave scale —from fourteen twenty to sixteen sixty-two megahertz—was actually a lead in and out to the main transmission—sort of like tuning a radio. I think the key message was in the blank parts."

"How can that be?" Lamb asked, confused.

"Well, I think—and it's only a theory—that the message is getting skipped about in time, somehow." Seeing a blank look on the others' faces, Levy continued. "When you transmit a message, you have several options in order to make it difficult for someone else to intercept and decrypt: You can vary the amplitude, the frequency, the message itself. But the best way would be simply to not have the message intercepted in the first place. If I had a way of transmitting where I could bounce the message back or forward a little in time, it would make it impossible for the person listening to pick it up."

"Is that technology possible?" Hawkins asked.

"We don't have it."

"Do the Russians?"

"Possibly, but not likely," Levy said. "Remember, that this only speculation on my part."

Her eyes took on the unfocused look that Hawkins was getting used to. "The key to it all is that microwave transmissions are made up of atomic matter.

This makes the possibility of being able to skip them about in time infinitely likelier than achieving the same end with larger objects. In fact, it is quite well accepted in the scientific community that there are a myriad of tiny wormholes—which are essentially time tunnels, or what you often hear about in science fiction as a warp tunnel—at the subatomic level.

"If you could surround the core of your message with negative energy matter, it would keep it intact through the hole. And since negative energy matter can be generated relatively easily, the real key to the problem is to generate a tiny wormhole—and of course to have a destination. Basically you would have a miniature tunnel through space, which means a small degree of time-shifting, since the message is not following a normal spatial path.

"The significance of such a message, though, is not that we can't intercept it in the first place, but rather that it is essential for an advanced race that is spread over the cosmos to be able to have what we would consider almost instantaneous communication over vast distances. Even at the speed of light a message from the nearest star system—Alpha Centauri—would take over four years to make it to our solar system. But if you could make use of these wormholes, you could get your message to your intended audience almost instantaneously across vast distances."

Levy halted, noting the way everyone was staring at her. "Well, that's what I think might be happening here, and not only can't I prove it but even if I could, there's not much you or I could do about it because we don't have the technology to receive it." She idly tapped her fingers on the desk. "If we did, space travel at a speed greater than light would be the next logical step, and we can barely put a satellite up into space. This technology is light-years ahead of what we have here on Earth now."

"Do you have any idea what such a transmitter would look like?" Hawkins asked.

"No. But, as I said, it would certainly be different from anything we've ever seen. Of course it might be so small that it could be easily concealed or it might be larger than the Great Pyramid. I have no idea. I only know the subatomic theories involved."

"You said that there was a part of the message that you think was directed to us," Fran noted. "Did you get that part at least?"

Levy nodded. "At the very beginning and the very end—beginning at fourteen twenty and sixteen sixty-two megahertz, where it would be likely that we would be listening, there were two words in the same digital form as the first transmission. It took me a while to decode it, because even with just the two words expressed digitally, the frequency was shifting. The binary code was spread over ninety megahertz in each case."

Hawkins restrained his impatience with great difficulty. "Could you please tell us what *that* message is?"

Levy turned and hit one key on the computer and pointed. Hawkins looked at the two words.

WELCOME DEBRA

"Is this someone's idea of a joke?" Batson demanded.

Levy shook her head. "No. That format is the same as the one used on *Voyager* and the first transmission." She pointed at the computer. "That's the Rock talking." She smiled dreamily. "It's just saying hi."

Hawkins reached into the desk drawer behind him and drew out several aspirin. With a swig of water he downed three.

THE ROCK

Central Australia
22 DECEMBER 1995, 0700 LOCAL
21 DECEMBER 1995, 2130 ZULU

HAWKINS WATCHED THE DUSTY TERRAIN FLIT BY UNDERNEATH as the helicopter banked slightly and then leveled. The other members of the team were peering out the side closer to them, looking at the sprawling Australian outback. The low-lying dunes that stretched to the horizon were an off-red color with an occasional sprinkling of rocks. It reminded Hawkins, though on a far larger scale, of west Texas, where water holes and places of civilization were few and far between.

"We'll see the Olgas in a minute or two," the pilot announced in their headsets. "Once we get over them you can see the Rock straight out on the horizon."

The seat bottom pushed up against Hawkins as the pilot increased altitude. A series of strange rock formations appeared ahead, like large isolated stones set on edge in the desert floor.

"There's thirty-six of them," the pilot commented as the hodgepodge assortment of rocks drew close.

The domes and pillars of the Olgas passed by quickly and then they had their first glimpse of Ayers Rock looming on the horizon. "It's beautiful," Hawkins heard Debra Levy whisper into her mike.

The sun was bouncing its rays off the eastern face, coloring the rock bright red. It looked like a hunched whale beached upon a flat plain of sand. It appeared totally improbable—a massive monolith rising out of what was otherwise, for miles around, flat terrain. As they drew closer, the color mellowed out to a lighter shade of red. From the distance it had looked deceptively small, but as the miles decreased, the Rock expanded to fill up more and more of the horizon until finally it *was* the entire horizon. The pilot gained altitude to crest the top.

Hawkins leaned over and looked down as the helicopter came to a hover, a thousand feet directly above. The humped side shape changed to that of a striated, cuddled-up fetus from the top. The surface was streaked with the results of millions of years of erosion by wind and the scant rain that falls in the desert. The streaks ran in parallel lines, looking smoothly cut from this far up, but as they descended, the convoluted dips and ridges that pockmarked the lines could plainly be seen.

The closer they got to the Rock, the more it surrounded Hawkins's consciousness. He'd seen larger and more spectacular views from a distance, but up close Ayers Rock was overwhelming. He found it hard to believe that this was all one solid rock, looming over the desert with a six-mile base. The most immediate thought one had on seeing it was to wonder how it had gotten there in the middle of the desert.

The sides were steeply sloped, dropping to a narrow fertile band all around the base. The rock itself was nonpermeable, so any rainfall poured off onto the surrounding sand, allowing growth there that would never have survived beyond a hundred feet from the base.

On top, in the center where the Rock was almost flat, large canvas covers were stretched, marring the beauty of the whole. Hawkins knew that the mine shaft and their new home were underneath that. The canvas was an attempt to partially defeat satellite investigation.

"We've got a helipad right on top, so I'm going to put down on that," the pilot informed them.

Hawkins saw the staked-down VS-17 panels marking the metal grating pitoned into the rock that made up the landing zone. He'd also noted the strong military presence in the area despite the attempts at hiding it. Brown camouflage nets dotted the desert around the Rock in a scattering unrecognizable to the nonmilitary mind. Hawkins overlaid the fields of fire from the positions in his mind's eye and nodded— Tolliver had deployed his men well. As they were about to touch down he spotted men hidden in the crevices of the Rock itself with shoulder-fired heat-

seeking antiaircraft missiles at their sides—a supple-
ment to the larger, tracked antiaircraft systems spread
out on the desert floor. He'd also spotted the ring of
Australian troops outside of Tolliver's perimeter, put
there to keep away the curious and the media. Two
Australian Cobra gunships were circling about to
keep aerial sightseers away.

The helicopter settled with a bump and Hawkins
slid open the cargo door. Several troops were there to
grab luggage. The team hopped out and followed
Lamb toward a large environmental shelter hidden
under the canvas covers. To the left Hawkins could
see a hastily put-together metal shack with numerous
cables running into it—the shaft entrance. The rumble of several large portable generators filled the air.
A high-pitched whining noise overlaid the sound of
the generators—the drill at work in the shaft.

Sweat was already staining the back of Hawkins's
fatigues as they entered the shelter. There was no relief inside; the dry, murderously hot air wrapped him
in a blanket of suffocating warmth.

"Sorry about the conditions. We've got some AC
units, but when the drills are running we have to keep
the power going to them," Lamb explained. "We're
having some more generators flown in later today."

A dozen or so metal folding chairs were placed
precariously on the hastily laid down plywood floor-
ing. There were three people already in the tent—
Hawkins recognized Tolliver. The second had on the
uniform of an Australian general. The third wore
nothing but a small cloth wrapped around his loins.

His skin was pitch black and wrinkled from both age and the sun. He sported a large bushy gray beard and two jet-black eyes that regarded the newcomers with suspicion.

Lamb did the introductions. "Ladies and gentlemen, this is General Anderson. He's the senior Australian representative here."

General Anderson shook everyone's hand with a distinct lack of warmth. He was a large stocky man with a florid face bathed in a sheen of sweat. His thinning hair was mussed and he looked none too pleased.

"And this is Tintinjara. He's the supervisor here at Kakadu National Park."

Hawkins considered the old man. He knew this was a farce—they'd been instructed by Lamb in no uncertain terms to say nothing to any Australians. Lamb was in very bad spirits—the content of the second transmission had not gone over well with him either. Even though Spurlock had validated the deciphering, it was clear to Hawkins that Lamb wasn't putting much stock in Levy or her theories.

It was also obvious to Hawkins that he wasn't the only one who knew this meeting was part of a political play—the Aborigine didn't shake hands, his dark eyes simply taking in each of them one by one as they sat down.

"I've asked General Anderson and Mr. Tintinjara here to give you an on-site briefing on the background to Ayers Rock," Lamb explained. "The Australians are very concerned with what we are doing here and—"

"Extremely concerned and very upset," Tintinjara interrupted. It was surprising to hear an Australian accent coming out of the man's mouth. "This is my people's land and it has been our land for countless generations since the beginning of time. We have filed our protest in the Parliament but that has not stopped what you are doing." His eyes were hard as he stared at Lamb. "It is very nice of you to *invite* me here. This is *my* land. You are the guests."

Lamb held up a placating hand. "I understand that. These are extraordinary times and I am sorry we must use extraordinary means to try to deal with them."

Tintinjara shook his head, not buying it. "I do not understand what is going on. You say Uluru has spoken, but my people have not heard."

Hawkins frowned and glanced at Fran. She met his look and shook her head slightly. Lamb nodded gravely. "Yes. But we have heard. And we need to find out who has sent the message."

"Aye," Anderson spoke for the first time. "But drilling into the Rock?" He shook his head. "I've been instructed to go along with you all on that, but I've got to tell you—"

"There will be no trace of what we are doing when we are finished," Lamb interrupted. "We are as concerned as you are about Ayers Rock and its role in your society."

"I doubt that very much," Tintinjara disagreed.

There was a long pause and then Anderson filled the silence.

"Well, we must deal with things." He looked at the members of the team. "What is it you wish to know?"

Hawkins knew they had everything they needed in the computer, but it was time for some public relations. He hated this.

"Some basic background information would be helpful," Lamb said.

Tintinjara's face was still, as if he knew the question was bogus. Anderson picked up a file folder from a briefcase next to his chair. "Well, basic stats you probably already know. Highest point 1,131 feet. A mile and a half wide. Two miles across. It's six miles to go around the base." Anderson wiped a hand across his soaked forehead. "It can get up to a hundred and thirty in the summer, which you all are just about in the middle of. That's fortunate in a way, though, because if you'd come in the winter, that would have been peak tourist season. We've had to turn some people away, but not too many. The media are abuzz about what's going on, but we've kept them in the dark also, although how much longer we'll be able to is questionable. We've already caught two reporters coming in out of the desert in a Land-Rover, trying to get around the roadblocks.

"The actual rock is feldspar-rich sandstone. It was uplifted from an ancient seabed millions of years ago." He pointed down at the wood planking. "The markings on the surface are the result of eons of erosion from wind and rain. The water hole here is the only active year-round one for hundreds of miles around.

"The first white man spotted the rock in 1873 and named it for Sir Henry Ayers, who was the Premier of South Australia at the time." Anderson inclined his head toward Tintinjara. "There is a movement afoot to change the name back to the original Aborigine name—Uluru. There are strong emotions on both sides about the issue."

Tintinjara took that as his cue to explain his perspective. His voice was a low whisper, almost drowned out by the rumble from the mine shaft. "Uluru rose out of the plain at the end of the creation period. In the beginning—before the world took on its present form—the carpet-snake people came out of the east and settled at the water hole here. Then came the venomous-snake men from the west and they attacked the carpet-snake people. At the close of the battle Uluru rose up, a symbol of all the fighting." He waved his hand slowly about. "Every pit, every outcropping, every mark on this Rock, has a special significance to my people."

"The spot at which we began drilling did not have any particular significance," Lamb interjected. "We have tried—"

"The entire Rock is significant," Tintinjara countered.

Anderson seconded that from his perspective. "Ayers Rock is called the 'heart' of Australia. You're drilling right into our heart, mate, and there's a lot of folks that aren't very happy about it."

Hawkins could tell Lamb was trying to maintain a diplomatic front. If this had been the United States and they were drilling through a Native American burial site, Hawkins had no doubt but that there would be no representative from a tribe present. National security would ensure that. Here, however, they had to try and placate.

"We understand," Lamb said. "Let me assure you that we will do everything we can to minimize any . . ."

Hawkins tuned out the political role-playing and walked out of the tent. If anything significant happened, the other members of the team would pick it up. He could feel the eyes of several guards on him as he walked over to the metal tower surrounding the drill hole. The marine at the door noted the access tag clipped to his fatigue pocket but still demanded to see Hawkins's ID.

Once inside, the temperature shot up a good twenty degrees from the sweltering heat without as two air-conditioner units strained under an impossible load. Four men stripped to their waists were working on a two-story platform that looked like a miniature oil-drilling derrick. One of the men noted Hawkins, searched his sterile uniform for any indication of rank, and, failing that, noted the 9mm pistol strapped in a thigh holster and the look on Hawkins's face. He came over, his black skin glistening.

"Can I help you, sir?"

Hawkins extended his hand. "Major Hawkins. How's it going?"

The man looked no more than twenty-five and seemed surprised at Hawkins's hand being thrust out. He awkwardly took it. "Captain Tomkins, sir. Third BLT Engineers." He glanced over his shoulder as a load of crumbled rock was pulled out of the borehole and loaded onto a small cart and hauled away. "We're over halfway down." Tomkins seemed to be trying to size Hawkins up. "Any idea what we're looking for, sir?"

Normally the inquisitiveness would have bothered Hawkins, but in this case he felt a strong affinity for the captain. "No. Wish I did." He walked over and climbed up the ladder to the platform where the other three engineers were, Tomkins following. Leaning over, he could see the drill pipe disappearing down into a three-foot-diameter hole in the red rock. There were no lights, so he could only see a few feet into the hole. He ignored the whine of the drill, the rumble of the rock shards coming up the small conveyer, and the presence of the men around him. He felt himself drawn to the hole, going down five hundred feet, to what? Hawkins shivered and broke his gaze away.

"How long before you get there?"

"Forty-eight hours, working this way. Whatever 'there' is," Tomkins replied.

22 DECEMBER 1995, 0800 LOCAL
21 DECEMBER 1995, 2230 ZULU

"WE KNOW ABOUT THE TRANSMISSIONS," FRAN SAID, "BUT what about the disappearance of *Voyager*? How could that have happened?"

Their new place of business was a government-issue nuclear-biological-chemical (NBC) shelter, designed for MASH units to be able to operate inside while deployed in severe climatic conditions. Central Australia certainly fit that bill, Hawkins thought, as the unit's air conditioner strained to keep the temperature barely tolerable inside the inflated white walls.

"I've studied what happened there," Levy answered, her eyes taking in the entire team from behind her thick glasses. "I've done some consulting work in the past for JPL—Jet Propulsion Laboratory—which runs *Voyager,* so I have some background on the subject."

"Do they have any idea at JPL what happened to it?" Fran asked.

"No." Levy shrugged. "Their best guess is that *Voyager* hit another object, perhaps a small meteor or comet. At the speed it was moving, such contact would have been disastrous."

"What do *you* think happened to it?" Hawkins asked.

"I don't know," Levy replied. "There is no data to work off, other than the lack of a bounce back. It could have been destroyed in a collision with another object, but the odds of that are slim. The fact that the message was sent using data off the plate from the probe indicates that perhaps there was some other agent at work."

"Some other agent?" Hawkins voice was sharp. "What do you mean by that?"

"I don't know."

"Can I throw something out?" Don Batson asked.

"Go ahead," Riley said.

"I don't think we should get closedminded here and totally focus on the four items you've listed on that chart. Those are the four things we've been given, but they don't stand alone. Each is part of a larger scheme or tapestry, if you prefer to look at it that way."

Hawkins frowned. "What do you mean?"

"Take the nuclear explosion at Vredefort Dome, for example," Don said. "You say there's a second bomb missing, right? Well, you have to factor that second bomb into the situation. The same with *Voyager*. Where was it located when it disappeared? What was its last message? What about the entire history of *Voyager*—maybe there's something there that has a bearing on the situation. Do you see what I mean?"

"You're saying let's not get tunnel vision," Hawkins replied.

"Right."

Hawkins briefly drummed his fingers on the table-top. "All right. Don has a good point. Let's get back to work and keep in mind that there's a hell of a lot more to all this than is readily apparent." The four went back to their hastily installed computer terminals, each lost in his or her own direction.

Hawkins was tapped in to the secure line to Orion headquarters, updating himself on the search for the remaining bomb and also going back over all the intelligence they had previously obtained, looking at it in light of present circumstances. Batson was studying all the geological data on Ayers Rock and the other sites, trying to determine possible links. Fran was reworking her projections, trying to figure out how all that had just occurred could affect things.

Debra Levy cleared her screen and sat in thought for ten minutes, her mind flitting over the information. She glanced up at the little diagram Hawkins had drawn and considered it in light of what Batson had said. She leaned forward and her fingers flew over the keyboard.

>*ACCESS* MILITARY RECORDS.

<*ACCESSED.*

>*REQUEST* INFORMATION AS FOLLOWS:
LOCATION: AUSTRALIA.
DATE: AUGUST 6, 1945.

<*ACCESSED.* SIX HUNDRED AND FORTY-TWO ENTRIES. TO BRING UP FIRST RECORD, HIT F-1.

>*SEARCH:* KEY WORDS: RADIO TRANSMISSIONS.

<SEARCH COMPLETED. ONE HUNDRED AND SIX EN-
TRIES. TO BRING UP FIRST RECORD, HIT F-1.

>SEARCH: KEY WORD: INTERFERENCE.

<SEARCH COMPLETED. THREE ENTRIES. TO BRING UP
FIRST RECORD, HIT F-1.

Levy tapped the uppermost key on the left side of
the board.

<ENTRY ONE: USPACCOM, SYDNEY, REPORTS INTER-
FERENCE WITH TRANSMISSIONS TO FLEET ELE-
MENTS OPERATING IN SOLOMON ISLAND AREAS.

ENTRY TWO: USPACOM, SYDNEY, REPORTS INTEFER-
ENCE WITH TRANSMISSION TO KWAJALEIN ISLAND.

ENTRY THREE: 14TH SIGNAL COMPANY, 23RD REGI-
MENTAL COMBAT TEAM, REPORTS LOSS OF RADIO
COMMUNICATIONS DURING UNIT MANEUVERS VI-
CINITY TOWN OF KATHERINE, NORTHERN TERRI-
TORY.

Levy used the cursors to highlight the third entry.
She hit the enter key to bring up more information.

<ENTRY THREE: 14TH SIGNAL COMPANY, 23RD REG-
IMENTAL COMBAT TEAM, REPORTS LOSS OF RADIO
COMMUNICATIONS DURING UNIT MANEUVERS VI-

CINITY TOWN OF KATHERINE, NORTHERN TERRI-
TORY.

1LT O'HENRY, 14TH SIGNAL COMPANY, FILED A
MIJI REPORT AS FOLLOWS:

UNIT: 14TH SIG/CO. *ALPHA:* (REPORT NUMBER):
6/8/45-12.

BRAVO: (POSITION OF TRANSMITTER/RECEIVER): 23
MILES SOUTHEAST, KATHERINE, NORTHERN TERRI-
TORY, GRID AKH238765, MAPSHEET AUS354.

CHARLIE: (AZIMUTH OF INTERFERENCE): 173 DE-
GREES.

DELTA: (DATE AND TIME OF INTERFERENCE):
6AUG45/0823.

ECHO: (DURATION OF INTERFERENCE): 16 MINUTES.

FOXTROT: (TYPE OF INTERFERENCE): BROADBAND.

GOLF: (COMMENTS): ALL TRANSMISSION AND RE-
CEPTION CAPABILITY WAS OVERWHELMED FOR DU-
RATION OF INTERFERENCE.

Levy leaned back in her seat and stared at the
screen, then began typing again, doing the same
search, only this time for 9 August 1945. When she
had that information she quickly scanned it, then left

her computer and looked at the atlas. She flipped
open to Australia and made a few calculations before
announcing, "I have something interesting here."

The other three members paused in their work
and looked at her.

"I've found two military reports of similar radio
disturbances of great power. When I draw a line along
the azimuths from the two reports, the lines intersect
at Ayers Rock."

"So this wasn't the first transmission out of the
Rock?" Fran asked.

"Apparently not," Levy replied.

"When did these two disturbances occur?" Hawkins asked.

"Six August 1945 and nine August 1945."

"Nineteen forty-five!" Hawkins repeated. "Are
you sure?"

"It's in the computer," Levy said.

"But—" Batson shook his head. "I don't get it.
Why then and now?"

Fran was looking at Levy intently. "What were
those dates again?"

Levy repeated them.

"You know what happened on those dates, don't
you?"

Levy nodded. "On six August 1945 the United
States dropped an atomic weapon on Hiroshima, followed by a second bomb on Nagasaki on nine August.
In each instance, approximately three hours after the
explosion, a very powerful radio transmission over-

whelmed all military radio receivers within eight hundred miles of Ayers Rock."

A long silence ensued, finally broken by Hawkins. "That's almost fifty years ago. Surely . . ." He paused and shook his head. "Are there any other records of transmissions out of Ayers Rock?"

"Those are the only two I could find," Levy said. "There might be more. I went specifically to those two dates."

"Why?" Hawkins asked.

"Because it occurred to me that maybe the arrows you drew on that diagram were correct, and, if so, the nuclear explosion under Vredefort Dome might have precipitated the transmission. I decided to check the only other time in history where man has used nuclear weapons against humans."

"What about all the nuclear testing that's gone on over the last fifty years?" Fran asked. "Have there been transmissions after each of those?"

In response Levy sat down at the computer. "I'll check."

The sound of her fingers hitting keys lasted for five minutes, then she looked up. "I can't find any other indications of transmissions out of Ayers Rock, but you have to remember that we're accessing only U.S. records. The only other time we had troops present here was during World War II."

"What about this station?" Batson asked. "It's been here since the fifties. Surely it would have picked up any other broadcasts."

Levy looked at her screen. "The one three days ago was the only one recorded here."

"If whatever is in the Rock transmitted right after the Hiroshima and Nagasaki explosions, then it's been in there for fifty years and it had the same capability that long ago. If it is a touchstone," he said, looking at Levy, "then it's been activated before."

"Yes, but we never knew it was activated," Levy noted. "And we never tried digging down to it."

Hawkins thought of the chill he'd felt looking down the shaft, into the darkness. What were they uncovering here?

"For God's sake, let's not get paranoid," Batson said.

"I'm not paranoid," Levy said calmly. "I'm just looking at the facts as they exist."

Hawkins held up both hands. "We need to—" He paused as the flap to the tent opened and Lamb walked in, followed by an old woman leaning on a cane.

PENCAK

Ayers Rock, Australia
22 DECEMBER 1995, 0815 LOCAL
21 DECEMBER 1995, 2345 ZULU

FRAN FORCED HERSELF NOT TO LET HER SHOCK SHOW AS DR. Pencak was introduced by Lamb. They'd been briefed that the older women had been severely injured as a teenager in a car accident, but Fran had never seen anyone so scarred. Surely modern plastic surgery could have corrected some of the deformities, Fran thought as she viewed the older woman.

Pencak took a seat and her single gray eye took in each of them, one by one, betraying no emotion. She laid her finely engraved cane with a large silver handle across her knees. "So. You went through quite bit of trouble to get me here. What do you wish to know?"

"You were briefed on the transmission?" Hawkins asked.

"Yes. But my name was not among those on the message. So why am I here?"

A voice snapped across the room. "You know why." Fran was surprised at Batson's testiness. He seemed uneasy with Pencak, and the information Levy had uncovered just prior to Pencak's entrance had upset him. "One of the reception sites was very close to, or actually in, Meteor Crater."

Hawkins stood and gestured at the geologist, trying to calm things down a little. "Don says you're the world's foremost expert on Meteor Crater. Is there something there like what we have discovered so far in Ayers Rock?"

"From what I've been briefed, you haven't discovered anything in Ayers Rock yet," Pencak replied calmly. "All you have is a radio transmission and sonar and EM reading of an anomaly in the Rock indicating there may be an open space down there."

She waved her withered hand as Hawkins started to reply. "No, no, young man. Don't get all excited. You have a problem and you are approaching it in the manner almost everyone in the population approaches problems. That's by butting the top of their head against the wall they perceive the problem to be and hoping that sooner or later they will break through and the solution will be on the other side."

She graced Hawkins with a twisted smile. "But that's not the way it should be. You need to use what's inside your head. Let me see your analysis of the reception sites."

Lamb put the overlay on the overhead projector

and turned it on. Pencak looked at it for a moment and then picked up an alcohol pen. She circled the site in North America.

"Meteor Crater. My home. You have all the numbers about size and depth and all that gobbledygook. All I can tell you is that there is nothing in the crater to receive the transmission from Ayers Rock. Nothing at present in the crater, that is. The bottom has been extensively swept over with various types of sensing devices—all searching for the core of the meteor that supposedly made the crater. It has never been found. Nor has anything like what you think you have in Ayers Rock."

She waved the dead hand again, once more cutting off Hawkins. She tapped the projector. "Despite its name it is not certain that Meteor Crater was created by a meteorite hitting the earth. That is simply the most widely accepted theory. There are others."

She circled the site in South America. "Campo del Cielo, Argentina. Actually, there are several craters there. All very close together. The theory is that several meteors hit, or one broke apart prior to impact and produced the same effect.

"Ah—Ries Basin." She put an X over the site in Europe. "Very interesting. Very large. Diameter almost fourteen miles. They've found boulders over thirty-five miles away that were ejected from that crater. Some think Ries was formed by volcanic action. Others by multiple meteor strikes." Pencak idly rubbed the dead side of her face. "People are so secure nowadays. They think it has all been solved. All the riddles of the world. Many even think most of the puzzles of space have also been solved."

She tapped the overhead. "Ries Basin hasn't been solved conclusively either. By the present school of thought sixty percent of researchers regard meteors as the agent that formed Ries Basin; forty percent volcanic action. Correct, Dr. Batson?"

. Don was startled to be called on. "Well . . . yes, that's true."

"Thank you. The bottom line is neither answer fits exactly." The marker crept south to Africa. "Vredefort Dome. Here the experts are very confused. The topography and the geology fit no existing pattern. No crater there, but the earth around the dome appears to have been buckled and in many places literally inverted by some massive force a long time ago. Unexplainable?" She laughed. "Of course not. The accepted theory is multiple meteor strikes.

"Funny, isn't it? Multiple meteor strikes. Throughout recorded history we have never had even the slightest mention of a single large-scale meteor strike. But here they are saying several major strikes occurred at approximately the same time on the cosmic scale."

Pencak pointed down at the tent floor. "Do you know that less than twenty miles from here there's a place called Henbury Craters? Twelve craters of various sizes. The explanation was a shower of meteorites. All landing within a half mile of one another and a hair's breadth away from this very spot, when you consider the surface area of the Earth."

Pencak sighed. "Ladies and gentlemen, this is the point at which I am usually asked to shut up and the class professors give their students the information they need to ingest to get an A on their next test."

"This isn't a test," Hawkins said quietly. "We need to know what the connection may be among these sites. What *you* think the connection is."

Pencak regarded him for almost half a minute and then nodded. "All right. I think there is little doubt but that meteors have occasionally hit the Earth over the course of millions of years. But most of those strike sites have traces of the meteor somewhere in them. Others occurred so long ago, or are so massive, that it is impossible to tell. Indeed it was only when we were able look back down on the Earth from space that we were able to see some of the patterns.

"There are those who believe that a massive meteor once hit Earth near what is now the east coast of Hudson Bay. There is a four-hundred-mile-long indentation in the Earth's crust, called the Nastapoka Arc, that suggests an impact. This might even have been the meteor that scholars have postulated helped cause the extinction of the dinosaurs. But that occurred much longer ago than the sites we are concerned with here.

"Our atmosphere eats up well over 99.9 percent of all meteors that come close. Those that get through have to be rather large and on a very direct azimuth; otherwise the atmosphere bounces them back into space.

"That latter occurrence happened back in 1972,

although most don't know about it. On August tenth
of that year a meteor traveling at about ten miles a
second and estimated to be about fifteen feet in diameter and weighing almost a ton hit Earth's atmosphere. The first visual sighting was over Nevada, although I would assume that NORAD in Colorado
Springs had been tracking it for a while.

"Ninety seconds after being seen over Nevada it
was over eastern Canada and then bouncing back out
into space. A meteor of that size—if it had had the
slightest change in trajectory and actually hit the
Earth—would have had the explosive force of about
twenty kilotons. If it had landed on Las Vegas you
could have said good-bye to the entire city and an
area twenty miles around it.

"The government kept word of this secret for over
two years and then released it in a manner calculated
to generate as little attention as possible. Think about
it!" Pencak leaned forward and Fran found herself
drawn in by the older woman. "Las Vegas came within
a hair—at least by astronomical measurement—of being obliterated and nothing was mentioned for two
years.

"So what else hasn't been said? The sad thing is
that when we can't explain something by knowns, we
throw out the possibility of the unknown. We ignore
it." Pencak then proceeded to outline the same theory
about the physical evidence concerning Meteor
Crater that she had for the class the previous week.
That made Hawkins sit up and take notice.

"You're saying that the most likely cause of Meteor Crater was a nuclear explosion?"

"It is the only thing that fits all the evidence—the intense heat; the silica; the fused quartz sandstone; the lack of meteor fragments; the shape of the crater—all of it. The same is true of Campo del Cielo, Ries Basin, and Vredefort Dome. All explained away so glibly as the result of meteor strikes, yet there isn't sufficient evidence to conclusively demonstrate it."

"Vredefort Dome is *not* a crater," Don Batson pointed out. "How can you link it with the other sites?"

"The Dome itself is not a crater," Pencak agreed. "But what do you know of the Bushveld Igneous Complex?"

"It's one of the richest, perhaps the richest, mining area in the world, most particularly for diamonds."

"And what forms diamonds?" Pencak asked.

"Intense heat and pressure," Batson replied testily.

"And what is the shape of the Bushveld Complex?"

"An elongated circle," Batson replied. "But that doesn't mean—"

"Patience, young man. How was the Complex formed?"

"Well, that's not quite certain. Some suggest massive lava flows along with strong magnetic effects in the area." Batson shifted uncomfortably in his seat, used to being on the other side of the questioning.

"And the Dome?" She turned her attention from

Batson when he didn't answer. "It's been called one of the most unique geological structures in the world. About sixty miles southwest of Johannesburg a ring of hills rises, surrounding an almost flat plain. Research has shown that the subsurface rock of the plain has been upturned to a depth of almost seven miles, thus forming the Dome. Imagine the forces involved to do that! Again, no one can quite explain this phenomenon occurring naturally."

"But how could all these formations have been caused by nuclear explosions?" Fran wanted to know. "How old are they?"

"Estimates vary from site to site. Anywhere from five to thirty thousand years old; some perhaps much older. That sounds like a large span of time, but when you balance it against the age of the Earth, in astronomical terms, it's almost the blink of an eye."

Fran shook her head. "Then I repeat my question: How could these craters and formations have been caused by nuclear explosion? That doesn't occur spontaneously in nature."

"No, it doesn't," Pencak agreed. "My theory is that the explosions were caused by some extraterrestrial life-form."

"What!" Batson could no longer sit still. "You're saying Earth got nuked thousands of years ago by aliens?"

"Putting it in layman's terms—yes."

Fran looked at the other members of the team. Debra was just staring at the old woman, as if soaking in her words. Don was shaking his head angrily. Hawkins was looking between Pencak and Lamb, whose face indicated his obvious disbelief. Fran wasn't sure how she herself felt.

Pencak explained herself further. "Originally, I'm not sure whether the explosions were deliberate—by which I mean weapons; or accidental—perhaps mishaps aboard nuclear-powered spacecraft. Based on the events you have witnessed here, though, I now believe the majority of the explosions to have been deliberate."

"But"—Hawkins paused and shook his head—"I'm just a dumb soldier. I don't quite understand this."

Pencak gave her twisted smile. "I'm sure you are anything but a dumb soldier, Major, or else you would not be here. I don't understand it either. Mind you, I am not saying I am certain that these craters were formed by extraterrestrial life-forms or even that they are the result of nuclear explosions. It is simply the solution that most closely fits the facts.

"Look at it logically based on the additional information you now have: You have an unknown entity—whether organic or purely mechanical—inside this Rock that is communicating with you using the data off the record on *Voyager 2*. The probe was out of the solar system proper when it disappeared. No one on Earth could have caused the destruction of the probe."

She tapped the overhead. "This entity attempted communication with these sites—perhaps there was a series of colonies at each of those locations thousands of years ago. Or more likely just research facilities. Perhaps what is in the Rock is simply an automated relay site, left behind by a race that might not exist any longer."

Fran glanced at Levy, thinking about her touchstone theory.

Pencak waved her good hand about. "It's a good place to hide a site, don't you think?—in the middle of the world's largest rock in the middle of one of the world's harshest deserts. The Aborigines certainly have numerous legends about Ayers Rock, don't they? It has long been theorized that many ancient legends might be based on the reality of extraterrestrial visitors."

Pencak shrugged, her one shoulder lifting and the other remaining dead. "I don't know the answer. I can only offer possibilities. I would suggest that the Henbury Craters that are so close by here may be the results of near misses caused by weapons that were meant for Ayers Rock. Maybe there was an interstellar war a long time ago and these were military bases."

Fran saw Hawkins swing his gaze to Lamb at that last sentence and then back to Pencak. She knew what he was thinking—if Lamb had had an idea that this was true, that explained the obsession with secrecy. Had Lamb given them the entire message? What did Lamb really hope to find in the Rock?

"Excuse me." Debra spoke for the first time.

"Yes, dear?" Pencak twisted in her seat.

"You've talked about only five of the six sites. You

haven't said anything about the one in Russia. Is there a crater there?"

Pencak stood up. "Ah, yes. Russia. That is the one I've been thinking about ever since Mr. Lamb briefed me. Could you put the overhead with the Russian site on the screen, please?"

Lamb sorted through the slides and then slid the correct one on top of the glass and turned on the power. A map showing the central part of what used to be the USSR was lit up with a circle drawn in the south-center.

Pencak walked up to the screen. "You have narrowed this down to a diameter of what?" she asked Lamb.

"Four hundred kilometers."

She ran her finger along the map, below the top edge of the circle. "The Trans-Siberian Railway runs here along the southern edge of your circle. North of that—stretching for thousands of miles up to above the Arctic Circle—is the Central Siberian Uplands, one of the most least populated and most desolate places on earth. To the south, Mongolia and the Gobi desert."

She looked at Lamb. "I believe I know the exact spot that message was sent to."

"How do you know?" Lamb demanded.

"Because there is only one place out there that makes any sense."

"Where?" Hawkins asked.

Her finger stabbed the screen. "Here. Tunguska."

She nodded at Lamb. "You thought perhaps the Soviet facility at Semipalatinsk?"

Lamb was startled. "No. That's farther to the west."

"Yes." She pointed a few hundred miles to the left of the circle. "Semipalatinsk is where the Soviets used to test high-energy lasers and charged-particle weapons," she explained to the others in the room. "Also, quite a bit of underground nuclear testing went on there. I imagine it is still open for business by the new people in charge. But, no, I believe the message was aimed at Tunguska."

"What's at Tunguska?" Fran was impatient with Pencak's sparring with Lamb.

"It's not so much what *is* at Tunguska—it's more what *happened* at Tunguska and what may have been there," Pencak replied cryptically.

"Please tell us," Debra asked.

"This is crazy," Batson said. "I don't think we need to sit here and—"

"We need to explore every possibility," Hawkins quietly interrupted. "If you don't want to listen to it, you can leave."

"I'll listen," Batson grudgingly said.

"Go ahead," Hawkins said to Pencak.

Pencak sat down with a sigh and was quiet for a moment. When she started, her gravely voice was very low and Fran had to lean forward to hear her over the rumble coming from the mine tent a hundred meters away. "The Trans-Siberian Railroad was completed in 1906. Four thousand miles long, it opened up perhaps the loneliest place on earth. Siberia is half again as big as the United States and in the first decade of this century the population in that area was well below one million people.

"In 1908, on June thirtieth, a little after seven in the morning local time, passengers on the railroad saw something sear across the sky and disappear below the horizon to the north. There was an explosion. Thirty-seven miles from the epicenter, at the trading station called Vanavara—the nearest populated location—the shock wave knocked buildings down and people in the open were dosed with radiation. At the site itself trees were obliterated for miles around and blown outward in a concentric pattern for dozens of miles. Herds of reindeer were blasted.

"In London, five hours after the explosion, instruments picked up the shock wave in the air—that was after it had already traveled twice around the world. They thought nothing much of it until that night, when there was a strange glow, bright red in the eastern sky. For two months afterward the night sky over England—indeed all of Europe—was much brighter than normal.

"Yet no one immediately made the connection with what had happened in Tunguska. The site itself was not formally investigated for twenty years. You have to remember that that was a turbulent time in Russian history. You also have to understand the remoteness of the Siberian tundra. It is the most godforsaken place on Earth. Miles and miles of pine trees growing in permafrost. You can travel for thousands of kilometers without any noticeable change in the terrain or any relief from the monotony. It is horrible!"

Fran was surprised at the rise in Pencak's voice and her strong emotion. "You sound as if you've been there."

"I have. I visited Tunguska in 1965 as part of an international team investigating the site. Although it was fifty-seven years after the explosion, the actual area still had not recovered. You could see the old deadfall blown outward with the new trees struggling to grow among it."

She sighed. "Ah—again they say it was a meteorite that caused the explosion. This time, though—no crater. So they say it exploded in the air instead of in the ground. The ice in the meteor head overheated and caused it to blow apart just before impact.

"Fools." Pencak shook her head. "Any ice would have been gone shortly after entering the atmosphere. Amazing how they will try to jam the data into the solution rather than find the solution that fits the evidence."

"What did you find?" Hawkins asked.

"We found the signs of an air-burst nuclear explosion. I would say the equivalent of a thirty-megaton blast. That is ten times the size of the bomb that destroyed Hiroshima.

"We found traces of the radioactive isotope cesium one thirty-seven in the ring structure of trees on the outskirts of the blast that corresponds to the year of the explosion. We found no sign of a crater. In fact, the trees at the very center of the blast were found still to be standing—the shock wave propagated outward from there, knocking the trees down in concentric rings. It was impossible to do any sort of soundings in the ground with the instruments we had available because of the permafrost.

"But despite all that evidence my colleagues agreed that it was a comet. All the non-Russian scientists, at least. The Russians themselves said nothing. They had their own theories."

"What did they think?" Hawkins asked.

Pencak got up and walked over to the coffee machine and poured herself a cup. Fran caught Hawkins's eye and mouthed, *What do you think?* to him. In reply Hawkins shrugged and tapped his ear, indicating, *Listen.*

Taking a sip of her coffee, Pencak continued. "The Russians are a strange people. We look down on their technological and scientific capabilities, but they did quite well for themselves working under an intolerable system that did not promote innovative thinking.

"The Russians have always been very interested in Tunguska—especially in the years since the Great Patriotic War. In 1946, after seeing what happened at Hiroshima and Nagasaki, Gregori Kazakov said that the explosion at Tunguska must have been nuclear and suggested that it had been caused by the nuclear engine of a spacecraft exploding. He said that traces of metallic iron found in the area were fragments from the skin of the spaceship. Other metals found there were from the ship's wiring. He based his theory on the fact that a spacecraft exploding in midair would leave no crater and form the effect that was noted in the area.

"In 1959 Professor Felix Zigorski, an aerodynamics expert from the Moscow Aviation Institute, also said the explosion must have been nuclear." She looked over at Lamb. "As you probably know, Felix was the head of the Russian team that went with us to the site in '65. Later on he was one of the men in charge of training their cosmonauts. He continued to claim, until his death four years ago, that there was no doubt but that extraterrestrial spacecraft have been active in the skies over Russia.

"Korkorov, a Russian aircraft designer, introduced a new angle on the Tunguska incident. He examined eyewitness reports of the object that had been moving across the sky and concluded that it had to have been under intelligent control. His calculation based on the reports show it slowed to around point six kilometers per second prior to the explosion, indicating an attempt to perhaps land—a meteorite would have continued to accelerate and been going much faster than that. Also, he laid out the route according to the various accounts and it appears, if the accounts from 1908 are to be believed, that the object actually made a significant course change prior to exploding."

"I'm a little confused," Hawkins said. "What does an explosion in 1908 have to with these craters that you say are at least five thousand years old?"

Pencak regarded him for a few seconds. "I would say the likelihood that whatever is in the Rock has tried to communicate with Tunguska ties them together. Obviously, they are all part of some sort of alien system. I suppose we will find out what kind of system when we complete the tunnel and come face to face with whatever is down there."

"Unless we communicate with it first," Debra said.

"That's another thing that makes me think we are dealing with aliens," Pencak commented.

"What's another thing?" Hawkins asked, the confusion plain in his voice.

"The frequency the initial transmission from the Rock was sent on. Fourteen twenty megahertz, correct?"

Lamb flipped open a file folder to check. "Right."

"Zigorski investigated material he called 'angel's hair' found at the sites where UFOs were reported in the former Soviet Union. These were metal needles about twenty-one to twenty-three centimeters long, wrapped together in a strange pattern. The needles were extremely thin and usually disintegrated or were blown away shortly after the sighting. Needles twenty-one centimeters in length, if used as antennas, would be broadcasting and receiving on a frequency around fourteen twenty megahertz."

"When and where were these needles found?" Lamb wanted to know.

"Zigorski investigated several reports all over the Soviet Union in the late sixties and early seventies."

"Maybe it was chaff used by their Air Force," Hawkins suggested. "Designed to throw off radar tracking at various frequencies. Maybe the UFO itself was an experimental aircraft. Like our Stealth fighter that was spotted out West for several years before the Air Force went public."

"Possibly," Pencak acknowledged. "I don't know. But I find it very interesting that it is the same frequency as that used by the Rock. Also, angel's hair has also been found at reported UFO sites in the United States."

"So now we have UFOs," Batson commented. "And prehistoric nuclear explosions combined with one in 1908 in Siberia. Come on, people. Let's get real here."

Lamb stood. "All right—that's enough for now. We have a lot of theories but no real answers. I've requested permission for us to transmit to the Rock. I haven't received an answer yet, but if it's a go, I want you people to give me a message to send. It has to be nonthreatening and noninformative. Basically we need to know if we *can* communicate with it. Is that clear?"

"Clear," Hawkins answered for the team.

TUNGUSKA

Ayers Rock, Australia
22 DECEMBER 1995, 1030 LOCAL
22 DECEMBER 1995, 0100 ZULU

AFTER PENCAK WAS ESCORTED AWAY BY A MARINE TO GET some sleep after her long journey from America, the team was left to consider the information and theories she had imparted. Hawkins looked around the room, trying to judge by the expressions where each stood. Levy maintained her wide-eyed, deep-in-thought look. Fran's face intimated nothing. Batson was shaking his head to himself slightly. Lamb was looking at a file folder with a secret cover sheet he'd just been handed by the marine, ignoring everyone.

"Any comments?" Hawkins asked.

As he'd expected, Batson was the first to voice his opinion. "I don't buy it."

"What don't you buy?" Lamb looked up from his papers.

"The conclusion Dr. Pencak has drawn from the available data. To begin with, a lot of her analysis is flawed." Batson walked over to the map on the wall. "She's linking together these sites because of the transmission. Then she's explaining the craters at or near the sites as having been caused by nuclear explosions. But it *is* just as likely that they were caused by meteors, based on the scientific studies made of each site. I should know that—geology is my field of expertise and I've studied several of those sites."

His finger slid across the map. "Campo del Cielo is estimated to have been formed a good twenty thousand years before Meteor Crater in Arizona. And Ries Basin and the Vredefort Dome complex well before that. We're talking a span of many millennia."

"Thousands of years to us might seem like just a few years to an alien culture," Levy quietly replied.

Batson snorted in irritation. "If you think that way, then you can say any damn thing you want to. If extraterrestrials had built something on Earth so long ago, don't you think we would have had some sort of contact with them before now?"

"Maybe we have," Levy said. "The data on that are incomplete. Certainly there are a multitude of reported sightings of—"

"Hold on." Lamb held up a hand. "Let's not get too far astray and start discussing whether UFO's exist."

"I agree," Batson said. "I think everything we need to know to understand what is going on is here right in front of our noses but we aren't looking at it from the proper perspective. People always have a tendency to make problems much more complicated than they really are."

Fran spoke for the first time. "So what perspective should we take, Don?"

Batson shrugged. "I'm not sure. Let's assume the six locations are connected, but not in the way Dr. Pencak said they were."

"You mean no aliens?" Fran asked. "But who would have put something in the Rock, then? We're back to square one."

"Not really," Lamb interjected. He flipped open one of his ever-present file folders. "I think for the first time we may have a line on who is behind all this."

Hawkins frowned. As usual they hadn't received all the necessary information up-front. "What have you got?"

Lamb gave a thin-lipped smile. "Dr. Pencak visited the former Soviet Union six times. She had a relationship with this Felix Zigorski fellow she mentioned. A relationship that spanned twenty years with quite of bit of communication between the two."

Hawkins couldn't quite imagine Pencak having a "relationship" with anyone—at least not in the way that Lamb's tone of voice indicated. But he had to admit that the Earth bogeyman was a lot more credible than an alien one. "So you're saying this is a setup?"

"It's possible—in fact, likely," Lamb replied.

"Oh, come on, now!" Fran exploded. "Are we going to see the Soviet Union behind every tree? Hell, the country doesn't even exist anymore. Being paranoid is what's gotten us to the crappy state of affairs the world is in right now. Besides, the Rock—whatever is in the Rock—hasn't done anything threatening."

"It took out *Voyager 2*," Hawkins reminded her.

"All right." Fran ceded the point, then twisted it. "But how could the Russians have destroyed *Voyager 2* and why?" She looked at Batson. "I don't agree that we have everything we need to know to figure this out. We need to get inside that chamber in the Rock. And even then I'm not sure we'll know what is going on."

"There's something else," Lamb said.

They all turned and looked as he laid out a large glossy photograph on the tabletop. "This is satellite imagery of Tunguska, taken less than ten hours ago."

They crowded around and peered down. Used to dealing with such enhanced photos Hawkins quickly made sense of what he was seeing. Large tarps were stretched over a piece of land in the middle of the pine trees that filled the photo. Snow covered the trees and earth but not the tarps, indicating they were recent additions. Fresh gouges in the snow showed where heavy equipment had torn new roads through the forest.

"You have thermal on this?" Hawkins asked.

In response Lamb slapped down another photo. In this one the forest was a mass of blue, but the area where the tarps were blazed bright red. "They've got heavy machinery under those tarps working very hard to be so hot," Hawkins explained to the others who were looking at him questioningly.

"Where is that exactly?" Fran asked.

"Dead center of where the Tunguska meteorite was supposed to have exploded." Lamb pointed at the normal-light photo. "If you look closely you can see old deadfall blown outward between some of the trees, just like Pencak described it. Also note the piles of freshly uprooted trees here, here, and here. And the pile of earth and snow here."

He put another photo down and looked at Hawkins. "We caught this at one point. What do you make of it?"

Hawkins leaned over and studied it. He could make out several vehicles—bulldozers, armored personal carriers, and dump trucks—parked around the tarp. Men were crouched on the sides of the vehicles away from the tarp. "They're blasting."

Lamb nodded. "Correct."

Fran was the first to verbalize what the others were realizing. "They've found their Rock!"

"And they're not wasting time digging through the frozen tundra," Batson commented. "They're blasting. They're trying to get to it as quickly as possible."

"We think they've already gotten to it," Lamb said. "Latest imagery shows the earth-moving equipment parked out from under the cover of the tarps. Thermals show numerous generators running underneath but no other equipment working."

"How large an area is covered?" Hawkins asked.

"Two hundred meters by a hundred and fifty."

Fran spoke slowly, sorting her thoughts out. "If the Russians are digging up something similar to what we have here in the Rock, then Pencak is right. The most likely source is extraterrestrial."

Lamb shook his head. "They certainly have found it quick enough. My analysts think they may have abandoned something out there and suddenly discovered a need for it."

"Oh, come on!" Fran shook her head. "You're grasping at straws so you can find a known enemy you can focus on."

Lamb eyed her coldly. "That's what I'm paid to do. Dr. Pencak says she was all over that area but they didn't find anything. Seems very convenient. Of course, the Russians were supervising the whole expedition, so maybe they steered them in the wrong direction. Or maybe she did see something and is lying."

"She also said that they didn't do any digging because of the frozen tundra," Batson noted.

Lamb stabbed a finger at the pictures. "They're digging now."

Hawkins held up a hand. "The critical question is, what have they found—or rediscovered?"

Lamb looked up and met Hawkins's eyes, and in that moment Hawkins knew what the other man was going to say next. He felt a churning anxiety begin in his stomach.

Lamb started picking up the folders. "We should know very soon what's under that cover."

"How?" Batson was perplexed.

"When did they go in?" Hawkins asked, his voice tight.

Lamb looked at his watch. "Four hours ago."

Hawkins quickly calculated in his mind. Several hours before dawn in Siberia. "How?"

"Combat Talon originating out of Pakistan. Low-level flight across western China. Over Mongolia and LALO almost on top of the target site."

Hawkins knew that was the only way to get in there without getting caught: low altitude, low-opening parachute-drop out of the Air Force's deep-penetration special-operations' modified C-130. "Did you get an initial entry report?"

Lamb nodded. "They're on the ground in the proper place and everyone is all right."

"Who?"

"Richman, Brown, and Lee."

Hawkins winced—he and Richman had been the two original forming members of Orion. He was also the acting commander, with Hawkins spinning his wheels out here in the desert. On top of that practical consideration, though, was a personal one: Lou Richman was his best friend, the man who had seen him through the accident and all those years sitting in the hospital at Mary's bedside.

"What are you two talking about?" Fran demanded.

Hawkins turned to look at her. "We should know very shortly what is under those tarps. Three men from my team jumped into Tunguska to take a look."

Fran blinked. "Into Siberia?"

Lamb tapped the satellite photos. "Despite all our technology there are some things that only a man on the ground can do. One of them is tell us what the Russians have dug up under that cover. I had recon teams forward-based as close as possible to all transmission reception sites as soon as we triangulated them. I ordered the Tunguska team in when we saw that the Russians were working there. I've also got teams on the ground in Germany, Arizona, and Argentina. The one for South Africa is on board a carrier task force in the South Atlantic."

"When is Richman's estimated TOT? Time on target," Hawkins added for the benefit of Fran, Batson, and Levy.

"They went in four klicks away. They estimated two hours to get a visual sighting on the target." Lamb glanced at his watch again. "Anytime now."

Hawkins turned and pointed to Levy. "Tell him what you found about the previous transmissions after nuclear blasts."

Lamb looked confused. "What previous transmissions?"

Levy succinctly went through the information. When she was done, Hawkins leaned forward, getting close to Lamb. "Now, if there were transmissions out of the Rock in 1945, that sort of casts doubts on your Russian theory, doesn't it?"

"It doesn't matter," Lamb said. "If the Russians have uncovered whatever is there, we need to know."

Tunguska

``THIS IS FUCKED, BOSS MAN,'' LEE WHISPERED TO RICHMAN.
Lee had his slight frame crammed under a dead tree,
his MP5 submachine gun pointing out, taking security
on that side. His night-vision goggles were hardly necessary, due to the reflected glow from the high-power
lights under the tarp less than fifty meters away.
Brown was to Richman's left, covering the other side.

Richman didn't bother answering. He agreed, but
telling his two teammates that wouldn't do much for
whatever little morale they might have left. The jump
had been bad enough—letting the drogue chute of
their parachutes suck them off the back ramp of the
Talon at less than two hundred feet—barely enough
time for the specially designed low-altitude main
chute to deploy before they crashed into the upper
branches of three pine trees.

Luckily their hazardous-terrain protective gear
had worked as intended and they'd all managed to
climb down to ground level and assemble without in-
jury. It had been a nightmare moving across the frozen tundra to the target, climbing and slipping over
snow-covered deadfall, the freezing night air clawing
into their bones. They'd spotted the lights a half hour
earlier and spent the time slowly working their way in
closer. The thickly packed pine trees surrounding the
target were great camouflage, along with the pitch-
black night. They'd already slipped past two rings of
security. Richman had had a Russian soldier almost

step on top of him forty meters back. Fortunately, the Russians were not equipped with night-vision goggles.

Richman tried focusing his PVS7 night-vision goggles on what was under the overhead cover. There were several tents set up, smoke billowing out of their stovepipes at the edge of a large pit. Richman estimated the temperature to be about twenty below, which helped explain the lack of people moving around who absolutely didn't have to. He could see three guards armed with AK-74 automatic rifles standing near steel grating that sloped down out of sight into the hole the Russians had just recently dug.

"We're going to have to go in," he whispered to Lee, then Brown. It was a credit to their discipline and belief in him as their team leader that neither uttered a word of protest. He reached inside his white parka and flicked on the portable SATCOM radio strapped to his back.

Ayers Rock

"HOW ARE THEY GETTING OUT?" HAWKINS ASKED.

"MH53 Pave Low helicopter," Lamb replied.

"Bullshit," Hawkins fumed. "They're in too far for the Pave Low." He pointed at the world map they'd been using to locate the transmission sites. "It's almost two thousand miles from Pakistan to Tunguska."

"It'll have a Talon escort for in-flight refueling," Lamb patiently replied.

Hawkins wasn't pleased with that answer, but there was nothing he could do—a feeling he was uncomfortably used to.

A marine appeared in the doorway. "We have communications with Phoenix, sir."

"Switch it in here," Lamb ordered as he turned on the SATCOM radio set up on top of the table.

There was a brief hiss of static from the speaker and then a voice could clearly be heard whispering, "I say again. Angel, this is Phoenix. Over."

Lamb keyed the microphone. "Phoenix, this is Angel. Over."

"Roger. We're about fifty meters from the edge of the tarps. We can't see down into the pit, so we're going to move in closer. Out." The radio went dead.

"We'd have known in twenty-four hours what's in the chamber in the Rock," Hawkins said. "Why did you have to put those men on the ground?"

Lamb kept his eyes focused on the radio. "Because we need to know what's there now. Twenty-four hours may be too late."

Tunguska

RICHMAN COULD HEAR VOICES TALKING LOUDLY IN RUSSIAN as he slid along the back side of one of the tents, weapon held at the ready. Lee was right behind, covering him. Brown was back in the tree line with the Stoner machine gun to provide support fire. A conveyer belt was set up about twenty feet to Richman's right front, leading over the edge of the pit. Richman decided that would be the best place for him to see in without being spotted by security.

Using hand signals he indicated for Lee to stay by the tent and cover him. Richman lowered himself into the mushy snow and low-crawled forward, keeping an eye on a bundled-up guard standing near the edge of the pit to his left. He jammed himself under the stanchions holding up the conveyer belt where it turned from vertical to horizontal and caught his breath. He looked back. He couldn't see where Brown was in the tree line and, shifting his eyes closer, Lee was nothing more than a dark shadow against the tent.

Richman turned his gaze to the pit and down. As his eyes focused on what was down there, he blinked and tried to make sense of it.

Ayers Rock

"ANGEL, THIS IS PHOENIX. OVER."

Hawkins could tell Richman must be in an extremely exposed position because he was barely whispering into his mike. Hawkins's heart was thumping more quickly than it would if he were there himself. A drop of sweat slipped over his upper lip and splashed against his chest unnoticed.

"Phoenix, this is Angel. What have you got? Over."

"I don't know." There was a pause, during which Lamb looked at Hawkins as if to blame him for his man's confusion. Richman's voice came back, low and tentative. "The hole is about forty meters around and thirty meters deep. In the center there's a half sphere with a flat face on this side. The outside seems to be some sort of metal that doesn't reflect light but the side that faces me, it's—well—it's just this black wall. But it's not a wall. I don't know what it's made of. It's sort of shimmering. The Russians have video cameras and other instruments facing the wall. There's something strange about the wall. Over."

"What's strange about it? Over." Lamb was gripping the mike tightly.

Richman's voice was tense. "It's not . . . well, it's not like anything I've ever seen. It doesn't look solid. Over."

"What are the Russians doing? Over."

"Hard to tell. There are some boom arms that look like they might be used to push something through—maybe a video camera or some other sensor, but I can't tell if they've been used. I don't think . . . wait one—there's some movement up here. I need my hands. I'm going to lock down on transmit. I'm going on FM too."

Hawkins gripped the back of the chair next to the table where he was standing. Richman was now broadcasting to his two partners on FM radio as well as on the SATCOM. Hawkins could hear some rustling as Richman moved. The man's breathing sounded loudly through the speaker. When he spoke it surprised everyone. "There's a patrol moving out. I think they're changing guard shifts. Lee, they're coming up on you. Shit." The last word was said sharply. Two seconds later the deep roar of automatic weapons resounded through the tent, startling Fran and Levy.

A new voice sounded tinnily—Lee as heard by Richman over the FM radio and fed back into the SATCOM. "I've got four down. Two still moving. Let's get the fuck out of here, boss man."

Richman's voice was hurried and short of breath. "We've got tracers out of the north. Brown, you got them? I'm going to try and disengage. Lee, to the right! The right!" Richman was screaming now. A deeper roar sounded in a long-held burst. Hawkins recognized the sound of the Stoner—Brown firing in support.

A deep grunt—Lee. "I'm hit, boss man. Two, maybe three rounds. Chest. Right arm. I can't move."

"I'll get you. Hang tight. I'll get you. Cover me, Brown."

The crump of an explosion and a scream that was cut off. Hawkins looked up. Fran's face was white. Batson looked stunned. He couldn't tell what the expression on Lamb's face was as he held the useless microphone.

"Brown's dead." Richman's voice was labored. "I confirm. Brown is dead. They blew the shit out of the tree line." He grunted and they heard Lee's sharp intake of breath. Dimly Hawkins could hear the soft chugging of Richman's silenced submachine gun spewing out death. "I've got Lee. I'm pulling back into the pit. They're all around us. I'd say they got at least a company's worth."

Over a hundred men closing in. Hawkins stared at the radio, wishing he were anywhere but here.

"We're down the ramp." Richman's voice sounded loudly. "Hey, buddy. Come on, buddy. Don't lose it on me." A roar of semiautomatic fire. "Fuck!" Richman screamed. Hawkins heard a long, sustained rattling of the sub firing and then the distinctive sound as Richman switched magazines. "Time to don berets and stack magazines."

Hawkins winced. That was a grim joke between him and his team members. They'd always talked about what they would do if caught in a hopeless situation. Surrender was out of the question. Any person —no matter how well trained—could be made to talk, and the men and women of Orion knew too much to have that happen. Hawkins had been the one to say that that was the time to put on the green beret most of them had worn when they were in Special Forces and stack magazines for ready access and fight it out to the death. The fact that Richman was wearing a sterile uniform and didn't have a beret didn't matter.

"Lee's dead. That last burst got him. I'm down to two mags. They're in no rush. They know they've got me cornered. I think they're worried about shooting up their equipment down here, otherwise I'd be Swiss cheese. Maybe they're worried about hitting the black wall." There was a short pause. "Angel, I don't know who you are, but tell my wife I love her and always will."

Hawkins wanted to grab the mike from Lamb and assure Richman he would, but there was no way they could talk to him—once Richman had gone hot with his mike he could only transmit, not receive.

"Fuck dying in this hole!" Richman's voice was strong. "I'm moving." They could hear him as he ran, the thunder of the Russians firing, and Hawkins recognized the flat crack of near misses. "I'm going to—"

The transmission cut off in midsentence. The signal was gone.

Lamb slowly placed the mike down on the table-top.

"You've got a shimmering black wall." Hawkins spoke with barely restrained anger. "Was that worth three good men?"

SECOND CONTACT

Ayers Rock, Australia
22 DECEMBER 1995, 1015 LOCAL
22 DECEMBER 1995, 0145 ZULU

"WHERE'S DEBRA?"

Fran's question caught everyone off-guard. Hawkins swung his gaze up and met hers. She'd rarely seen such profound sadness in a person's eyes. There was more to Hawkins than the cold-blooded military man he liked to present the world with, she realized. She regretted her mercenary comment earlier in the cafeteria.

"She must have left when things got hairy on the radio," Batson replied. "She was here when it all started."

"Help me find her," she said, taking Hawkins by the arm and shuffling him toward the tent flap.

They stepped out, the bright sun causing them to blink for a few moments to allow their eyes to adjust.

"Did you see Miss Levy?" Hawkins asked one of the marine guards.

"Yes, sir. She headed for the communications center a few minutes ago."

Fran led the way along the top of the Rock to the shelter that bristled with antennas. Entering, she spotted Debra seated at a console, typing.

"Debra, what are you doing?" Fran asked.

Levy glanced over her shoulder. "I'm letting them know that what just happened at Tunguska is a mistake."

"Letting who know?" Hawkins asked, his mind still echoing with the screams of dying men.

Levy tapped the enter key. "Whoever is in, or behind whatever is in, the Rock."

"What did you do?" Hawkins asked, startled.

Levy pointed at the screen. "I just transmitted."

Hawkins and Fran looked over her shoulder. The screen was an unintelligible mass of 0's and 1's.

"What's the content of your message?" Hawkins asked.

Levy hit another key and the screen cleared. "Just what I said—that we mean no harm and that we wish only peace."

Hawkins glanced at Fran and grimaced. Across the van, Spurlock was sitting at another console, headphones on, oblivious to what had just happened.

"Do you know if the Rock received your message?" Fran asked.

Levy smiled. "We should find out shortly."

22 DECEMBER 1995, 1140 LOCAL
22 DECEMBER 1995, 0210 ZULU

"WHAT DO WE HAVE IN COMMON THAT WHATEVER IS IN THE Rock would want us four here?" Fran asked the question that had been bugging her ever since she'd been told of the message at the end of the initial transmission.

Levy was still with them, although Hawkins had had to argue fiercely with Lamb to keep him from locking her up. She still refused to divulge the exact contents of the message she had transmitted. A chagrined Major Spurlock could confirm that a message had been sent—the automatic logs at least had that recorded, but Levy had erased the actual contents. She'd sent it out in the same manner as the second transmission had been received—on a sliding wavelength moving up from fourteen twenty megahertz. Whether the Rock had received it, no one knew.

The members of the team were sitting in the operations shelter with Lamb, trying to regroup from the double shock of the military action in Siberia and Levy's attempt at communication.

Lamb shook his head in reply to Fran's question. "I've asked that same question and my people have cross-referenced your backgrounds, looking for a common thread. We've come up with nothing for all four." He looked at Hawkins and their gazes locked— Lamb was convinced Levy had crossed some mental line and "no longer had both oars in the water," as Lamb had scientifically put it.

As if she had intercepted that look, Levy's low voice cut across the room. "You think I'm nuts, don't you?" When no one answered, she continued. "I assume you know about my therapy? And my institutionalization?" This time she didn't wait for an answer. Her voice took on a slightly mocking tone. "The doctors believe what happened to me happened because my rapid academic advancement outstripped the emotional skills I needed to cope with it." She laughed. "I assure you, gentlemen, and lady," she said, nodding her head at Fran, "I am probably the sanest person in this room right now."

"Then you know about my breakdown too," Fran quietly commented, looking at Lamb. That brought a look of surprise to Hawkins's face.

"Yes, we know about it, but you've been cleared by the doctors," Lamb replied.

Batson was vibrating in place. "What about you?" He was looking at Hawkins. "Did you have a breakdown too?"

"No. I just kill people," Hawkins replied, his eyes glinting dangerously.

Batson was caught up in the confusion of the situation. "Well, I haven't had a breakdown, nor have I had to get regrooved in a nuthouse. Nor have I killed anyone. So why am I here?"

The sharp crump of an explosion derailed any answer. "What's that?" Fran asked.

"We're blasting to get to the chamber," Lamb explained.

"I thought you weren't going to do that," Batson said.

Lamb's reply was brief. "Things have changed."

"Afraid they're going to beat us to the punch?" Hawkins asked.

"They've already beaten us to the punch, as you put it," Lamb replied. "Either the Russians are behind this thing or they're as confused as we are. Either way, they've already uncovered their site. We can't waste any more time."

"What are you going to do when you get to the chamber?" Fran asked.

"It depends on what's there." Lamb shrugged. "It might be the same as what's in Tunguska, but we have to remember that Tunguska never transmitted. We're sitting on the transmitter. Maybe the one over there is just a receiver."

A man poked his head in the tent and gestured for Lamb, who stood. "If you come up with anything that you all have in common that my people might have missed, let me know. I've got other pressing matters that I need to attend to." He walked out, taking his folders with him.

Fran looked at Hawkins and then Batson. The latter sank into a chair with a sigh. "Listen, Fran, I think I know why I'm here. And probably why you're here. I can even understand why you're here." He jerked a thumb at Hawkins. "But I don't understand why Levy is here."

"Why do you think you're here?" Hawkins asked.

"I'm one of the top experts in the world in geology. This thing—whatever it is—is in the middle of the largest homogeneous rock in the world." Batson waved a hand, to forestall Hawkins's comment. "On top of that, though, is that I'm a member of the Hermes Project. As is Fran."

"I've heard that referred to several times," Hawkins said. "What is this Hermes Project?"

Batson rubbed the stubble of beard on his chin with a shaking hand. "It was formed about two years ago. Some bright light in D.C. figured that the President should have a scientific think tank that he could call on when he needed answers. Not knowing what the potential questions would be that he might need answers to, the government recruited one or two of the top people in every possible scientific field and made them part of what they named the Hermes Project. I was tapped to be part of it eighteen months ago. In that time I've been to five orientation meetings in West Virginia, but this is only the second time I've ever been called to actually work on something."

"What about you?" Hawkins shifted his gaze to Fran.

"I was one of the original members of Hermes. Last I checked, there were eighty-seven full-fledged members. I've done a lot more work under the auspices of the project than Don has, though. As a matter of fact, all I've been doing for the past sixteen months is running projections for Lamb and his people."

"A scientific soothsayer."

They all turned in surprise at the unexpected voice. Dr. Pencak stood in the tent doorway, leaning on her cane. She made her way over to the table and sat down in a chair.

"I've never heard statistical projection called that," Fran remarked. "Quite frankly, the way my projections run, they are far from being soothing."

"How does this event merge with your projections?" Pencak asked.

"It doesn't," Fran said.

"So are they still valid?"

"It depends," Fran replied. "You need to look at the course of history as a deep-running river. You can throw stones in the river, but it will still run in the same course. You need something very significant to be able to change the direction. No pun intended, but so far this is just a stone. A very puzzling one, but still just a stone."

"What direction are we headed in now?" Batson wanted to know.

"Not a very good one." Fran closed her eyes briefly, really not wanting to get into it, then opened them. She knew the numbers by heart. "There's a very strong probability we will have a severe worldwide economic depression in the next few years. The destruction of that mine in South Africa can only hasten that event. There's also a very strong probability we may have another world war, as the world's economy reaches critical mass—this one oriented more north-south, industrialized nations against the underdeveloped. The shapers against the suppliers of the raw materials."

"Not a very strong chance we will live happily ever after?" Hawkins asked.

Another explosion rumbled through the Rock.

"No. If we don't screw ourselves up by setting off nuclear bombs, then what we are doing to the environment will most likely do us in."

"Is that why you had your breakdown?" Hawkins quietly asked.

Fran considered him for a few moments, then nodded. "You can only deal with so much negative information before you need a release. I had no support in my marriage, so I picked the easiest thing I could find. I started drinking too much. I thought I could handle it all, but it finally caught up with me after a year."

"And the information hasn't gotten any more positive, has it?" Pencak noted.

"No, but I deal with it better," Fran replied.

"Yes, you may deal with it better," Pencak said. "But the people who are in power don't. Why does this entire mission here have to be classified? Why can't we share what we have found?"

Fran looked at Hawkins and knew what he was thinking. If Pencak knew about the men who'd just died at Tunguska, she'd really have something to talk about.

"What do you think about the second transmission?" Batson asked the question Fran had already considered in her mind.

"What message?" Pencak interrupted Fran's answer.

Fran quickly explained the strange transmission that had faded out and in. "I think Debra might have a point," she ended up admitting.

"Hold on," Hawkins said. "We're getting too caught up in the details here. Let's get back to the big picture. We've had a lot of things happen in the past week—most of which don't make much sense. Let's back up a little bit and see if we can find any pattern to all this."

Fran hid her smile as Hawkins went to the easel and started writing on the paper with a marker. She liked his way of always trying to draw things out to make them easier to see.

When he was done, he had seven blocks listed:

**Nuclear Bombs
(Vredefort Dome/one still loose)**

**Transmissions Ayers Rock
(most recent/two in 1945 after nuclear blasts)**

**Voyager
(data plate/destruction)**

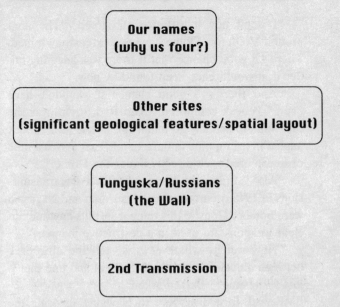

Our names
(why us four?)

Other sites
(significant geological features/spatial layout)

Tunguska/Russians
(the Wall)

2nd Transmission

Hawkins tapped the paper. "The nuclear bombs may have nothing to do with the Rock. All we know is that a transmission was directed at Vredefort Dome shortly after that bomb went off. If we assume there was something under the Dome, similar to what we have here and what the Russians have uncovered at Tunguska, we might also assume that the transmission was an attempt to contact whatever it is. Perhaps what's here in the Rock monitored the blast and wanted to check on the status of the site at Vredefort Dome."

"And it failed," Fran noted, "because the nuke destroyed whatever was under the Dome."

"I don't buy it," Batson disagreed. "The area around Vredefort Dome has been extensively mined. There's a good chance that if there was anything under it, it would have been found by now."

"And there's a good chance it wouldn't have been," Pencak countered. "The Red Streak was the first mine to actually go under the Dome itself, and it angled in over a mile underground. That leaves a mile of unexplored rock directly under the Dome."

"Also," Fran said, "remember that the transmissions in 1945 occurred when Hiroshima and Nagasaki were bombed. Maybe this thing transmits anytime nuclear weapons are used in a destructive manner."

"How can it—whatever it is—tell the difference between a nuclear blast that's for real and one that is just for testing?" Batson asked.

Pencak turned her eye to Hawkins, ignoring the geologist. "I have not been kept up-to-date on everything that's happened. What do you mean when you say 'similar to what the Russians have uncovered at Tunguska'?"

Hawkins showed her the satellite imagery and explained what had happened with his team. Fran watched the older woman's face for any sort of reaction. If Lamb was correct, the Tunguska information should come as no surprise to her. Her face betrayed little, but her voice was excited as she ignored what had happened to the men and focused on what had been found by the Russians.

"This is amazing! We never did any probing into the ground when we were there. Maybe Felix did know something, but I doubt it. They would have dug this up a long time ago if they had suspected it existed. If there is something at Tunguska, then I think we definitely have to believe that there was something under the Dome."

"What about the other three sites?" Fran asked.

"Destroyed long ago, most likely."

"Fine," Batson said. "Say we buy into that. What about *Voyager 2*? How did it get destroyed only yesterday?"

Pencak shook her head. "I don't know. But I think that fact also points very strongly to extraterrestrial involvement."

Hawkins disagreed. "The Russians have particle-beam weapons that might have destroyed *Voyager*."

"That far away?" Pencak wasn't buying it. "If they had a particle-beam weapon that could reach from Earth to beyond the orbit of Pluto, I think we would have seen it deployed here on this planet or at least heard something about it."

Hawkins wasn't going to give up so easily. "Maybe they've got it deployed on board their space station. That would remove any interference from the atmosphere."

Pencak gave a soft laugh. "You still prefer the enemy you know to the unknown, don't you?"

"I prefer it to worse-case scenarios," Hawkins retorted. "To me the worst case is if the Russians are behind the destruction of *Voyager;* the transmissions out of the Rock; and, ultimately, the use of those two nuclear bombs." He tapped a finger on the easel.

"The one common denominator that I can come up with is Russia."

Fran had to admit his logic made more sense than anything else they'd heard so far. She felt the jet lag of the long flight finally starting to kick in and she also sensed that they were spinning their wheels and going nowhere.

"You have no concept of what we might be dealing with, do you?" Levy asked rhetorically. "It's not like in the movies and on TV. An extraterrestrial civilization that could cross space to other star systems would most likely be of a magnitude we could not comprehend." She looked around the room. "Has anyone here ever heard of the three levels of civilization based on energy as postulated by the Soviet astronomer Kardashev?"

Seeing that no one was ready to reply, she continued. "Kardashev laid out three levels of civilization—we here on Earth are at the first level, which is the burning of readily available fossil and planetary nuclear fuels. A level-two civilization would be one that could tap the energy of its star, which most scientists on Earth concede is the next logical step for us in the next millennium if we make it that far. Tapping in to a sun increases the power potential by trillions. A level-three society would be able to tap the entire energy of the galaxy of which it is a part. That amount of energy is almost incomprehensible."

"All right," Hawkins said. "If this is a message generated by a non-Earth source, what level of civilization do you think is sending it?"

"Obviously a level-two civilization," she said. "Whoever it is must have interstellar travel and it is most likely a carbon-based life-form."

"Why do you say that?" Fran asked.

"Because of the frequencies—bouncing between fourteen twenty and sixteen sixty-two—the water holes of interstellar communication. The hydrogen line is at fourteen twenty megahertz and the first hydroxyl line is only two hundred forty-two megahertz higher at sixteen sixty-two. Between the two lies the quietest part of spectrum. But it also is quite interesting that it lies between the lines of the molecular building blocks of carbon-based life—water.

"In fact," Levy said, "I think that—" She paused as Major Spurlock and Lamb appeared in the doorway to the shelter.

"We've picked up a third transmission," Spurlock explained as he quickly made his way to the computer. "Just like the second one, except shorter."

He typed in some commands and then gestured for Levy. "You broke out the first one. See what you make of this."

The rest of the team gathered around as Levy sat down at the keyboard and her fingers flew over the keys. She kept the others up to speed as she worked. "It's in digital format, sliding up the scale, from fourteen twenty just like the second one. In fact, it is exactly like the second one, with a disappearing center."

She hit the return key. "Here's the initial part that I can decode." Her face lit up with a wide smile as four words appeared.

DEBRA COME TO US

"Great," Hawkins muttered, glancing at Lamb.

Lamb turned to Spurlock. "Can you confirm that message?"

In response Spurlock replaced Levy at the computer. After a few minutes the same words came up.

"What does it mean?" Fran asked. "How do they expect you to come to them?"

Levy shrugged. "They will provide."

"Still nothing on the middle part?" Lamb asked.

Levy shook her head. "It disappears."

Hawkins pressed a hand against his left temple. "How long until we're through to the chamber in the Rock?"

Lamb checked his watch. "Six or seven hours."

Fran stood. "I don't know about all of you, but I'm beat. We can sit here all day and speculate and argue, but until something happens we might as well get some rest. We're going to need it once they get into whatever is in the Rock."

As she left the operations tent she was surprised to find that Hawkins was right behind her. "Let's go for a walk," he suggested.

Together they walked along the top of the Rock, the summer heat rising off the pitted surface. Hawkins halted near the edge, where concertina wire blocked the drop. Out in the distance, on the desert floor, the camouflage nets of Tolliver's marines dotted the landscape.

"What do you think of Levy's theory?" Hawkins asked.

Fran sighed. "I don't know. I do know I can't offer a logical solution for all that's happening."

"Do you think Levy's lost it?" he asked, twirling a finger next to his head.

"Maybe. If we buy the aliens theory, why would they contact her and not any of the rest of us? It's all too weird."

"Maybe because she is the only who seems to believe," Hawkins mused. "What about Don?" he asked.

"What about him?

"He's on edge."

"He does seem pretty high strung," Fran admitted.

Hawkins's voice was sharp. "Is that a nice way of saying he's drying out? You worked with him in Hermes. Did he dry out there, too, or did they let him drink?"

Fran remained silent.

Hawkins finally sighed. "All right. I guess I'm on edge too. We've all done the best we can with what we have. It's hard on all of us." An explosion reverberated through the rock under their feet. "Hopefully, we'll get some answers when they break through," Hawkins said. "You're right in saying there's not much we can do at present. I just hate waiting."

That was the first time Hawkins had ever expressed a personal opinion in front of Fran. She sensed he was uneasy about something and wanted to talk. "Do you have *any* idea why the four of us were chosen?"

Hawkins shook his head. "None. And I'm not sure I agree with Don about his being here because he's a geologist. And why would I be chosen—a military man? I think there's something else involved."

Fran studied Hawkins's face in the bright sunlight. "I don't mean to pry, but you made a very odd comment in the mess hall back at DSCC 14 about your wife. You said—"

"I know what I said," Hawkins snapped. He turned from her and stared out into the desert for a long moment. Fran shifted uncomfortably from one foot to another, not sure what to say.

"My wife's been in a coma for the past four years. She's essentially brain dead."

"I'm sorry," Fran said quickly. "I didn't mean to . . . well, I just wondered if . . ." She trailed off into silence, surprised to see what she could have sworn was a tear merge with the lines of sweat on Hawkins's face as he turned back toward her.

"No. You have a right to ask anything. We're all in this together." He sighed. "We were in a car crash. Hit the back of a semi that was stopped on the road."

"You weren't hurt?"

"No. I had my seat belt on. Mary didn't." There was a pause. "The next question most people ask is, who was driving?"

"You can't blame yourself, can you? It was an accident, right?"

Hawkins closed his eyes briefly. "Yes, it was an

accident." He opened his eyes and looked directly into hers. "But do you think that makes any difference in how I feel?"

"You said she didn't need you," Fran remembered. "Is that true?"

"I don't know."

"Do you see her?"

"I visit every evening when I'm not deployed. She's in a government hospital. They keep her body alive." Hawkins eyes lost their focus. "Sometimes I wonder if there isn't some part of her still alive in there—something of who she was. The doctors say the damage was too extensive, but if you're alive, then who's to say? Who's to say she isn't trapped in there by a body that won't respond and by a brain that's been damaged and not killed?"

A long silence ensued, broken only by the whine of generators and the distant thump of the guardian helicopters. Finally, Fran spoke. "You looked surprised when I said that I had had a breakdown."

Hawkins blinked, his mind returning to the present. "I was."

"Why?"

"You seem like someone who, pardon the expression, has her shit together."

"So do you," she noted. "I would have never imagined that I would see you get emotional like you just did."

Hawkins had no response to that.

"I lost it—completely lost it," Fran said quietly. "I calculated so many different ways the world could get screwed up. No one was very interested in projecting ways we could get our act together. That would have required action and upsetting the status quo. It just overwhelmed me—something I couldn't control, but was there present in front of me every day."

"Yeah," Hawkins said. "I understand the feeling."

"But my problem," Fran continued, "was that I started taking responsibility for it all. As if I alone should somehow change things. Yet I also knew I couldn't. I drank so I didn't have to think, and when that didn't work, I flipped out. Just withdrew from the entire world. Locked myself in my room for three days before my husband broke down the door and had me committed. The one thing those people at the institute taught me, and the only thing that helps me get out of bed every morning, is that I am responsible for me and for doing all I can do, and that's it. That's all that can be expected of us as human beings. To do our best."

"If only more people thought that way, we might have a better world," Hawkins noted.

"If you thought that way, perhaps your life would be a bit happier," Fran said.

Hawkins stared at her for a long moment, and then the trace of a smile crossed his lips. "All right, *Doctor* Volkers. I'll keep that under advisement. Now, I'd advise you to get some sleep. You're going to need it."

Fran turned for her tent. "You get some sleep yourself," she called over her shoulder.

Hawkins waved at her and then turned back to

stare out over the red sand. When Fran looked out the flap of her tent ten minutes later before lying down on her cot, he was still there, a lonely figure etched against the brilliant blue sky.

22 DECEMBER 1995, 1145 LOCAL
22 DECEMBER 1995, 0215 ZULU

``WHAT KIND OF FALLOUT ARE WE GOING TO GET OVER those three men from Orion?" the President demanded.

"Should be minimal," Lamb replied. "They were completely sterile, so nothing can be gleaned from their equipment. The Russians will suspect we were behind it but they won't really have anything to show. I don't think we need to worry about them trying to expose the mission. I think our main problem now will be that they'll try to infiltrate our site here. We've upped the stakes and they could answer quite readily."

"You have no idea what it was that those men saw before they were compromised?"

"No, sir."

"No idea if the Russians know what they have uncovered or even if the Russians are behind it?"

"No, sir."

The President shook his head. "I need some answers, Steve. You've got a mess there and I've got one here." The President frowned as he looked down at some papers spread on the desk in front of him. "Things are not looking good. Volkers's projections are running true to form. Congress is battling me to a standstill on my aid plan to those countries hardest hit economically because of the loss of the mine."

Lamb could understand Congress's reluctance. Why spend desperately needed dollars overseas? He also knew that the few Congressional leaders briefed on Volkers's statistical projections had not been impressed. Long-range planning was not a strength of the American political system.

"What about the other bomb?" the President asked.

"I haven't heard anything. Still searching, sir."

"How long until you're into whatever you have there?"

"Six or seven hours."

"All right. Let me know what you come up with."

Lamb watched the television screen go blank and then called for Colonel Tolliver. Perimeter security needed to be tightened. He hadn't told the President about the last two broadcasts from the Rock. Lamb figured that this was his own problem right now—not something he should burden the President with.

Done with Tolliver, Lamb had one of the marines track Hawkins down.

"What more did you pick up on Levy?" Hawkins asked, slumping into a chair.

Lamb snapped open one of the ever-present file folders. "I have a copy of the transcript of her last meeting with her psychologist a week ago in New York."

Hawkins didn't bother asking how Lamb had gotten hold of that privileged information—in fact, it didn't occur to him to ask. He took it for granted that Lamb would get such information.

"What are the highlights."

Lamb studied the fax paper for a few seconds. "Her doctor is Michael Preston. Ten sixty-five Fifth Avenue. Does quite a bit of work with people like Levy—they call them intellectually accelerated personalities. She's been seeing him for eight months, ever since she was released from the hospital. All previous work focused on her trying to adapt socially to a world she did not emotionally feel a part of. This last session, however, took a different turn, with Levy terminating the relationship."

"Was she on any sort of drugs? Antidepressants or any of that?" Hawkins asked.

"No. Just therapy."

"Why'd she terminate?"

"It would be easiest if I read you the transcript," Lamb said. "It's not very long."

Hawkins leaned back and closed his eyes. "Go ahead."

"She started the session: quote, Levy: *I'm afraid this simply isn't going to work.*'

"Doctor: *What isn't going to work?*'

"Levy: *My seeing you. I don't think you can help me.*'

"Doctor: *Why not?*'

"Levy: *'Because you can't understand me. It's not your fault. No one has ever really understood me. And you can't even understand that, can you?'*

"Doctor: *'You can help me understand, Debra.'*

"Levy: *'No, I can't. I've tried that before and it didn't work. My head is my enemy. And I can't get rid of it without getting rid of me.'*

"Doctor: *'Is that why you tried to kill yourself?'*

"Levy: *'I tried to kill myself because I'm dangerous and I will become more dangerous as I learn more.'*

"Doctor: *'Learn more about what?'*

"Levy: *'You wouldn't understand. My work.'*

"Doctor: *'Dangerous to whom? Yourself?'*

"Levy: *'No. To the world.'*

"Doctor: *'Oh, come now. Why do you say that? How can you be dangerous to the world.'*

"Levy: *'Wouldn't you say the men who worked on the Manhattan Project were some of the most dangerous men the world has ever seen?'*

"Doctor: *'But they also gave us nuclear power.'*

"Levy: *'And that's not very safe either. No, Doctor, I don't think you can help me. If you can't think like me, then how can you hope to help? Don't worry. I'll be all right.'* ''

Lamb closed the folder. "And that was the end. She walked out of his office and never went back."

"What was she working on?" Hawkins asked.

"She consulted for a few of the teams working on some SDI projects, but nothing particularly earth shattering," Lamb replied. "She was mainly working theoretical stuff at MIT."

Hawkins rubbed his chin. Not earth shattering now, but Levy was only twenty-three. In another decade who was to say what she would be working on and whether her theories might turn into reality? Hell, Lamb had told him that they had her on the list to be added to Hermes during the next selection—at only twenty-three!

Hawkins looked across the desk. "I'm starting to think we've got this thing by the tail and it's going to turn around and bite our head off." He thought of the deaths of the members of his team in Tunguska. He had grown used to death a long time before—at least he thought he had. But there was a feeling in his stomach and chest that didn't agree with that cold logic. He remembered Fran's recent advice and stood. "I'm going to try and get some sleep."

THE RUSSIAN II

Vicinity Rokitno, 200 Kilometers Northwest of
Kiev, Ukraine
22 DECEMBER 1995, 0700 LOCAL
22 DECEMBER 1995, 0400 ZULU

THE TRUCK'S ENGINE WHINED IN PROTEST AS THE RUSSIAN
negotiated the steep logging trail. The wheels spun in
the virgin snow, spewing it out to the rear in long
plumes. Easing off the gas, the Russian downshifted
and continued on, the multiwheel drive finally finding
purchase.

The Russian's limbs felt the weariness of the past
thirty-two hours of driving, but his mind fueled his
muscles with the elixir of revenge. Once he made it
over the mountains, he'd rest for a few hours—only
enough to gather strength for the last leg of the journey.

Reaching a relatively flat area before the next up-
grade, the man rolled to a stop and put the parking

brake on. He pulled out a map case and checked his location. The winter weather was slowing him down and he'd already had to revise his estimate of time on target, adding perhaps half a day. He had enough fuel loaded in the rear to get to the target and beyond— not that there would be any beyond.

Putting the maps away, he picked up an AK-74 and checked to make sure a round was in the chamber and it was functioning properly. He did not believe he would run into anyone this soon, but as he got closer there might be guards out. He had no doubts about his ability to deal with that. In thirty-two years of military service he had done more than his share of killing. It didn't matter anymore. Nothing mattered except the final revenge. The world was not a place worth living in. Concepts such as duty and loyalty were carrots and sticks to be used by less scrupulous men to control men of honor. But no more.

He put the weapon down and released the parking brake.

THE CHAMBER

Ayers Rock, Australia
22 DECEMBER 1995, 1830 LOCAL
22 DECEMBER 1995, 0900 ZULU

HAWKINS ROLLED TO HIS RIGHT, OFF THE COT, INTO A KNEEL-ing position on the floor. The muzzle of the pistol he'd retrieved from under the pillow was centered on the figure standing in the darkened tent. The intruder froze, eyes fixed on the large black hole pointing between his eyes.

"Sir, Mr. Lamb sent me to inform you that we've broken through in the Rock."

Hawkins forced himself to relax, sliding his finger off the trigger. The marine hurriedly left, glad to be out of sight. Throwing a shirt over his sweat-soaked chest, Hawkins made his way to the shaft building, trying to clear his mind of a jumble of sleep-induced dark thoughts. He vaguely remembered cloudy visions of Richman, screaming for help, and running toward his executive officer, firing a weapon from his hip, but never able to get any closer and the cries growing weaker and fading, then reemerging from another direction in a never-ending cycle.

Hawkins squinted at the horizon as he walked on the sandstone top of the Rock. The sun was sinking in the western sky, giving slight relief from the blistering heat of daytime. The view from the top of the Rock was magnificent—the Olgas on the far eastern horizon and the Gibson Desert stretching out in all other directions—but Hawkins's eyes didn't see the beauty.

He met Fran, Debra, and Pencak as they went into the metal building. No words were exchanged as they entered the steam bath inside. Batson was already up on the platform, along with Lamb. The silence was unsettling—even though they'd been at the Rock less than twenty-four hours, they'd all grown used to the sound of the drills and explosions. Now only the rhythmic mutter of the generators filled the air. The President's aide turned as they clambered up the stairs.

"We're running a fiber-optic cable down there." He pointed at a small TV screen perched on the platform. "We should get our first view shortly."

"Another thirty feet," Tomkins advised as the twin cable ran over his gloved hand and disappeared into the hole. "One's the fiber-optic line, the other is the light." He gestured down with his free hand. "We punched through into something open. The drill suddenly dropped a good five feet. I ran it down from there and we hit something solid ten more feet down.

It's at the depth the EMR sounding told us there was an open area."

The winch stopped and Tomkins let go of the cables. He moved over to a control panel and glanced at Lamb. "Ready, sir?"

"Go ahead."

Tomkins threw a switch. The TV screen went from dark to a hazy black-and-white picture. Tomkins fiddled with the controls and a smoothly cut rock wall came into focus, approximately ten feet from the cable end.

"That's not natural," Batson murmured.

"I'm rotating," Tomkins announced.

The view shifted, the rock wall coming slightly closer and then moving out again, suggesting an elliptical shape. It grew farther away and then suddenly ended.

"The black Wall," Fran whispered to Hawkins. He peered at the screen as the scene continued to shift. The black Wall extended directly across the chamber, looking as if cut in half, although there was no guessing what was on the other side—or if there was another side. Hawkins could tell why Richman had been vague in his description. Even in the two-dimensional screen of the black-and-white TV it was obvious there was something very strange about the texture of the Wall.

"It's empty except for the Wall," Tomkins noted.

"Let's go," Batson said.

Lamb looked at Hawkins, who nodded. "How do I get down?"

Tomkins pointed at a small, waist-high cage that was suspended by cable on a winch. Hawkins stepped into the cage. Lamb handed him a small radio that was hooked into the cable and Hawkins put the headset on, then grabbed the cable for support.

Tomkins maneuvered the levers on his control panel and the cage swung out over the narrow hole. Hawkins glanced down once, then looked at Tomkins and gave him the thumbs-up. With a slight start the cage slowly settled into the hole. Hawkins watched the lip rise up and then he was completely surrounded by rock pressing in on all sides. He looked up and watched the opening grow smaller and smaller. Down below, the faint light from the fiber-optic cable made a small pinprick of brightness at the end of a long, dark tunnel.

The cage was surprisingly stable, so Hawkins released his grip on the cable and relaxed. It was a tight fit—if he'd wanted to, he could have touched either side of the tunnel by just moving his arms a couple of inches or so out of the cage. Because of that he knew they were going to be limited on the equipment they could bring down here. After what he estimated to be about a minute the light below appeared to be closer than the one above. The temperature dropped rapidly as he went down. The descent slowed and Hawkins watched the end come up. He slid into the chamber and the basket touched the floor with a slight jar.

"I'm down," he announced into the boom mike.

"Is it clear to send the others?" Lamb wanted to know.

Hawkins looked around. This part of the chamber looked as if someone had taken a football and sliced it first horizontally with the rock floor and then vertically with the black Wall. The rock walls were smoothly cut, almost polished. There was nothing to indicate how they'd been made—no blast marks, no sign of drilling. The small pile of rubble from where the drill had bit through was the only thing that marred the antiseptic atmosphere of the chamber. The air was clear and the coolness was a welcome relief from the heat above.

Hawkins peered at the black Wall. It seemed to shimmer in the glow of the optic-cable light. His skin felt tight, the hairs standing up, as if he were close to a powerful electrical field. This close, he could very much understand Richman's lack of clarity about the Wall. It certainly did not look like anything Hawkins had ever seen.

"Looks all right. I'm clearing the cage."

Hawkins took off the headset and put it on the floor of the cage and watched as it rose from the floor and disappeared above. He took the opportunity to walk up to the black Wall. Standing right in front he felt very uneasy. He had no desire to touch the glistening black material. Hawkins had a feeling there was something on the other side—maybe even someone. Hawkins wondered if it was a sophisticated version of those one-way mirrors that police used in interrogation rooms. He didn't like the idea that he might be under observation. Beyond that, though, he sensed a tremendous power and energy inherent in that wavering black surface. The air had a charged feel to it, as if a powerful electric current was running close by.

Hawkins started as he caught movement behind him. The cage settled in and Lamb stepped off and the cage started back up immediately. Lamb stepped up next to Hawkins and stared at the Wall, wordlessly. Batson was the next to arrive and he checked out not only the black Wall but the stone too.

"I don't know what cut this chamber out of the rock, but these walls are smoother than anything I've ever seen done in a mine. Maybe a laser with a hell of a lot of power, but I haven't heard of anything yet made that's powerful enough to do this." He looked about. "And there doesn't seem to be any access to even get machinery in here." His voice dropped almost to whisper. "It's like it just appeared here."

"What do you make of this?" Lamb gestured at the black Wall.

Batson shook his head as he stepped up to it. "It's not rock. At least not any rock that I've ever seen. It might be some sort of metal," he said dubiously. He started to reach out his hand.

"I wouldn't do that!" Hawkins snapped.

Reluctantly, Batson pulled his hand back. "It almost looks like it's permeable."

"Yeah, but if it is, we don't know what it's permeable to, nor do we know what's on the other side."

Fran had arrived by now, holding a portable video camera. She started to film the entire chamber. Levy was next down, followed by Pencak and then Captain Tomkins.

The basket went back up and Hawkins turned to Lamb. "What now? We know we've got what appears to be the same thing that the Russians have at Tunguska, but that doesn't do us much good."

Tomkins was tying in a power line that he'd brought down with him and hooking in some small portable lights. Lamb didn't answer Hawkins right away as he continued to stare at the black Wall. Finally he turned to the members of the team. "Anyone have any ideas what this is?"

There was a brief silence, then Pencak spoke. "I'd say it was a door."

Lamb frowned. "A door? To what? The other side?"

"Of course the other side," Pencak replied. "The question is, what's on the other side? Or more appropriately, *where* is the other side?"

"What do you mean, where?" Lamb asked, but Pencak ignored him.

Hawkins rubbed a hand through his hair. "Maybe it's some sort of force field to protect the equipment that made the transmission."

"Maybe it *is* the equipment that made the transmission," Fran threw in.

Lamb turned to Tomkins. "Can we rig some sort of device to touch this Wall?"

Hawkins noted that there now seemed to be an unspoken agreement among all in the chamber that no person was going to make contact with the Wall.

"Yes, sir. I've got some remote arms that we ought to be able to break down and get through the shaft."

"All right." Lamb turned to Hawkins. "We're going to—"

Fran's yell cut him off and Hawkins stared in amazement as the black Wall flickered. Patterns of searingly bright light flowed across the surface for almost five seconds, then suddenly stopped. It went back to black for two seconds, then glowed bright white for a split second and Richman tumbled out, sprawling to the floor, blood pumping from his right shoulder, his MP5 gripped tightly in his right hand. Just as quickly, the Wall turned black again.

Hawkins sprinted to his executive officer and knelt beside him. Richman was conscious, looking up at Hawkins with disbelieving eyes. The muzzle of his submachine gun wavered uncertainly about the chamber, his finger pulling fruitlessly on the trigger with the bolt closed on an empty chamber.

"Are you all right?" Hawkins asked as he carefully extracted the weapon from Richman's hands and then put pressure on the wound.

Richman looked about in confusion as the others in the chamber gathered around. "Where am I?"

"Australia," Hawkins replied. "Ayers Rock."

Richman lifted his head and looked at the black Wall and then back at Hawkins. "I don't understand."

"What happened, Lou?" Hawkins pulled the dressing out of the case on Richman's combat vest and tore it open. "The last transmission we heard from you was that you were moving. You went off the air in the middle of it. We thought you were dead."

Richman shook his head. "I don't know what happened. They were closing in on me. I didn't have any choice. If I'd stayed, I'd have been dead." He lifted himself up on his good elbow and nodded his head toward the black Wall. "That was the only place I could go. I ran into the Wall—I didn't even know if I could go through or if I'd bounce off. But that was in Russia!"

The chamber went silent as everyone's eyes shifted from Richman to the black Wall and then back. Pencak was the first to break the silence. "You went into the black Wall in Tunguska and you came out here?"

Richman shrugged, the move bringing a grimace of pain to his face. "Yes."

"But you went off the radio over eight hours ago!" Hawkins said. "Where were you in between?"

"Eight hours! But I just went through!"

"Tell us what you do know," Lamb snapped.

Richman glared up at the presidential advisor. Hawkins wrapped the bandage around his XO's shoulder and whispered in his ear, "It's all right. Go ahead, Rich."

"But I can't tell you anything more than I have. I ran into the Wall—it was like suddenly stepping into molasses—everything slowed down. Once I touched it, there was no way to pull back. It sucked me in. It was all bright for a second and then dark. Then it was bright again and I was falling out here. I don't know where the eight hours went. For me it was—"

"Hey!" Tomkins's yell startled everyone. Hawkins looked up and was surprised to see Levy standing next to the Wall, reaching out with her hands.

Fran stepped forward. "Debra! What are you doing? I don't think you should—"

She stopped in midsentence as Levy stepped into the Wall. Her body started to melt into the black. Hawkins was on his feet and moving. Levy was halfway gone when he grabbed her right shoulder and pulled. To his amazement the effort seemed to have the opposite effect. He was drawn in, feeling the black surround him like a warm, wet blanket. He was blinded by a flash of white and then was gone.

QUESTIONS

Ayers Rock, Australia
22 DECEMBER 1995, 1900 LOCAL
22 DECEMBER 1995, 0930 ZULU

FRAN IGNORED THE YELLING AS SHE HELPED BATSON TIE Richman into the wire stretcher that had been lowered in place of the cage. Lamb was in Tomkins's face gesturing at the Wall, venting his frustration at a situation that had gotten far out of his control.

Certain Richman was secure, she gestured at Tomkins for his men to bring him up. The basket slid up into the dark hole and was gone. Only then did Fran turn her gaze back to the chamber. Lamb had finally fallen silent and was now standing shoulder to shoulder with the others, staring at the Wall.

"Maybe they're in Tunguska now?" Batson postulated.

Fran considered that. "Maybe. But maybe they're wherever Richman was for eight hours."

"He said he didn't remember being anywhere," Batson countered.

"That doesn't mean he wasn't someplace. It just means he doesn't remember," Fran said.

"It just sucked them in," Pencak marveled, standing a respectful five feet away from the Wall.

"What do you think it is?" Fran asked the older woman. "Do you still think it's a door?"

"Of course," Pencak replied. "But a door to where? I don't think it's a direct line to Tunguska. Maybe they're in Meteor Crater. Or in South America. Or farther. Who knows? We'll just have to wait until they come back. In fact, I think it might be more than a door."

"You seem very certain they are coming back," Lamb noted, eyeing Pencak with suspicion.

"The soldier came through unharmed, except for what the Russians did to him. There is no reason to believe that whatever force is behind this Wall is malevolent."

Lamb turned to Tomkins. "I want you to send a remote camera through ASAP. Do you understand?"

"Yes, sir." Tomkins whispered into his microphone for a few seconds and the cable began moving. A few minutes later a large steel suitcase appeared in the hole and hit the ground with a slight bump. Tomkins disconnected it and opened the case. He set up the small TV they'd used above, hooking it into the power line. Then he placed the reel holding the fiber-optic cable near the Wall.

"Ready to go, sir."

Fran frowned. She wasn't sure this was a good idea, but she had nothing concrete to base that feeling upon and she could sense that Lamb was not in a mood for any dissension.

"Go ahead," Lamb ordered.

Tomkins slowly unwound the reel and the optic cable, small camera in front, snaked across the floor toward the Wall. It touched the black and slowly melted in, until suddenly the Wall flashed white. The cable spun off the reel faster than the eye could see, disappearing, and dragging the TV and suitcase with it. Tomkins leapt away, almost getting smashed as the TV flew by. The entire system was gone in less than half a second.

Tomkins stared at the Wall in disbelief and then back at Lamb, speechless. Fran glanced at Pencak, who was as expressionless as ever.

"Send the cage down," Lamb ordered. "I need to make some calls."

After he had disappeared up through the hole, Fran turned to the other two scientists. "What do we do now?"

Batson simply shook his head. "I don't know."

Pencak sat down on the rock floor near the black Wall, her bad leg stretched out in front. "We wait. I think they"—she nodded at the Wall—"whoever they are, have the initiative now, along with Major Hawkins and Ms. Levy."

"Shit," Batson muttered, walking away from the two of them and sitting down in the far end of the cave, where the ceiling curved down. Fran moved over and joined him.

"How are you doing?"

Don eyed her suspiciously. "All right."

Fran stared at him for a couple of minutes until he finally spoke again. "What? What are you looking at me like that for?"

"I know what it feels like," she said.

"What what feels like?" he snapped.

"At least you don't have the shakes too bad," she noted.

Don glared at her. "I don't need any shit from you."

"No, you don't. You do a good enough job of that yourself." She reached over and grabbed his right hand, wrapping it in both of hers. "It will be all right."

Don kept the angry look in his eyes for several minutes, then it gradually faded and he leaned back against the smoothly cut wall. "I'm sorry," he whispered. "I just don't feel too hot."

"I know," Fran said. "Like I said, I've been through it. It gets better."

He looked up at the Wall. "I don't think so."

Fran followed his look. "I do. I have to."

22 DECEMBER 1995, 1910 LOCAL
22 DECEMBER 1995, 0940 ZULU

LAMB RUBBED HIS FOREHEAD NERVOUSLY AS THE SCREEN
wavered and then cleared up. When the President appeared, Lamb gave a dispassionate recital of the events of the previous hour.

When he had finished, the President sat silent for a few minutes, his gaze turned away from the camera. Finally he looked at Lamb. "All right. You've got two people missing. One of the men you thought was lost at Tunguska came through this thing. So we know for sure it's some sort of transporter, correct?"

"Yes, sir."

"And nobody but this soldier has come through, right? No Russians, correct?"

"Yes, sir."

"And we don't know where these two people who went through your side have gone?"

"No, sir. I'm having imagery taken at Tunguska, but we have the same problem of not knowing what's happening under the tarps out there."

The President drummed his fingers on his desktop, eyes lost in thought. "If the Russians have them, they'll ID Levy very quickly. And Hawkins knows too damn much." He slammed his palm onto the desk in frustration. "Dammit, Steve, this is a screwup. We still don't know who or what we're dealing with. Do you, or any of those people you have with you, have any idea of what to do next?"

Lamb shook his head. "No, sir. I'm thinking of

sending a remote camera with a SATCOM transmitter through. Maybe we can get pictures of the other side then."

"Do you think Levy is a Russian agent? That she knew what this Wall is, and has been using these transmissions for her own purposes?"

"It's possible, sir." Lamb shrugged in frustration. "I just don't know."

"If the Russians were behind this, why would they send this fellow Richman through?"

"I don't think they would have done that on purpose. Maybe there was a mix-up. But maybe they aren't behind it."

The President considered that for a few seconds. "What about Pencak?"

"She's made no overt actions."

"You have no idea how this Wall works?"

"No, sir."

"We don't have anything like it in the pipeline?"

"No, sir."

"Not even on spec?"

"No, sir."

"Nothing from intel that anyone else might have such a thing?"

"No, sir."

The President glanced past the camera at someone who must have entered the office with him. "All right. What about the Russians? Anything on the fleet movement?"

"It's in position south of here, sir. They're just holding in place. I am concerned that if they really aren't behind this, they may try something in response to our recon team in Tunguska."

"I've received nothing about that through diplomatic channels," the President noted. "Either they haven't IDed the two bodies as ours, or they have a reason to keep it quiet. With all the trouble he's having with his own Parliament, Pamarov can't afford to cause any waves." He glanced down at the notes on his desk. "Anything on the other bomb?"

Lamb had checked that with his assistant before getting on the air. "No, sir. Not a word."

"Sending that team into Tunguska was a mistake, Steve. Letting Levy and Hawkins go through was too. Let's not have any more."

The screen went blank.

THE OTHER SIDE

HAWKINS BLINKED, TRYING TO ADJUST HIS EYES TO THE DIM surroundings after the flash of white light. He was completely disoriented and his senses shifted into focus slowly. The experience of going through the Wall had run from the feeling of sinking into molasses—as Richman had said—to feeling as if every cell in his body was being stretched, to a sudden snapping back to normal.

He felt no immediate threat, so he took it one sense at a time. He was cold, colder than he'd been in the chamber. Hawkins estimated it was in the high forties, yet the air had a very curious texture to it— almost like a humid summer day. The first thing he could clearly see was Levy standing at his side, peering about. Directly behind them a shimmering replica of the Wall stood. He scanned outward, trying to keep his brain moving with his eyes.

As best he could make out, he was inside some sort of massive cavern or building. Metal struts loomed up from the nearest wall and disappeared overhead into darkness. Hawkins strained his eyes into the dimness, trying to make out the exact dimensions, but he could only see the solid wall closest to them and another directly across. There were numerous large, blocky objects scattered about on the floor, the exact purposes of which were indeterminable. To the far left there appeared to be a bright light glowing. Unable to determine the scale of the light Hawkins had no idea how far away it was, but he estimated at least two to three kilometers.

A sudden snap caught his attention and he whirled, hand reaching down for the pistol on his hip. He caught the last of the black Wall fading into nothingness. Then just as quickly it was back, hanging there, shimmering.

One thing he knew for sure—they weren't in Tunguska.

"Where do you think we are?" His words were muffled by the thick air and swayed about by a skittish wind, a strange feeling in what his senses told him was an enclosed place. The place felt old and abandoned, with a thin layer of dust covering the floor, which appeared to be smoothly cut black rock.

Levy had put a hand over her eyes, trying to keep the grainy dirt from blowing in them as she peered about. "We're there."

"Which is where?" Hawkins repeated.

"This is where the Makers are from."

"The Makers?" Hawkins asked.

"Of the Wall."

"But where exactly is here?" Hawkins wanted to know. He'd traveled extensively throughout his military career and this place bothered him deeply, as it didn't fit in his known catalogue of locations and climates. Underlying all that was the inherently disturbing fact that the air simply didn't feel right as it ran across his skin.

"We're not on Earth," Levy quietly replied.

"How do you know that?" Hawkins snapped.

Levy simply looked at him. "Do you feel like you're on Earth?"

Hawkins didn't respond to that. "How can we breathe, then?"

"Because they wouldn't have said come if we couldn't."

Hawkins frowned. "Who said come?"

"The Makers."

Hawkins tried to control his emotions. "Who are the Makers?"

Levy met his eyes again. "I don't know. They told me to come and I have."

Hawkins took a deep breath. "What do you think is going to happen?"

Levy shook her head, her eyes bewildered behind the thick glasses. "I don't know. I just had to act, after seeing your man come through and thinking of those who have died. It is all so foolish and terrible that men should die like that. We put the best of ourselves —our heroism, our intelligence—into the worst of ourselves." She shook her head. "I didn't expect you to join me."

"I didn't either," Hawkins muttered, looking about cautiously.

Levy didn't bother replying to that remark. She was staring off into the distance. "Look!"

Hawkins looked in the direction she was pointing and then shifted his eyes in small arcs, coming back toward their position, and spotted what Levy was pointing at. There were four figures moving among several of the large objects that Hawkins assumed were some sort of machinery, about eight hundred meters away, moving off toward the light.

Hawkins instinctively grabbed Levy and pulled her to the ground. The figures were out of sight now, behind something. Hawkins thought furiously. He hadn't been able to see that well through all the blowing grit and darkness, but the four had appeared to have human form. "Let's go back," he suggested.

Levy sat up and regarded him curiously. "Back where?"

"Back to the Rock."

"How?" she asked.

Hawkins jerked a thumb over his shoulder. "Through the Wall."

Levy shook her head. "We don't know where we'd end up if we went through again."

"But we came out here," Hawkins argued.

"Yes," Levy acknowledged, "but your man went through in Tunguska and came out at the Rock. We went through at the Rock and came out here. I don't think there is a direct one-to-one linear connection among these Walls. You saw it disappear and come back—what if that was some sort of realignment and it now has a different connection?

"Someone or something is controlling these Walls. We might go through here and end up someplace where we *can't* breath. Or at least not without equipment."

Hawkins sat up himself. She had a point. If they weren't on Earth, then this was totally out of his scope of reality. If they were on Earth, then the odds were those four figures out there might have some answers. He stood. "Let's go."

Levy didn't ask where this time, she simply joined him and they moved out in the direction of the figures. Hawkins wished he'd been better prepared as he flipped open the cover on his hip holster. He had the 9mm but that was it, other than a survival knife strapped inside his shirt in a shoulder sheath.

He led them among the machinery, some of which hummed with power, crossing open areas only when necessary and then by keeping low and moving quickly. He caught a glimpse of the four figures as they crossed what appeared to be a wide-open thoroughfare among the machines. They were now less than four hundred meters away.

Definitely two arms and two legs on each, which comforted Hawkins somewhat. They were wearing helmets and dark full-body suits. One thing he had definitely noticed were the weapons in the hands of each one of the figures. They were nothing he'd seen before, but he had no doubt that they were weapons —they were as long as an M16 and the way the figures handled them, ends pointing out, left little question as to their function.

Hawkins slithered to the edge of the next machine on his stomach, Levy crawling up beside him. Looking ahead, he could see two of the figures about eighty meters ahead, halted and silhouetted against the light source, which appeared to be no closer. He wished he had a pair of binoculars.

"They look human," Levy whispered.

Where were the other two? Hawkins thought. His instincts were on fire. "Let's get out of here," he ordered, grabbing Levy by the arm. Turning, he froze, looking into two wicked-looking large-bore muzzles. Hawkins looked from the muzzles to the heads—the faces were hidden behind tinted visors but just above those faceplates was something that confirmed what Hawkins had been fearing. Each figure had a name stenciled there in Cyrillic writing.

"Nyet strelyat," Hawkins yelled, moving his hands away from his holster and getting to his feet.

One gestured with the weapon at Hawkins's holster. Using his left hand he unsnapped the belt and thigh catch, letting it drop to the ground and then kicking it toward the two. One picked it up and slipped it into a pack. The two figures inclined their helmets slightly at each other, as if exchanging an unseen glance. Hawkins assumed they were speaking on a com-link. He turned slightly as the other two appeared from behind and joined their partners. The four stood together, ten feet away, regarding Hawkins and Levy. He desperately wished he could hear what they were saying on their radio.

He was surprised when a voice echoed out of a speaker on one of the men's helmets, speaking unaccented English. "You have no trouble breathing?"

Hawkins relaxed slightly. That simple question told him a great deal about the present situation. *"Nyet."*

"You can speak English, Major Hawkins," the man replied, gesturing at the name strip on his uniform. "I have heard of you, although we did not know what you looked like." The man lifted the shaded visor and a leathery face peered out the clear plastic at the two of them. "I am Lieutenant Colonel Tuskin of the Russian Army. You are either very brave or very foolish to be here so poorly equipped. Or perhaps you know something about all this"—the weapon made a small arc—"that we do not know?"

Hawkins shrugged. "I was about to ask you the same question."

Tuskin's face showed no emotion. "What about your man who went through the portal in Tunguska? Do you not know of him?"

Hawkins hesitated, not sure how much information to divulge. "I don't know what you're talking about."

Tuskin shrugged. "Then I suppose I ought to just kill you both right now and continue on with my mission. We know those two bodies we have in Tunguska are American. We can't prove it, and the politicians don't want to make a fuss, but *I* know. That's good enough for me."

Hawkins could understand Tuskin's thought process. He'd be saying the same thing if he were on the delivering end of the weapon and Ayers Rock had been infiltrated by an obviously well-trained Russian team.

Tuskin shifted his gaze to Levy. "Who are you?"

She answered without hesitation. "Debra Levy."

"What are you?"

"I am a physicist."

Tuskin showed some surprise for the first time, looking back at Hawkins as if trying to figure out what the two of them were doing here, wherever here was.

"Do you have to keep pointing those guns at us?" Levy continued.

"Your major is a very dangerous man, if all I have heard about him is true," Tuskin answered, but he lowered his muzzle, his men reluctantly following suit. The move surprised Hawkins.

Levy gestured back the way they'd come. "Did you come out the same Wall we did?"

Tuskin frowned. "Wall? You mean the portal?"

Levy nodded.

He pointed past the massive jumble of machines to the opposite wall. "No. We came out back there." Tuskin regarded the two of them for a long minute. "Are you saying you are not responsible for all this?"

Levy shook her head. "No."

Tuskin looked at Hawkins. "I almost believe that, because I do not think you would be here so ill prepared if you knew what was happening. How did you get here?"

Before Hawkins could stop her, Levy answered. "I went through the portal in Ayers Rock and Major Hawkins tried to stop me and ended up here with me."

"Ah! So there is one in Australia! We thought that's what you might be digging for after we intercepted the transmission and then saw the imagery. So, if I am to believe you, then you do not know where we are either?"

Hawkins shook his head. "I've never seen this place before."

"You have lied to me once already. Why should I believe anything you say?" Tuskin asked.

"All right," Hawkins acknowledged, accepting the strangeness of the situation. If this was a Russian setup, it was by far the most complicated and sophisticated he'd ever imagined. "Those were my men. The one who escaped and went through the Tunguska portal, as you call it, came out in Ayers Rock."

Tuskin shook his head. "How can that be? We went through the Tunguska portal over an hour ago and we ended up here."

Hawkins spread his hands. "We went through the Ayers Rock portal fifteen minutes ago and ended up here."

Tuskin looked worried for the first time and Hawkins could understand his consternation. The Russian was realizing that perhaps he could not simply return through the portal he'd come out of and end up back in Tunguska. It must have taken extreme bravery for him to bring his men through the portal in the first place—that or a very strict order to do so.

Hawkins was about to say something when a distant noise caught his attention. It was a hissing sound, almost like a steam jet, and it appeared to be coming closer. Tuskin heard it too. He suddenly turned and his three men deployed in a defensive line, facing the noise.

With a great blast of dust a large airborne vehicle appeared, hovering over the nearest machinery and clearing it. The vehicle's four large thrusters pointed to the ground as it slowly settled down and came to a halt ten meters in front of them.

Tuskin's men stood there, pointing their rifles at the dull gray sides of the craft. It was fifty feet long by twenty wide, flat on the bottom except for the thrusters, with the sides sloping up to a slightly rounded roof. The front was blunted, with no apparent cockpit, although a wicked-looking barrel mounted on three arms portruded from above the front—obviously a weapon of some sort. It wasn't pointing at them, but Hawkins had no doubt that whoever or whatever was inside could readily make up that deficiency. He also had little doubt that Tuskin's rifles would probably have little effect on this craft. The dull sheen of the metal sides had that same tough, unyielding look as the armor on a main battle tank.

Obviously, Tuskin was thinking the same thing, too, because his men lowered their weapons for the second time. He looked over his shoulder at Hawkins. "Any suggestions, Major?"

"No, Colonel."

The weapons swung up immediately as a crack appeared on the nearer side of the craft. A section of metal folded down to the ground, making a ramp. A low red glow pulsed out of the inside. The tableau stayed frozen for a long minute and it was Levy who broke the spell. "I suggest we go on board, since it seems no one is coming out. I think this is our ride."

Hawkins started forward, only to come to an abrupt halt as Tuskin swung his weapon around at him. "How do I know this is not a trap set up by you to catch me and my men?"

Hawkins smiled grimly. "How do *we* know it's not a trap set for all of us?" He continued toward the craft, past Tuskin. Glancing over his shoulder, Hawkins watched the Russian consider the situation and then bark orders into his radio. With one of his men he headed for the ramp behind Hawkins and Levy. The other two Russians held their position on the rock floor.

The inside of the craft consisted of benches all along the walls, facing inward. The front was blocked off—if there was a pilot, he, or it, was behind that wall. Hawkins settled down on the bench, Levy at his side. Tuskin walked up to the front and studied the bulkhead, looking for a door. As he was doing that, the ramp picked up without a noise and slid back into place, closing them off from the world outside.

Tuskin stumbled slightly as the craft lifted and

then banked hard to the right. There was hardly any sound inside from the thrusters underneath, and Hawkins briefly allowed his mind to wonder what was propelling them. He'd been on Hovercraft, but this was different. He certainly didn't want to waste any brainpower guessing where they were going or what they might run into. Since coming through the portal he'd taken things one step at a time, and even then he'd been overwhelmed by events.

He glanced across the compartment at the Russian officer. Tuskin was seated uncomfortably on the far bench, his headgear still tightly in place. Hawkins recognized the cylinder on the man's back as some sort of rebreather—lighter and easier to carry than oxygen. Despite Levy's and his apparent good health Tuskin was obviously not going to trust himself to the strange atmosphere. Hawkins didn't blame him—for all they knew, there was some slow-acting particle in the air that might have already passed a sentence of death on the unprotected.

That train of thought was interrupted as the craft settled with a slight thud and the thin whine of the thrusters was silenced. The ramp folded out again and Hawkins stood quickly, looking out. He brushed past the hesitant Russians and stepped down to the ground. They were inside a smaller room off the large open area—he could see the ceiling about fifty feet above, and the walls were eighty meters away on the near sides. There were two other craft similar to the one they had just ridden in parked nearby, but no sign of life.

A door on the nearest wall slid open. Hawkins glanced at Levy, who started forward without a word. Hawkins followed and Tuskin and his trooper brought up the rear.

They entered a twenty-foot-by-twenty room. The door slid shut and the floor practically jumped from beneath their feet as the room hurtled downward. Within ten seconds the process reversed and Hawkins's knees almost buckled as they rapidly decelerated and the elevator came to a halt.

The door slid open, leading to a small room with eight chairs set in a row facing a raised platform with a large flat white surface. In front of each chair was a curved arm, rising from the floor, looking like the equipment tray a dentist uses, except thicker, with two openings in it, each about four inches across and spaced shoulder width apart.

The elevator door shut just as silently and quickly as it had opened. Tuskin was nervously fingering his rifle, the cold steel giving him scant comfort.

"Well, we know they've got to be similar in size to us," Hawkins observed, his words sounding abnormally loud in the room.

"Why?" Tuskin asked.

Hawkins pointed at the chairs. "They're the right size."

"They could have specially made those for us," Levy observed.

"The benches in the craft were the right size also," Hawkins continued. "I doubt they built those just for us."

Levy was surprised at that; she was accustomed to being the knowledgeable one. "You're probably right." She looked up at the ceiling. "How far underground do you think we are?"

Hawkins shrugged. "A long way."

"Why do they want us?" Tuskin asked.

The light in the room dimmed. The arms on the front of the chairs swung out, leaving the chairs invitingly open. A dim red glow emanated from the holes in the arms.

"What do you think?" Hawkins said, his voice unconsciously dropping to a whisper.

"I think we should sit," Levy said, and she did just that, settling into one of the center seats. As soon as she had settled down, the arm swung back in. Levy looked at it for a second and then extended her hands, one into each hole.

Hawkins looked at Tuskin, who shrugged and took a seat. Hawkins followed suit. As soon as he sat down, the arm swung back in over his lap. He extended his hands into the holes. He felt a slight crackle of static as his fingers penetrated into the red glow.

Hawkins felt a calmness settle over him. It was a feeling he was used to. The worst part of any combat mission for him had always been the preparation and the waiting. Once things started happening, he'd always felt strangely calm and had a sense that time slowed down and everything was moving in slow motion.

The room went totally dark and a single point of light appeared directly ahead, just in front of the white wall, hovering in the air. Hawkins felt something prick the back of his right hand and he tried jerking it away, but neither hand would move. He no longer had control of them. He heard a startled yell in Russian and assumed that Tuskin or the other Russian had just experienced the same thing he had.

He felt a coppery taste in his mouth and his vision blurred for a brief second and was clear again. Hawkins blinked, still focusing on the white point of light, the only thing he could see. He suddenly realized he couldn't hear anything—there was a deep, echoing silence in his ears, as if he'd put on an expensive pair of stereo headphones but no sound was coming out of them.

Taking a deep breath, Hawkins settled back against the chair, waiting for whatever was coming, his eyes focused on the white point of light.

THE RUSSIAN III

Don River, 80 Kilometers South of Pavlosk,
Russia
22 DECEMBER 1995, 1500 LOCAL
22 DECEMBER 1995, 1200 ZULU

THE TRUCK ROLLED DOWN THE FROZEN DIRT ROAD AND
halted, front fender facing the slowly flowing waters
of the Don River. The Russian looked to his left at
the well-constructed log house built into the river-
bank. The front door opened and a man with a long,
flowing black beard stepped out, looking quizzically at
the military vehicle.

"Can I help you, comrade?"

The old ways died hard in the countryside. The
Russian opened the door to the vehicle and stepped
down. "I need to cross."

The man looked at the truck, then down at his
large flatbed barge drawn up on the crossing site.
"Can you pay?"

Some of the new ways had made it out here. The Russian reached into his overcoat and pulled out a wad of bills. "Yes."

The man nodded. "Let me get my coat." He disappeared into the house and when he reappeared, his son was at his side, a strapping youth who looked sullenly at the Russian soldier.

"My son will load your vehicle onto the barge. If you'd like a cup of tea, my wife has some inside. We'll be ready to go in a minute."

The Russian's stomach twisted at the thought of putting anything into it, but he kept his face expressionless. "Thank you, comrade." He left the two to maneuver the truck onto the barge and walked into the cabin.

A woman of indeterminate age, her features withered by the harsh living here in the forest, greeted him without a word, simply extending a chipped mug of steaming tea.

"Do you three live out here alone?" The Russian asked, cradling the mug in his hands, allowing the warmth to sink in.

The woman nodded. "Yes, General."

The Russian smiled. "I am only a colonel." He glanced over his shoulder. The truck was on board the raft. The old man was starting the two ancient outboard engines. The son was walking about the truck, going to the rear and peering over the back gate, trying to see what was tied down beyond the canvas.

The Russian gently set the cup of tea down. The old woman was back at the fire, stirring something in a large blackened kettle. He pulled his pistol out and shot her in the back of the head, the body pitching silently forward into the fire.

The Russian strode out of the cabin and down the sloping bank toward the barge. The youth stepped away from the rear of the truck and made his way over to his father, to take control of the second engine. The Russian hopped on board and they were on their way across, the engines fighting not only to make it to the other side but to keep them from being swept downriver.

Up to this point all the lesser rivers and streams had posed no obstacle, as the fierce winter weather had frozen them over with enough ice to be negotiated even by the ten-ton truck. The Russian had known the Don would be a major obstacle and in preparation for his final mission had studied crossing sites, finally settling on this one. The bridges were to be avoided—they were choke points with the potential of being closed off. Here, more than a hundred kilometers from the nearest tar road and bridge, this family was one of several that operated along the river, giving access to the other side for those willing to pay the freight.

In five minutes the far bank drew up and the father and son expertly maneuvered the front end of the barge into the landing site. The son laid down the two squeaking metal ramps and gestured for the Russian to drive off. As he stepped up to the cab of the truck, the old man appeared.

"If you don't mind, comrade, I'd like my payment now before you drive off."

The Russian reached into the cab and pulled out his AK-74. The old man's eyes widened. "Forgive me, comrade, you do not have to pay."

The Russian fired a three-round burst, the rounds producing a triangular pattern in the old man's chest and blowing him off the barge into the swirling frigid waters of the Don. The son turned and ran, leaping off the barge and scrambling up the snow-covered bank. The Russian flipped the selector lever to single shot, nestled the folding metal stock into his shoulder, aimed, and fired. The son tumbled down the bank into the water, and was washed away, a streak of red on the snow the only sign of his futile escape attempt.

Clambering into the cab, the Russian started the engine and carefully rolled off the barge, up the far bank, and into the cover of the woods. He knew he'd be long gone before anyone found the bodies, and even then the authorities would most likely conclude it was the work of bandits and not pursue the matter aggressively or quickly enough to affect his mission.

He felt no emotion over the death of the family. In fact, he felt he had done them a favor. At least they had died quickly—if all went as he planned, in forty-eight hours they, and millions more, would have begun to die slow and painful deaths.

THE COALITION

The Other Side

A DISCORDANT SOUND REVERBERATED IN HAWKINS'S EARS, like the sound coming out of a car's speakers as you try to tune in to a distant station. The spot of white light in the center elongated and pulsed. Hawkins started as the static suddenly disappeared and words echoed in his head. "You can call me the Speaker. It is my role to communicate with you."

A red dot appeared to the left of the white light, followed by a blue one to the right. The white image remained elongated, pulsing as the words came. "I am joined by the Mediator and the Defender. We represent the Coalition."

Another long silence filled Hawkins's head.

"It is the Defender's message I will communicate first." A multicolored glow appeared in the air between Hawkins and the others and the far wall. It fluctuated briefly, then coalesced into an intricate system of numerous glowing dots. With great effort Hawkins twisted his head and looked to his left. He could now see the others in the reflected glow. Levy's eyes were focused ahead and she seemed unaware of anything except the lights in front of her.

Hawkins tried to speak and nothing came out. He concentrated hard and tried again. "What is it?" he managed to croak out.

Levy blinked and only her eyes turned, acknowledging his words. "That's a star map," she replied.

"I will orient you," the voice in his head said. The left center section of the map glowed bright green. "That is the Coalition." On the outer edge of the Coalition a spot started flickering. "You call the third planet of your system—the planet you live on—Earth. I will use the same term. Earth is there."

Hawkins licked his lips nervously. If that one dot was the Earth, the Coalition consisted of thousands of star systems.

A large section outside the Coalition suddenly turned bright red. "That is the Swarm. For three hundred and twenty thousand of your years there has been war between the Coalition and the Swarm. It is not a war we wish. It is a war we must fight for survival."

One factor stood out to Hawkins immediately: The tiny flickering dot that represented Earth stood at a point where green and red surged up against each other.

"Although we are not of your species, we are similar. We are able to communicate with you in this manner and through our transmissions. The Swarm is different. You would not understand their thinking. They would most definitely not be interested in understanding yours. And they would not attempt any form of communication other than death. They hold nothing outside of themselves"—for the first time the Speaker, hesitating, seemed to be searching for words, —"they hold nothing outside of themselves worthy of respect. They are not individual entities as you understand life to be. They have what you might call a race consciousness that supersedes the individual life-forms that make up their race. We have never been able to speak to them. The only communication between our races has been death.

"We first encountered the Swarm over three hundred thousand of your years ago. To that point we had not known interstellar war. The last planetary war in the Coalition had ended millennia previously. Once a planet was accepted into the Coalition, it was past the point of aggression—otherwise it would not have been allowed in."

A large section of the red area bordering the green was highlighted. "For six hundred of your years the Swarm overwhelmed us before we were able to make adjustments and defend ourselves. We lost all those systems marked and all the life in them in that time. Billions of life-forms perished in the fighting. Entire species were obliterated.

"Since then we have been able to keep the Swarm at bay." A brief red glow showed on the far side of the star map. "We believe that the Swarm has expanded in the other direction away from the Coalition, but no probe through Swarm space has ever returned. Over the years the Swarm has continued to attack our border at sporadic times, at points seemingly chosen at random."

A bright white line suddenly glowed, dividing the red from green. "To contain the Swarm, two hundred thousand of your years ago we developed a defensive boundary. Because the border was too vast to patrol constantly, we devised a static planetary surveillance line to be supplemented by mobile Space Forces."

The map swirled and the glowing dot that was Earth expanded. Hawkins realized that the area around Earth had been blown up for clearer viewing. He could see small representations of the sun and the other planets, hovering in the air in front of him.

"Your solar system was chosen to be incorporated in that surveillance line for two reasons. Primarily because of its location. But also because of the presence of life on the third planet. Deep-space sensors and weapons were placed at the edge of your system and oriented outward." A series of small glowing dots appeared outside the orbit of Pluto.

The air cleared and then there was only Earth hanging in the air, slowly rotating. "The control system and master relay were placed on the third planet." Six small spots glowed on the surface of the globe. Hawkins could immediately place each spot as the continents came into view: Tunguska, Ayers Rock, Ries Basin, Vredefort Dome, Meteor Crater, and Campo del Cielo.

"The Swarm attacked in force through this part of the Coalition approximately one hundred and ninety thousand years ago. The defense system succeeded in its primary task of giving sufficient notice, and Coalition Space Forces responded. A great space battle was fought three hundred parsecs from your solar system and the Swarm was beaten back despite heavy losses to the Coalition. The defense system only partially succeeded in its secondary mission of protecting this solar system."

Half the lights winked off on the globe—Ries Basin, Meteor Crater, and Campo de Cielo. "Three of the relay sites were destroyed by the Swarm. There were near misses at the ones you call Vredefort Dome and Ayers Rock."

The scene expanded again to take in the solar system. Many of the small red dots around the rim of the system disappeared. "Forty-three percent of the deep-space sensors and automated weapons were also destroyed. Despite those losses, though, the system remained functional, as the original had had redundancy built in." There was the briefest of pauses. "With the recent loss of the relay under Vredefort Dome the system is no longer functional to the satisfaction of the Defender."

There was a long pause. Hawkins stared through the display at the three points of light. He glanced down at his hands and could see the wrists where they disappeared into the red glow. He again tried to withdraw his hands and failed. He forced himself to relax and slow his heartbeat.

"The Defender has proposed to Council three options. The first option is to repair the defense system." The lights in the Solar System blinked back on. Then the lights shifted back to the star map. "The second option is to expand our border beyond the vicinity of your planet and build a new defense system here in what you call the Sirius Alpha and Beta system and another here in the Epsilon 2398 Alpha and Beta system to adequately defend the new area." The green sphere crept outward a tiny fraction. "That would move your solar system from being on the border to being inside our border.

"The third option is to contract our border and build a defense system here in the Barnard's star system." The green sphere edged back a fraction of an inch. The small flashing dot representing Earth stood alone between the red and the green.

Hawkins glanced to his left. Levy was staring at the star map. Beyond her Tuskin turned his head and met Hawkins's eyes. They were both military men and understood immediately what the three proposals represented in strategic terms. The Speaker's next words confirmed what Hawkins had feared.

"The Defender recommends option three."

In the silence following these last words Hawkins could hear the sound of his own heartbeat thudding through his arteries. He was startled when Levy spoke for the first time.

"Why?"

There was no indication that she was heard. The star map disappeared and only the three lights remained. The center one continued to pulse in rhythm to the words spoken.

"I will now speak for the Mediator. All factors have been considered as presented by the Defender. Option one would require the least cost, but is considered too risky because the native life-forms on the third planet have proven themselves a threat to the defense system by having destroyed part of it.

"Option two would require the highest cost, but would only be done if the Council considered the natives of the third planet as potentially worthy of membership in the Coalition. It would require a lengthening of our internal lines of communication, which is not recommended.

"Option three is recommended because it can be immediately implemented and requires no interaction with the natives of the third planet. Additionally, it reduces our internal lines of communications, always a desirable military goal.

"The Mediator's role is to observe and then present to the Council the perspective of all parties involved. The Defender's perspective has been presented. The Mediator has studied the data on your planet. The Mediator has tentatively concluded that the natives of Earth are not yet ready for inclusion in the Coalition, nor are they on a developmental path that would lead to it."

In place of the lights was a swift flickering of images, most gleaned from Earth news reports. Despite the rapid shifting of scenes Hawkins recognized all of it—Lebanon, the Gulf War, Somalia, Yugoslavia,

Northern Ireland, all the hot-spots of the world flashed before his eyes in a distressing series of pictures.

"The Mediator has also tentatively concluded that the natives of Earth are responsible for the destruction of the relay site under Vredefort Dome and that there is a statistically significant probability that there may be future damage to the defense system caused by the natives, even if the present damage were to be repaired—especially now that our relay sites at Ayers Rock and Tunguska have been detected and uncovered."

Again the scenes shifted, this time showing pictures of missile silos, submarines, bombers, and other military hardware.

The images disappeared. "The Mediator believes that the natives of the third planet should be given a chance to present their perspective. There is some information we require to clarify the situation. Why are only three of the eight personnel we requested present? You may now speak."

Hawkins blinked and looked at Debra, then down the line at Tuskin. The Russians must have been given a list of four names also.

"We did not understand what the message meant," Debra offered.

"You understood enough to uncover our relays at Tunguska and Ayers Rock," the voice replied. "You understood enough to send some personnel across. We examined the man who came through alone—he was injured and disoriented and appeared simply to be fleeing the site where he had been. He was not one of those we requested. We sent him onward to where our scanners indicated he desired to go. Where are the other personnel we requested?"

"Our other two members are waiting for us to report back on what we have discovered," Hawkins said. "We had no idea what would happen when we went through the Wall in your relay site."

"What about your other three, Colonel Tuskin?"

That was the first indication that the voice knew whom it was addressing. That also explained the eight seats lined up. Hawkins wondered what sort of information might be getting drawn from him through whatever had pierced his skin. Was it some sort of lie detector? What had he been injected with?

Tuskin seemed at a loss for words for a few seconds. "My people also did not know what would happen. Your Defender should understand that a reconnaissance is in order before committing oneself to a course of action. As the military man listed, I was sent across first."

"Your distrust and unwillingness to comply with a simple request does not indicate favorably. We selected the two most powerful group entities on your planet to communicate to. Between your two entities you control the vast preponderance of military might —and most of the destructive weapons that pose a threat to our relay sites.

"More important, you are the only two group entities on this planet that have projected personnel into space. That is normally considered one of the first steps in proving eligibility to join the Coalition. We were disappointed to discover that you have managed to do that, yet still remain riven as a species entity on your planet."

"Did you destroy the *Voyager 2* probe?" Hawkins asked, trying to steer the conversation away from the failings of the human race.

"Yes. When it passed out of your star system, it was detected by the sensors and examined. The main computer allowed it to continue until the Vredefort Dome relay was destroyed. At that time automatic defensive measures destroyed it. The initial reaction was that the Vredefort Dome relay had been destroyed by a Swarm attack, and all systems responded accordingly until the data could be examined."

"How could a Swarm attack have made it through your defensive system to attack Earth?" Tuskin asked.

"The Defender has shown you that the system has been degraded. The Swarm has the capability to make attacks of limited size that might evade the external sensors."

"Has this happened before?" Hawkins wondered why Tuskin seemed so concerned about this.

"Most recently, in the time count you call 1908, a Swarm Splinter ship infiltrated this system. It reached the third planet and launched an attack on the Tunguska relay. We were able to destroy the ship just prior to destruction of the relay. We were not capable of doing that at Vredefort Dome because the attack came from the planet natives and not the Swarm."

"The explosion at Vredefort Dome was not done

by either of our governments," Hawkins tried explaining.

"It was done by a native of the third planet."

Hawkins went into detail, talking about the two missing bombs and the fact that he had been part of a team trying to recover them. He felt shackled with the inability to use his hands and by the total lack of response from the three points of light. There was no indication that he was even being heard, until he had finished. The reply was not what he had hoped.

"We are not interested in the factionalism among the natives of the third planet except as they directly affect the Coalition. The destruction of the relay site at Vredefort Dome did so affect us. We wish to avoid such occurrences in the future. For that reason we have shown you the three options we are considering, along with the perspective the Defender and the Mediator have on those options.

"The fact that you have a weapon still missing and uncontrolled that is capable of such power as that which destroyed the Vredefort Dome relay was a very significant factor when we considered your species on the scale for acceptance into the Coalition or even simply protection by the Coalition.

"We carefully selected four personnel from each of your two factions in terms of the skills of those personnel so you could understand the options and the relative merits of those options. We chose one military person to be able to understand the Defender's analysis. We chose a statistician to understand the risk-and-benefit projection of each option.

A geologist to be able to help you uncover the relay sites so we might bring you here. And a physicist to understand scientific matters as they might come up to affect your decision."

"Where are we now?" Tuskin asked.

"Our present location is classified," the Speaker replied.

"Are we on Earth?" Tuskin persisted.

"No."

"How did we get here?" Tuskin asked.

"Through what you call the portals or Walls."

"We know that," Tuskin replied. "I want to know how we traveled through space to get here."

"Even if we told you, you would not understand."

Hawkins was frustrated. He had the answers to many of the questions they had been struggling with prior to going through the portal. But those questions were no longer important in the face of what the Speaker had presented. "You have shown us your three options. You have also indicated which option you are inclined to pursue. You say you want our perspective, yet you seem to know all you need to know about humans to make your decision. What true options do we have? What can we do to influence your decision? You must have brought us here for some reason other than simply to explain the situation to us."

"We felt we must apprise you of the situation out of respect for you as sentient beings. The Mediator also desired to hear from you should there be anything that might change the analysis of the situation."

There was a long silence and Hawkins was surprised when Debra was the one to break it. "You said you wanted our perspective, but you ask it only after presenting us with information we were not aware of, and which in itself would change our perspective. Our race is still very young as compared to yours. We need time to develop and we need time to adjust to this new information."

Tuskin stirred. "You chose us, but we are not the ones that make decisions for our species. We can bring your message back to those who do. That may change things on our planet enough so that your first or second option may be feasible. If our governments cooperate, we can make this planet a worthwhile place to defend."

"We will consider this. Wait." The room went totally dark and Hawkins was left with the image of the lights etched on his retinas, slowly fading away.

Hawkins was sweating despite the cool temperature. He directed his question in the general direction of Tuskin. "You were sent four names?"

Tuskin's voice sounded very far away. "Yes. A message to our space lab. Very directional. It came up from Tunguska. That, along with the message out of Ayers Rock, led us to dig. We have long known there was something strange about what happened at Tunguska so many years ago."

"Why didn't your government send the four people named in the message?" Levy asked.

"Why didn't yours?" Tuskin countered. "Why did you infiltrate our country to try and find out what we were doing? We can ask questions all day, but if they come back through that door and say they want nothing more to do with us, everything as we know it may be over!"

"The last time this Swarm attacked Earth was 1908," Hawkins observed. "It may be a long time before they do it again."

"The simple fact that they are out there is enough!" Tuskin spoke harshly. "You know as well as I do that the Coalition's most feasible military option is to pull back and shorten their defensive line."

"I take hope from the fact that they didn't simply do that," Debra said. "That they chose to speak to us is important."

Tuskin seemed not to have heard. "We have been groveling in the dirt fighting each other since the beginning of civilization, yet now suddenly we look up and realize that we have been so infantile!" His voice lashed out at Hawkins. "I kill you because you are American. You kill me because I am Russian. Yet we are all human." Hawkins heard him spit. "Stupidity. It is too late. It is all over."

Hawkins could understand where the other man's anger came from. Tuskin had spent his life dedicated to fighting for a government that had fallen apart at the seams just a few short years before. The carefully cultivated myth of duty, honor, and country in the Russian military had had the rug pulled out from under it. Now what had happened to Tuskin's country was happening to the planet. If a trained military man like Tuskin was affected this way, Hawkins wondered how others would react when they learned what he had just been told in this room.

He was still pondering that when the lights reappeared. "You will have twenty-four hours to return to us with both a proposal and actions completed to indicate that we may consider options other than number three."

"What?" Debra exclaimed. "This system has existed for hundreds of thousands of years and you give us only twenty-four hours to do something? We must have more time."

"The relay sites you came through will return you to where you started. In twenty-four hours the portals will shut down." The lights disappeared. With a rumble the elevator door slid open behind them and the light from it spilled out into the room. Hawkins again felt a flicker of pain on the back of his hand. He pulled and this time his hands came out without any resistance. The arm swung away and he stood and turned for the elevator.

RETURN

ON THE SURFACE NIGHT HAD SETTLED IN, BUT IT MADE NO difference to Fran down in the chamber. She sat on the rock floor, her eyes staring at the Wall as if simply by looking long enough, she could see through and discover what had happened to Hawkins and Debra.

Tomkins had gone off shift an hour before, replaced by a young lieutenant whose presence was an irritating buzz to Fran as he worked on the remote gear that would be sent through as the next probe. Don Batson had stayed down here, joining her in the watch, his eyes reaching to hers every so often for encouragement in his own personal trial. A few feet away Dr. Pencak sat as still as the floor she was on.

"Debra seemed to know what she was doing." The

words came out before Fran even realized what she was saying.

She looked over at Don, who was running his hand along the smooth stone wall, for perhaps the fiftieth time in the past hour, taking comfort from the rock itself, something he understood well. "For all we know she was crazy," he commented. "Maybe she's on her own form of medication," he added wryly, holding out his own hand, which shook slightly. He jerked a thumb up toward the surface. "Lamb's convinced Hawkins and Levy came out in Tunguska and the Russians have them."

"The Russians!" Fran said bitterly. "Always the Russians. Or the Iraqis. Or the Cubans. Or the Libyans. Or whoever our enemy of the week is."

Don shrugged, glad to be thinking about something other than his own problem. "You've been at the Hermes meetings. They spend most of their time trying to worst-case things and looking at everyone as an enemy." He looked at her. "Hell, Fran, that was your job—worst-case things. Correct me if I'm wrong, but it seems to me that a large spur for us even being at some of those meetings was your analysis of present trends and where they are likely to lead us."

Fran leaned forward. "Those were statistical projections based on what was happening. Those projections will come true if nothing is done to avert the disastrous course we are on."

"Yeah, I know," Don said. "Hell, the last tasking I got from Hermes—along with a hundred-and-sixty-thousand-dollar grant—was to work on finding natu-

ral underground shelters that could be developed by
the military into bunkers for minimum cost. They
even had me do up a study on how Mammoth Caves
could be converted by the military in a crisis."

"Bomb shelters!" Fran exploded. "They want to
handle the world's problems by building bomb shelters? That kind of thinking belongs back in the fifties."

"Then I guess I belong back there too," Don said
quietly.

"Thinking like that is more concerned with surviv-
ing than living," Fran continued as if she hadn't
heard.

"What's the difference?" Don asked.

"Animals survive," Fran replied. "Humans live."

"Animals don't build nuclear bombs and lose
them," Don retorted. "What do you really think is
going to happen if that second bomb is exploded?"

"It depends on where it goes off," Fran said.

"Regardless of where it goes off," Don persisted.
"What do you think will happen?"

Fran looked at him. "I think we're going to be in
even deeper shit than we know we are in now. There
are a lot of variables and therefore a lot of outcomes,
but over ninety percent of them are bad. And that's
the only number I'm concerned with."

Don nodded. "Well, listen, Fran. I may have had
my head up my ass for the past fifteen years working
for the government—I did what they told me to do
and took their money and didn't think much about it.
I didn't think much about anything. Hold it"—he held

up a hand as Fran started to interrupt—"let me finish." He pointed at the Wall. "But the events of the past forty-eight hours have opened my eyes. I'm not sure what's going on here, but I do accept that I have a responsibility beyond my own little world."

Pencak had been so quiet that it took both of them by surprise when she spoke. "Very good, but even now you still refuse to accept the possibility that the unacceptable may have to be accepted." Pencak's words hung in the air for a long moment.

"I can accept the unacceptable if I know what it is. This is all so—" Batson's words were cut off as the Wall suddenly glowed brightly and Hawkins and Debra stumbled through. They looked no different than if they had just gone through a revolving door. Hawkins had his hand on Debra's shoulder and was holding her, as they both blinked in the glare of the high-power lights pointing at the wall.

The lieutenant was yelling into his com-link as Fran, Batson, and Pencak gathered around the two travelers. "Are you all right?" Fran asked as the two tried to get their bearings.

"We're fine," Hawkins answered, looking back over his shoulder at the portal.

"What happened?" Batson asked.

"We met the creators of all this," Debra said, gesturing around at the chamber. The way she said it told Fran right away that she wasn't talking about the Russians.

Hawkins held up a hand as they were barraged

with questions. "We'll tell you everything, but I want to do it only once. We don't have much time."

"We don't have much time for what?" Fran asked.

In reply Hawkins pointed at the hole. "Let's go up. We need to brief Lamb so he can relay it to the President."

22 DECEMBER 1995, 2307 LOCAL
22 DECEMBER 1995, 1337 ZULU

FRAN LISTENED IN AMAZEMENT AS HAWKINS GAVE A DE-tailed account of what had happened to Debra and himself from the moment they went through the wall to the time they returned. Debra occasionally added a comment or small fact, but it was obvious to Fran that Hawkins was well versed in giving such reports. She imagined he had to do this after every mission he went on—she was also sure, though, that he'd never experienced anything like what he had just gone through.

When he told of the twenty-four-hour time limit, Lamb was shaking his head. Fran didn't know what to make of it all. Not having gone through herself, she thought it all sounded very distant and outrageous. Hawkins's dry and factual accounting of the events didn't lend them an air of credibility. They sounded like stories from a supermarket checkout tabloid rather than an army officer's after-action report.

"Did you see the Russians go back through their portal?" was Lamb's first question.

"No," Hawkins said. "We were let off the craft at our portal first. It lifted and headed toward where I presume the Russians' portal was—near the opposite wall."

"So for all you know, the Russians might still be there," Lamb said.

A look of frustration flashed across Hawkins's face. "That is a very slight possibility. I'm sure they would be in as much of a rush to get back to their superiors and report what happened as we were."

"Unless they set this whole thing up," Lamb returned.

Hawkins leaned forward. "They didn't set this up. There's no way they could have set it up." He pointed out the door of the tent toward the mine shaft. "How do you explain the portal? How were we transported? There's never even been a hint that Russia possesses such a capability. And where were we transported to?"

"That's what I'd like to know," Lamb said. "They said you weren't on Earth, but if these aliens could transport people that easily, how come they didn't come here?"

"Would you have come here if you were the one in control like they are?" Hawkins countered.

"What about Richman?" Batson wanted to know. "If you have to go through one Wall or portal to get here, and another to get to Tunguska, how did he get directly from Tunguska to here?"

"The Coalition said they had Richman for those eight hours," Hawkins explained.

"You said you were in some sort of large building —maybe underground. Why do you think it wasn't here on Earth?" Lamb demanded.

"It didn't *feel* like Earth," Hawkins said. "I know that sounds strange but the air, the building, the machinery, which I didn't recognize—the whole thing just felt very different, like nothing I've ever experienced before."

"Why did they hide from you?" Lamb asked.

"For all I know they weren't hiding," Hawkins said, his voice taking on an edge. "They probably weren't even on the same planet as us. It looked like a transmission. Maybe those points of light *were* members of the Coalition."

Fran spoke for the first time, trying to get the conversation back on a productive track. "What is it exactly that they want from us?"

"They didn't say they wanted anything," Debra said.

"Then why the twenty-four-hour time limit?" Fran asked.

"They gave us twenty-four hours because we asked for it—or to be more precise, Colonel Tuskin asked for it. I got the feeling that they were going to shut the system down in twenty-four hours anyway and were just letting us know that. We wanted a chance to come back and tell our leaders what the situation is. If any move is going to be made, then we need to be the ones to make it and then present it to the Coalition."

Lamb threw his hands up in the air. "This is the craziest thing I've ever heard. I can't go to the President with this. He'll think I'm insane. We have no evidence other than your story."

"If you don't go to the President with this immediately, then you might be dooming this planet," Hawkins returned hotly. "If he won't believe what he's told, then ask him to get on a plane and fly here." He pointed down. "There's hard evidence right below our feet. The President can make it in less than four hours aboard the X-27"—referring to the Air Force's super-secret spy plane capable of traveling at eight times the speed of sound. "He can go through with us and see for himself. If you wait too long, the portals will shut down and we'll never know if I was right or wrong."

Lamb looked at Hawkins incredulously. "How did you know about the X-27?" he demanded. "You weren't cleared for that!"

"I know a lot of things I'm not cleared for," Hawkins replied ominously. "I know if you decide to get off your ass and tell the President exactly what's going on *and* recommend he come here, that we can do something positive for once. Let's use our resources for good."

"There's no way he'll come here," Lamb argued.

"Well, he has to do something!" Levy blurted.

Batson tried mediating. "I don't understand why the aliens—if that's what they are—have to do anything. Why can't they just leave things alone? If this story is true, then things have gone all right for a very long time."

Hawkins shook his head. "The loss of their relay station under Vredefort Dome has apparently reduced the capability of their defense system below an acceptable level."

"Why can't they just fix it, then?" Batson asked. "If they can send you back and forth so easily, why don't they send someone through with a toolbox and fix the damn things? I'm sure the sites can be guarded from here on out from another incident like the one that happened in South Africa."

"You don't understand this from their perspective," Levy said. "We're a minor irritant to the Coalition. It's as if we put a radar site for our nuclear early warning system on some island in the Pacific in the middle of a war. And there's a bunch of monkeys on that island that threw coconuts over the fence around the radar. And finally one day one of those coconuts breaks the radar. What would our reaction be?"

"We'd wipe out the monkeys," Hawkins answered succinctly. He turned to Lamb. "I think Debra's point is valid. We should be thankful that they even bothered to talk to us. The twenty-four hours is their time line and they probably feel they don't have to explain their agenda to us. What we have to do is give them a proposal to make it worth their while to either fix the system here or extend their perimeter."

"I think it's much more likely that both of you were the victim of some sort of mind-control technique." Lamb looked at Hawkins and Levy. "Maybe these memories were implanted in your brains or were part of a computer simulation. Maybe you didn't go farther than three feet on the other side of that Wall." He pointed at the small red mark on the back of Hawkins's hand. "You were probably drugged and all this was implanted in your memory. We've had some success working with mind-altering substances and computer simulations that can do that."

Hawkins stood. "It was no computer simulation and it was no mind game. This is real. That damn chamber down there is real and that portal is real. Richman going through in Tunguska and coming out here is real. *Voyager* getting destroyed is real. The transmission is real. And we know for damn sure that second bomb out there is real!"

Lamb stood, looking anything but convinced. "I'll relay this to the President. We'll see what he wants to do." He left the shelter, leaving the team members to consider each other. Fran was surprised when Pencak broke the silence.

"There will be no action." She looked at Hawkins. "You know that, don't you?"

Hawkins reluctantly nodded. Fran felt her stomach churn with anxiety. When she'd first heard Hawkins and Debra tell their story she'd felt a breath of hope that her calculations might be overturned. Now she realized that hope was premature. In fact, if an adequate response wasn't presented in twenty-four hours, things could be even worse with a non-Earth threat added on top of all the man-made ones. The portals closing would simply be the exclamation point on Hawkins and Levy's story—with no chance to change the ending other than wait for the threat from the Swarm that might not materialize for generations or might appear in a day. Fran didn't think there would be anyone left in a few generations to face that threat anyway.

"Tell me about the place you were in," Batson said.

Hawkins described the cavern and machinery as best he could, the rest of the team listening raptly.

"Did you see any sign of life other than the Russians?"

"No."

"What about lighting?" Batson asked.

"As far as I can remember, there was just the distant light source," Hawkins said.

"We cast faint shadows in only one direction," Levy recollected.

"I think we were at a military base," Hawkins said. "There was the craft that picked us up and the other two in the hangar and they definitely had something that looked like a weapon system on the front. The room we were briefed in was very far underground, which indicates a desire for protection."

"I think we were on a planet close by," Debra said. "Perhaps one in the perimeter they showed us, near Earth. The amount of time you say we were gone corresponds to the amount of time we spent on the other side. So however we got there, the travel was relatively instantaneous."

"It was probably a staging area for the Space Forces they told us about," Hawkins suggested.

"All that's well and good," Pencak threw in, "but it doesn't help us with the immediate problem."

"Let's hold up here a second," Fran said. She walked across the tent to the easel where Hawkins had done his line diagrams in previous meetings. She flipped back through until she found what she was looking for. She ran her finger up the line diagram until it rested on NUCLEAR BLAST VREDEFORT DOME. "This is the event that started everything—if we're to take all that happened to Hawkins and Debra at face value." She held up a hand to forestall Hawkins's angry reply. "Listen—I'm going along with all this. This Speaker said that the fact that a nuclear weapon was still missing was one of the factors they considered when looking at the human race for eligibility to join the Coalition."

"A significant factor," Hawkins corrected.

"All right," Fran said. "Even better, a significant factor. That's understandable, because the other bomb is the one that started this whole mess. Well, wouldn't it be a sign of good faith if that one missing bomb was tracked down and brought under control?"

Hawkins nodded slowly, thinking about it. "Yes. I think that might make an impact on their consideration of the options."

"At the very least it might influence them to give us more time to get the politicians to support more positive steps," Pencak noted. "They might keep the portals open awhile longer. I think recovering that bomb would be an excellent first move."

"That's all well and good," Hawkins said. "Except

for the fact that I was part of the U.S.'s team to track that bomb down and we didn't have much of an idea of where it is."

"But maybe the Russians do," Pencak said. "Maybe this Colonel Tuskin might have a good idea."

"Except he's on the other side of the world right now," Batson said. "And he's probably getting the same chilly reception there from his superiors that you received from Lamb."

22 DECEMBER 1995, 2323 LOCAL
22 DECEMBER 1995, 1353 ZULU

DESPITE HAVING WORKED WITH THE PRESIDENT FOR OVER eighteen years—from his early days as a governor—Lamb was uncertain what the expression on the man's face in the video monitor meant. He'd just relayed Hawkins's story as briefly and as factually as he could and the President had listened without comment until now.

"Christ, Steve. What am I supposed to do? Do you believe this stuff?"

Lamb had been asking himself the same question ever since he'd listened to Hawkins. "No, sir, I don't. But I don't think we should dismiss this outright. Something is going on here—something that is very significant. There's a possibility that the Coalition story could be true, a possibility we can't afford to ignore. Even if it isn't true, we're dealing with some very advanced technology and if someone on Earth is behind it, we need to find out damn fast who it is. The most obvious answer is the Russians, but if they are, I don't understand what they're doing. None of it makes much sense."

The President's face drew in tight, a look that Lamb *was* familiar with—he was upset. "Then call me when you make some sense out of it, Steve, but don't dump all this nonsense on my desk and expect me to sort it out. That's your job! I've got half a dozen major crises and God knows how many minor ones that I'm dealing with—ones that I know are real. Am I supposed to call Pamarov over this? And have him throw what happened with the Orion team at Tunguska in my face? Am I supposed to go to Congress with it? And what exactly am I to tell them? What are we supposed to do? If these things shut down in twenty-four hours, maybe that's all for the best."

Lamb was silent. The President glared at the screen for a few seconds, trying to regain his temper. When he spoke again, the anger was gone, replaced by a deep weariness. "When you figure things out, Steve, you give me a call with some recommendations. If you think it's such a priority, then you work that much harder to solve it."

The screen went blank. Lamb turned off his communications set and sat still for almost five minutes. Then he pushed a button on his desk. "Come in."

Colonel Tolliver and Major Hawkins entered the communications shelter. Lamb looked at Tolliver first. "Report."

The Marine colonel worked from farthest threat in. "The Navy's got aerial and electronic surveillance of the Russian fleet off the coast. The Russians are holding in place. We've alerted the Australian authorities to be on the lookout for Russian agents. No reports from them of anyone suspicious. Our outer and inner perimeters are secure."

"I want a squad of your men detached to my direct command as of now. Have the officer in charge report to Captain Tomkins at the mine shaft."

"Yes, sir."

"That's all." Lamb waited until the marine was gone and then turned to Hawkins. "We've picked up some new information on Pencak," Lamb pulled a manila envelope out of his briefcase and handed it to Hawkins. "That's the dossier on Felix Zigorski—the Russian scientist she was involved with."

Hawkins pulled a sheaf of papers out and glanced at the cover sheet. "She volunteered that he worked with the cosmonaut program." He scanned down. "There's nothing that significant here. Looks like he was legitimate as a scientist, although that doesn't rule out his doing covert work for the old KGB."

Lamb pointed at the envelope. "There's a picture of Zigorski in there, sir. I suggest you take a look at it."

Hawkins reached in and pulled out an eight-by-ten glossy. He stared at the figure in the picture and then looked up at Lamb. "What the hell happened to him?"

"He was in a tank in the Great Patriotic War,"

Lamb said, using the Russian term for World War II. "It got hit during the battle of Kursk and burned up. They pulled Zigorski out and somehow he survived."

Hawkins looked at the photo again, noting the man's deformities. Zigorski's skin in the picture was bright red and looked freshly boiled. He was missing his right arm and was seated in a wheelchair. It was hard to tell from the picture what state his legs were in. "Well, I can certainly see now the attraction he held for Pencak," he said sarcastically. "But is there any indication that he and Pencak might have been part of some plan that has anything to do with what's going on now? We know they were both at Tunguska. Is there any record of either of them ever coming here to Australia?"

"No."

Lamb tossed the picture and dossier down. "What about Batson? How were his last psych and security eval for Hermes?"

"Good to go on both."

"His last polygraph?"

"Clean."

"He's clean?" Hawkins asked, surprised. "Your people gave an alcoholic a clean bill of health?"

"It wasn't that bad last time he was checked," Lamb said.

Hawkins changed the subject, realizing it was fruitless to talk about something he could do nothing about. "Anything more from Tunguska?"

Lamb shook his head. "Nothing. We checked the imagery from the time you went through to when you came back and there doesn't appear to be any unusual activity."

"What about the Russians going through?"

"We couldn't see what was going on under the tarps. There are more troops in the area now. At least a regiment of armored infantry. They're also flying Hinds around the clock in aerial surveillance. We couldn't get another team in to look under the tarps without compromise." Lamb paused and stared at Hawkins. "Give it to me straight, Hawk. Do you think you might have been mentally manipulated—that you really didn't travel anywhere and this was all implanted in your mind?"

Hawkins sat back in his chair and thought. He remembered the prick of something going into the back of his hand and the coppery taste in his mouth—what had been the purpose of that? Also the way the voice had sounded, as if it were inside his head, and not coming from the outside. But he had been able to converse with the others in the room.

"I have to admit it's possible," Hawkins conceded. "But I don't think so. I think this is for real. I also don't see any reason it shouldn't be for real. Who on Earth has anything to gain by doing this? Plus, I think we have a lot to lose if we don't accept that this is real."

Lamb shook his head of those thoughts and leaned back in his chair. "What about the other bomb?"

"Nothing. If Qaddafi has it, he's keeping damn quiet about it, and so are all our assets over there. My

Orion teams have nothing. What's the status on Libya?" he asked.

"The President is still holding off having the Seventh Fleet cross the thirty-third parallel. The Russians are still keeping quiet about whoever sold the bombs."

Hawkins stood. "What's the next step?"

Lamb waved a hand at him, dismissing him. "Let me think about it."

22 DECEMBER 1995, 2327 LOCAL
22 DECEMBER 1995, 1357 ZULU

HAWKINS STEPPED OUT OF THE MEDICAL SHELTER INTO THE warm night air and looked up at the stars, wondering if one of those was where he had been. Richman was doing well; the shoulder wound was clean and he hadn't lost much blood. Hawkins had pumped him for information concerning the missing eight hours and what he had seen at Tunguska, but had learned nothing new. Richman had no memory of a large enclosed space filled with machinery.

"Makes you feel kind of small, doesn't it?" Fran appeared out of the darkness into the glow of the arc lights from the perimeter security.

"What does?"

"All those stars, all so far away."

"Yeah, I suppose." Hawkins nodded his head in

the direction of the shaft building. "Are they still down there arguing?"

"Yes. I think Don is in over his head—he's got to put a lot of energy into simply staying straight. Pencak insists it's aliens and your story confirmed what she believed earlier. I'm not sure where Levy's head is at."

Hawkins peered at her in the dark. "Do you believe me?"

She didn't hesitate. "I've thought about it and I've decided that I want to believe you very badly. And if I want to, then I'm going to."

Not exactly the most supportive answer Hawkins had ever heard. "What do you think we should do?"

Fran stared out into the desert. "Lamb's talked to the President. I saw him a few minutes ago talking with Tomkins. They're working on sending the remote camera through with a SATCOM link. If it comes out anywhere on the planet, they ought to be able to keep contact with it."

"It won't work," Hawkins declared.

"I know it won't. But he has to try. He didn't say anything, but I got the idea the President wasn't too impressed."

Hawkins stepped away from the tent and walked over to where triple rolls of concertina wire surrounded the compound. The edge of the Rock was less than fifty feet away, dropping abruptly off to the ground. He could make out the silhouette of a marine right near the edge, highlighted against the moonlit night sky.

"I knew he wouldn't be impressed. We really didn't give him too much to work with, because the aliens didn't give us too much to work with. Pencak's idea is the only reasonable thing I've heard since I came back."

"Going after the other bomb?" Fran asked. "But you said that there are people already on that. What can we do?"

Hawkins sought her eyes out in the dark. "There's something I left out of my briefing to Lamb. When we reboarded the skimmer to return to our respective portals and go through, I talked to Colonel Tuskin. I told him that I didn't think we would get a good response to what we had seen and heard. At least not a timely one."

"What did he say?"

"He agreed."

A small smile played across Fran's face. "So what plan did you two come up with?"

"How do you know we came up with anything?"

"Because you told me yourself not to trust anyone, and I think you would have been calculating five steps ahead from the minute you came out of that chamber after hearing what the aliens had to say. And you would have known what would happen when you got back—as you just said you did. And I think you would have come up with an alternate plan."

Hawkins squatted down and touched the pitted surface of the Rock with his palms. He then peeled the camouflage cover from his watch and looked at the reflective surface. "We agreed that if we didn't get a positive response, we would go back through, eight hours after our return."

"And do what?"

"Get the bomb ourselves."

Fran sat down next to him. "But how are you going to do that?"

"Tuskin knows who the Russian general was who sold the bombs. And he knows where he's being held. That's something we didn't have before. He says the Russian authorities are keeping it quiet because it's a great embarrassment and would only add to their poor public image."

"How are you going to get to the general?"

Hawkins shrugged. "We didn't have enough time to figure that one out. It isn't the greatest plan, but it's a start. It beats sitting around here waiting for everything to close up."

"I don't understand you," Fran said.

Hawkins glanced at her in the dark. "What's not to understand?"

"How you can have done what you've done for the past several years, yet still seem to care so much about people and the world. How you can react so strongly about your wife, yet be capable of killing without a second thought."

"It's my job," Hawkins replied.

"Bullshit," Fran said without raising her voice. "I don't buy that."

Hawkins twisted on his knee and faced her. "All right. You want to know what makes me tick? I'll tell you the truth—I don't know. At first I did what I do because I thought I was one of those people that had their finger in the dike and kept it from breaking. But then I started realizing that maybe my side of the dike was just as screwy and fucked up as the other side. And that maybe there was some guy on the other side with his finger in the same hole I had mine in.

"But what was I supposed to do? It's all well and good to intellectualize it, but when you're waist deep in the swamp fighting the alligators, that isn't the time to be worried about draining the swamp."

"Maybe that's the best time to think about draining it," Fran replied. "Then you wouldn't have to be battling them."

"Fine," Hawkins snapped. "I'll go out and change the whole world by myself." His eyes glinted, the glow of the perimeter lights reflecting off them. "You want to know something?" He didn't wait for an answer. "On my last mission before coming here I killed a woman. Just put a round right between her eyes and walked away. Because she was in the wrong place at the wrong time with the wrong person. That's the way it goes. That's the world. I didn't make the rules. I just play by them as best I can."

"Is that what you feel about the accident with your wife? Wrong place, wrong time, and wrong person?" Fran quietly asked.

Hawkins went tense and was silent for a long time. Finally he spoke, his voice so low, Fran barely caught it. "No. That's not what I think."

"Then don't apply it to the rest of the world. You

can make a difference. You have a good plan with Tuskin. Believe in it and do all you can."

"I was going to do it anyway," Hawkins said.

Fran reached out and touched his shoulder. "But you'll do it better if you believe."

Hawkins suddenly stood. "There's some information I need to find out. Then I'm going to get some sleep." He glanced at his watch again. "It's Lamb's show for the next seven hours and twenty-five minutes. I suggest you get some sleep too." He strode off into the darkness, heading for the operations tent, leaving Fran alone in the dark. She looked up at the stars one more time, then went off to find Don and see how he was doing.

PROBING

FRAN RETURNED TO THE MINE SHAFT AND DESCENDED THE wire bucket for the second time, arriving in the chamber just as Tomkins was about to send through the remote camera. Pencak, Levy, and Batson were gathered there also, next to Lamb in front of the TV screen. A squad of marines in full battle gear stood fidgeting off to the side, weapons held in nervous hands.

The remote consisted of a video camera mounted on a small, tracked cart. A powerful built-in transmitter would beam back into space the images the camera picked up on a broad band that itself was capable of being picked up by one of the Keyhole satellites blanketing the Earth, thus averting what had happened to the camera linked by the fiber-optic cable.

"Ready to go, sir." Tomkins held the remote control in his hand.

"Go ahead."

Tomkins flicked a switch and pushed slightly forward on the toggle in the center of the remote control. The cart hummed and then slowly rolled toward the Wall. On the TV screen the Wall grew closer and closer. The cart touched the Wall and there was the flash of light and the cart was gone. The TV screen had gone totally white as the same time as the Wall and now showed solid black.

"What's happening?" Lamb asked.

"I've got it stopped," Tomkins said. "That's if I've still got contact with it," he added after a brief pause.

"How come we're getting nothing on the screen?" Lamb demanded.

"You're not going to get anything," Levy spoke quietly. "It's gone farther than any radio link man has devised can reach."

"Reverse it. Bring it back," Lamb ordered.

Tomkins played with the remote for a long minute. Finally he stopped and simply looked at Lamb. "I'm getting nothing on the satellite link. Zero telemetry."

Lamb turned to the man in charge of the marine squad. "Are you ready, Lieutenant King?"

The young officer's face was bathed in sweat despite the coolness of the chamber, but his eyes glittered with the blind obedience that had allowed marines to charge across open beaches under fire for generations. He stepped up to the group. "Yes, sir."

"You're not going to send them through, are

you?" Fran protested as she realized what was happening, placing herself between him and Lamb. "For what reason?"

"To verify Hawkins's story."

"But the Coalition might take that as an aggressive act!" Fran argued.

"The Russians sent through armed men," Lamb responded.

"They might not go where Hawkins and I went," Levy said. "Remember that Richman went in at Tunguska and came out here. What happens if these men come out at Tunguska?"

Lieutenant King fingered his M-16. "Then it's rock and roll time."

"What if they step out somewhere new?" Levy asked. "What if it's someplace where humans aren't able to survive?"

A couple of the lower-ranking marines exchanged worried glances.

"I'm in charge here," Lamb said. "I take responsibility."

"Your taking responsibility is great," Fran said bitterly. "It will certainly help the families of these young men feel better when they don't come back to know that you took responsibility."

The lieutenant's eyes had not lost any of their earlier intensity. "I go where I'm ordered, ma'am."

"Hey, LT." A large black sergeant, his crew-cut hair gray with twenty-three years of experience in the Corps, stepped forward. "Maybe we ought to talk to Colonel Tolliver first?" He shot a look over his shoulder at the Wall. "I think we're out of our league here."

Lieutenant King shook his head. "No, Sergeant Johnson. The colonel specifically said we were under the command of Mr. Lamb." The NCO reluctantly stepped back into ranks.

"When you cross, send one man back immediately so we know you're all right, and to tell us where you're at," Lamb said.

"Aye, aye, sir."

Fran slowly moved out of the way and the marines formed a wedge, point facing the portal. King was in the lead, less than a foot from the Wall. He glanced over his shoulder and looked at Lamb expectantly.

"Go," Lamb ordered.

Lieutenant King stepped forward and the Wall went white. As each man hit, there was the same brief flash and then they were gone, one after another in the intrepid spirit that had taken Mount Surabachi. It took less than five seconds for all ten men to disappear.

Those left behind watched the Wall, waiting for the promised report to come back. As the seconds ticked away, the mood shifted from one of expectation to one of uncertain dread.

The Other Side

KING WAS MOMENTARILY DISORIENTED AND THEN QUICKLY
gained his bearing, only to be further confused when
he saw his surroundings. He was bumped forward as
the next man came through and the procession continued until all ten men were milling in a large room.
The far wall was about thirty feet away and the side
walls were twenty feet apart. The walls were pure
white and appeared to be made of some metal alloy.
The ceiling was twelve feet above the floor and both
were made of the same material. Behind them was the
black Wall. There were no windows—only what appeared to be a door with no handle. The light came
out of thin strips of glowing material in the center of
the ceiling.

"Andersen, go back and tell Mr. Lamb that we're
in a room—not in a large enclosed area like Major
Hawkins described."

As the private turned to go back through, the
black Wall coalesced from a shimmer into a solid
black circle and then rapidly diminished into a small
dot and disappeared, leaving the same white metallic
wall as the rest of the room.

"What the hell?" King muttered.

"What now, LT?" Sergeant Johnson asked.

King licked his lips nervously, trying to regain control. "All right. Spread out. You make too good a
target clumped together."

"For who?" Johnson muttered, gesturing around
the empty room with his rifle. "There's nothing here."

King ignored him and walked over to the door. He pushed on it to no avail. "Everyone step back." He aimed his M-16 at the door as Johnson stepped forward. "I wouldn't do that, sir!"

King fired a three-round burst. The bullets ricocheted off the metal and flashed around the room, ricocheting several more times until they ran out of kinetic energy. One of the marines let out a surprised yell and stared in amazement as a pool of blood spread on his left thigh. "What happened?"

Johnson grabbed his arm and gently lowered the soldier to the ground. "You're hit, Pritchett. You don't feel it right now, but you will." He pulled the first-aid kit out of his load-bearing vest and began bandaging the wound, getting the flow of blood stopped. "It's not too bad. You're lucky the bullet bounced a few times before hitting you. You'll have a little scar."

"Will I get a Purple Heart?" the young soldier asked, staring wide-eyed as his leg was worked on.

Sergeant Johnson gave a fatherly chuckle. "We get back home, Pritchett, and you can have one of my Purple Hearts, okay?"

King was still standing by the door, sheepishly holding his rifle. "What do we do now, Top?" he asked quietly.

His hands covered in blood, Johnson spared his officer a brief glance. "We sit down and we wait, sir."

Ayers Rock, Australia
23 DECEMBER 1995, 0130 LOCAL
22 DECEMBER 1995, 1600 ZULU

THEY WAITED A SILENT HOUR, LOST IN THEIR OWN THOUGHTS as the Wall refused to disgorge any information. Finally, Fran turned and headed for the basket. Her words echoed through the chamber as she climbed in and gave the order to be lifted. She wanted to say something to Lamb but she realized it would be futile. She knew he'd been pushed to the edge by the events of the last couple of days and that had affected his thinking, as it had all of theirs.

As she rode up the black borehole, she thought of the young faces of the marines who had gone through. Her mind flashed a vision of them lying on the surface of some cold planet, the mouths wide open, frozen in a desperate gasp for air that wasn't there. Some of them probably trying to crawl to the Wall and come back, but none making it. She shivered despite the oppressive heat and felt tears well up. She'd had so much hope in that first briefing but it seemed that every move that had been made since then had only worsened things.

She went by Hawkins's tent and looked for him, to tell him what had happened, but he wasn't there. Physically and emotionally exhausted, she crawled onto her own cot and passed into unconsciousness.

THE RUSSIAN IV

100 Kilometers Northeast of Volgograd, Russia
22 DECEMBER 1995, 2200 LOCAL
22 DECEMBER 1995, 1800 ZULU

THE RUSSIAN VOMITED OFF THE EDGE OF THE TRAIL, HIS stomach spasming in agonizing ripples. The remains of the cold army ration he'd eaten earlier in the evening stood out clearly against the white snow. He stood and willed the pain to stay a hand's distance away. He sensed it, but didn't let it override his control. The sickness was coming quicker than he had expected. He walked slowly back to the truck and pulled out the large-scale military maps of the area.

He checked his location and then estimated how far he had to go. He'd misjudged the radiation poisoning, but he hadn't made much of a miscalculation on his rate of travel. He should make it to his destination in a day, give or take six hours. He put the maps away and reached into his rucksack, pulling out a small pill bottle. He shook out the painkillers and took several, swallowing them with great difficulty.

Stiffly, he climbed into the cab of the truck and started the engine. He was on the edge of the wilderness that stretched to the northeast of Volgograd, formerly known to the world as Stalingrad. He felt it was appropriate that that city, site of the greatest exhibition of will of the Soviet people in the Great Patriotic War and so casually renamed by those in power, should be the first to fall to his plan.

He looked out the windshield. Mile upon mile of pine forest stretched in a mind-numbing continuity in front of him. His target lay out there, long camouflaged and hidden among the trees and swamps. When he destroyed it, the action would most certainly make them aware of what they had done to his son and all the others. He was committed to all who had sworn to uphold Mother Russia and had had their faith shattered and their pride spit on.

He pushed the gearshift lever into first and the wheels started turning, crunching the fresh snow from the previous night beneath as he moved down the old logging road. His eyes flickered for a moment from the dull glow of the headlights on the trail to the old photo he had taped to the dashboard. The young man in the sharply cut uniform, with the pilot's wings proudly pinned on his chest, grinned back at him. The Russian's eyes closed briefly—this time the pain coming from a deeper source than the radiation—and then he opened them. He focused on the road.

ESCAPE

Ayers Rock, Australia
23 DECEMBER 1995, 1130 LOCAL
23 DECEMBER 1995, 0200 ZULU

HAWKINS FELT PHYSICALLY REFRESHED AFTER TWO HOURS OF sleep, but the news of the missing marines hit him hard. There seemed to be no end to the conveyer belt of stupidity that channeled young men to their doom. That event only served to strengthen his resolve to follow through on his own plan.

Hawkins met the other members of the team in the chamber, where a solemn-faced Captain Tomkins stood watch. He'd had Fran gather them together while he did some last-minute checking and gathering of supplies. He threw his duffel bag onto the rock floor, and looked at the other four people.

"Did Fran brief you?"

They all nodded. Tomkins looked over, curious as to what was going on.

"Are you all with me?" He stared hard at Batson, who fidgeted briefly before replying.

"What if we go where the marines went and not back to where you and Debra went?"

Hawkins shrugged. "For all we know the marines did go where we went. I don't know why they didn't send anyone back. The portal simply might have been closed off behind them."

Tomkins frowned, concerned, but held back from interrupting by the rigid lines of military rank.

Pencak slapped Batson on the back. "Come on, young man. Where's your sense of adventure?"

Hawkins picked up the duffel bag and slung it over his shoulder. "Let's go."

Tomkins finally reacted, stepping up to Hawkins. "What are you doing, sir?"

"We're going through."

Tomkins shook his head. "I wasn't told anything, sir. Do you have authorization from Mr. Lamb?"

Hawkins smoothly pulled his 9mm pistol out and pointed it at Tomkins. "This is my authorization. I'd hate to shoot you, Captain, but I think you know I will if you get in my way."

Tomkins swallowed, looked briefly at his M16 leaning against the rock wall, then moved out of the way in the opposite direction.

"Go," Hawkins ordered. Pencak stepped into the portal without a backward glance. Levy immediately followed. Fran grabbed Batson by the arm and smiled at him. "Off to see the wizard!" They stepped off together and the Wall flashed white and they were gone.

Hawkins threw a salute at Tomkins and walked into the portal.

The Other Side

THE STRANGE MIXTURE OF COLD AND MUGGY AIR WRAPPED itself around the members of the team as they stared about the dark cavern. Hawkins pointed to the light in the far distance. "That's the way we head."

"Is that where you were briefed?" Batson asked.

"I have no idea," Hawkins said. "But it's the only recognizable point in the place, and that's where Tuskin and I agreed to link up."

"What about the Russians' portal?" Batson asked. "Do you know where that is?"

Hawkins pointed. "Somewhere on the far wall, over there."

Batson held up his wristwatch. "I've got a small compass on the band. According to it that Wall is north of here. Of course," he added, "magnetic north here might not be aligned on the poles like it is on Earth—wherever here is. Plus all this machinery could be throwing the reading off. I could be picking up a strong electromagnetic field."

"This air is so strange!" Fran marveled. "And I've never seen any enclosed space so large—you can't even see the end," she added, pointing in the direction opposite to the light, where the open space disappeared into distant darkness.

"But the air is breathable to humans," Batson noted. "I don't know much about it, but that strikes me as something that would be extremely rare on another planet. Unless, of course, this is an artificial environment. That would help explain a lot."

Fran wrinkled her nose. "It may be breathable, but it certainly doesn't smell good."

Hawkins unfastened the end of the duffel bag and was pulling items out. He slid on a black combat vest decorated with a knife, ammunition pouches, and various other accoutrements of war. He took a pistol out of the bag and handed it to Batson.

"What's this for?"

Hawkins proceeded to hand one to each member of the party, including Pencak, who took hers with a look of amusement. Fran repeated Batson's question. "Why are you giving us these?"

"Because it's better to have them and not need them than to not have them and need them."

"Where'd you get them?" Batson asked, turning the pistol over in his hands.

"The marines weren't guarding their gear very well." Hawkins held his own pistol out in front of him. "Here's the safety. Forward is on. Back is off. Keep it on unless you need to shoot. You also have a safety built into the handle. If you aren't gripping the handle, the gun won't go off, even if the lever safety isn't on. There are fourteen rounds in the magazine."

Pencak held her pistol out. "Thank you, young

man, but I won't be needing this. I hardly expect my-self to be much of a help in a gun battle."

Hawkins took the gun back and put it in the bag.

"Me too," Levy said, holding hers out. Fran did the same. Don awkwardly put his in the waistband of his trousers.

"Let's go." Hawkins ordered.

"Do you think the craft will meet us like last time?" Debra asked as the moved out.

Hawkins shrugged. "Maybe. I don't know. We don't have the time to wait for them." He paused and cocked his head as sharp cracks reverberated through the air and echoed. "Did you hear that?"

Batson pointed. "Sounded like some shots among the machinery near the far wall."

"I heard them too," Debra confirmed.

Hawkins drew his pistol and cocked it. "You all stay here. I'll be back in a minute." Without waiting for a reply, he set off in a sprint in the direction of the brief burst of gunfire.

It was hard for him to tell how close he was, be-cause after the first few shots there was no further noise. When he turned a corner, he was surprised to see three figures in an open space near the far wall. One was kneeling, holding the other in his arms. The third was a bloody heap in the dust.

As Hawkins ran over, he recognized the first figure as Tuskin. The person he was holding was a young man and Hawkins could clearly see the large splotch of red on his shirt.

"What happened?"

Tuskin wasn't surprised to see Hawkins. "I had the other three members of the team assemble near the portal. That fool General Kolstavek had them there all along, but he would never send them through!" He gestured down at the man in his arms. "This is Potekin. He's the most brilliant physicist in my country. They would never have sent him through."

"Where are the other two?" Hawkins asked as he checked Potekin's wounds. Potekin was dying. He had two sucking chest wounds and another round had torn through his neck, nicking the artery there, the bright red blood pulsing out of a wound that only a surgeon in a hospital could close. His eyes were wide in shock and he didn't even move as Hawkins injected him with a morphine syringe from his vest.

"Dead," Tuskin answered. "They wouldn't move fast enough. They didn't think the guards would shoot."

"Who's that?" Hawkins pointed at the body.

"A guard. He followed me through."

Hawkins looked around. "Where's your portal?"

Potekin's breathing grew shallower. A small shower of red froth poured out of his lips and with a last rattle of breath he died. "You wasted your needle," Tuskin said, sliding the body off his knees and standing. He pointed at a particularly large piece of machinery that towered eighty feet above their heads, its dark surface humming. Several pipes extended from the machine at various heights, disappearing into the rock wall. "That's where it was. Just on the other side. The portal closed after the one guard came through." He gestured with his hands. "It dwindled to a little ball and then—poof—it was gone! The other two members of my team didn't even make it through. They were killed before we got to the portal." Tuskin pulled the magazine out his rifle and replaced it with a fresh one.

Hawkins walked over and picked up the guard's rifle. "They didn't believe you?"

Tuskin snorted. " 'An American plot,' they insisted. And your government?"

"They were confused and moving slowly." Hawkins looked at the Russian. "Did a squad of marines come through at Tunguska?"

Tuskin stared at him. "You sent marines through?"

"I didn't—the government did to see if I was crazy, lying, or both. We didn't hear back from them, so we don't know where they went."

Tuskin shook his head. "There was no activity at the Tunguska portal until I tried bringing my team through." He looked up as the rest of Hawkins's party appeared. "You seem to have had better luck with your people."

Hawkins waved the team over. "What happened?" Fran asked, her eyes taking in the two bodies.

As Hawkins started to give a quick synopsis of Tuskin's story, Levy gave a gasp as she got close to the two dead men. "That's Pyotr Potekin!"

"You knew him?" Hawkins asked.

"I never met him but I read his work and saw his picture in the journals. He is—was—brilliant!"

Off to the side, as Hawkins was talking to the rest of the team, Batson was staring at the wall closely. He walked over to it, running his hands along the gouged surface. Pencak joined him, leaning on her cane.

"What is it?" Pencak asked.

Batson pointed. "Do you see it?"

"What?"

"Look at the rock," Batson insisted.

Pencak looked, then returned her gaze to Batson. "What am I supposed to see?"

"You don't understand, do you?" he asked excitedly. "I had a feeling it was something like this!"

Pencak frowned. "What are you talking about?"

His answer was cut off as a noise came from the opposite direction. The skimmer appeared and settled down about a hundred feet away. They all stared in amazement as the door slid up, and the opening beckoned.

"Let's go!" Hawkins yelled. "Hurry up!"

Fran hustled forward as Hawkins took the lead, and they headed toward the skimmer. They clambered up the ramp and Hawkins helped them on board. As they settled on the benches, Fran looked around and then stood. "Where's Don?"

Hawkins shrugged off the duffel bag, dropping it on the floor. He counted heads and then looked out the door, back the way they'd come. The two bodies lay there, but there was no sign of the geologist. "Wasn't he with you when you got on board?"

"No. I lost track of him in all the confusion."

Hawkins started to step out on the ramp, but at

that moment it started to pull back in and he hurriedly got out of the way as the door slid down. "Where the hell did he go, then?" Hawkins demanded. He turned to the others as the skimmer lifted and banked. "Did anyone see Don?"

"We were over at the wall when the craft came. I thought he was behind me," Pencak offered. "But I can't be sure."

"Well, he couldn't have just disappeared!" Hawkins said.

"Then where is he?" Fran asked.

Hawkins looked at Tuskin. "Did you see anything?"

"No. I thought we had everyone."

The skimmer settled with a slight bump and the door reopened. They were in the same room as last time and the same door beckoned on the near wall.

"Maybe they'll know where Don is," Hawkins said as he stepped out. They filed across the floor and into the elevator.

Ayers Rock, Australia
23 DECEMBER 1995, 1200 LOCAL
23 DECEMBER 1995, 0230 ZULU

LAMB KNEW HIS RANTING AND RAVING WOULD MAKE NO difference in what had happened, but at least it made him feel a little better. Captain Tomkins was standing at stiff attention like a West Point plebe on the other side of Lamb's desk, his eyes focused on a spot about six inches above the other man's head.

"Why didn't you inform me when all of them gathered down there?"

"I didn't have any orders to, sir," Tomkins replied. "They were authorized to be there—just not to go through."

"Jesus Christ, man! This is the second time someone has gone through without my permission."

"Yes, sir."

"No one, I mean no one, even goes down there now without my explicit permission. Is that clear?"

"Yes, sir."

"Get the hell out of here."

After Tomkins had scuttled out, Lamb swiveled his seat around and looked at the SATCOM radio/video that linked him with the President. He shook his head. This was one piece of bad news he was not going to relay. Not only did he know nothing more than the last time he'd talked to the Old Man, but he'd also lost the marine squad and now the members of the team along with Pencak. Goddamn Hawkins! Lamb pounded a fist on the desktop.

"Sir?"

Lamb turned back to the entrance. His intelligence analyst stood there. "What?"

"We've got some strange imagery from Tunguska." He hustled forward and laid out a series of colored photos. "These are the thermals, hot off the down link from the INTELSAT."

"What am I looking for?" Lamb demanded, staring at the confusing array of color.

The agent pointed. "The dark blue here is the eastern edge of the target, where there's snow. No heat signature. These dark red splotches here are engines running—probably generators. This, with the haze of red coming off it, must be a stove, and the smoke that's coming out of it and cooling in the air."

"Yes, so?" Lamb said testily.

"Here, sir." The agent tapped groups of red circles. "These are people." He slid another photo in front of Lamb. "Here is the weird thing, sir. See these here?" His pointer skipped over several computer-generated figures. "These are people too. Except note that they are a different shade from these other ones."

Lamb nodded. "All right. What does that mean?"

"They're dead, sir. Those are fresh bodies and their body temperature is dropping quickly due to the subfreezing temperatures there in Siberia. The computer estimates they died about ten minutes before this picture was taken."

Lamb leaned forward and looked at the photos. "How many bodies?"

"Seven."

"The marines?"

The agent considered the question for a moment. "No, sir, I don't think that's our marines. There were ten of them and that lieutenant had his finger on the trigger when he went through. There should be a bunch of dead Russians, too, if the marines came out in Tunguska. Not enough bodies."

"Who is it, then?"

"Maybe the Russians also had some people go through who they didn't want to go through," the agent offered. "Or try to go through. Or someone came out that they didn't like."

Lamb rubbed his forehead. "Keep monitoring that. Let me know if there's anything more. Is that it?"

"No, sir." The agent slid another photo across his desk. It showed the flat deck of a large naval ship. "That's the *Minsk*—a Kiev-class V/STOL carrier. It's the flagship of the Russian fleet off the south coast." He used his pointer to indicate several aircraft on the deck. "Those are KA-25 helicopters—code-named Hormone by NATO. My analysts believe they're being outfitted for a long-range flight. Those round objects next to them are external fuel tanks—not normally used. We've also picked up photos of some Spetsnatz commandos test-firing weapons off the deck of the *Minsk*.

"There's only one possible target for them from the south coast of Australia," he added unnecessarily.

"Tell Tolliver to double his security tonight," Lamb ordered. "I want more surveillance put on the Russian fleet. If those helicopters launch, I want to know immediately. Alert the *Eisenhower* to be prepared to launch a protective air cover on a five-minute notice."

"What about the Australians, sir?"

"Don't worry about that. I'll take care of them."

"Yes, sir."

"Anything further on Hawkins, Levy, or Pencak's background?"

"No, sir."

"How about Volkers or Batson?"

"Nothing suspicious, sir."

"There's *got* to be some connection! Find it!"

"Yes, sir."

THE OFFER

The Other Side

THE ROW OF CHAIRS BECKONED AND HAWKINS, TUSKIN, and Levy quickly took their places, followed more slowly by Pencak, Fran, and Batson. The arms swung in and Hawkins again felt that slight prick on the back of his right hand. The room darkened and the three points of light appeared. The center one immediately expanded and a voice filled Hawkins's head. "We will listen."

Hawkins spoke first. "We have returned with an offer of goodwill."

"Is it goodwill that there is violence at one of our relays and we are forced to close it off?"

Surprisingly, it was Pencak who answered. "Let us be honest with each other. Our governments are not designed to react quickly—especially to the most astonishing development in the history of our species. They are still grappling with how to respond. We are here to show you that as a people we are worthy of being protected for the time being and that we have the seeds to develop into a race that will be worthy of membership in the Coalition."

"How will you show us?"

"We will recover the stolen nuclear weapon." Hawkins said. "The twin of the one that destroyed your relay at Vredefort Dome. You said the fact that that bomb was missing was significant. Recovery of that bomb ought to be significant also, then."

The red and the blue lights suddenly expanded and pulsed. It seemed as if they were communicating, yet nothing was heard until the side ones returned to their original state and the Speaker replied. "The Defender is not impressed. The Defender points out that your various factions have thousands of nuclear weapons—all capable of interfering with our defense system."

"We have to start somewhere," Hawkins replied.

"You have had generations to start," the voice replied.

Fran jumped in. "Our governments have a hard time believing that all this is really happening. They did not want us to come through to talk to you until they could be more certain. You did not allow them the time to be certain. It was your time limit that precipitated the events in Tunguska.

"You said it took the Coalition six hundred years to react to the Swarm attack. Yet you give us only twenty-four hours. Three of the four people whose names you listed for the Russians are dead because they tried to come to you. That sacrifice must mean something.

"The fact that all of us standing here have sacrificed everything to come to you and make this offer—and that we are willing to give our lives to retrieve this other bomb—that should mean something to you. Surely your Defender can understand the importance of a race whose individuals are willing to sacrifice themselves for the common good. And we are individuals—we are not like this Swarm that we have been told about that you are fighting. The most precious thing to each of us is our own individual life. Yet we stand here and offer those lives to you. Three of us have already given their lives up. If that is not enough, there is nothing more we can give."

The last sentence seemed to hover in the air during the long silence that followed. Finally, after a minute's wait, the Speaker's voice echoed. "You have twelve hours. We will consider what happens in that time with regard to our final decision." The three points of light started to fade.

"Hold it!" Hawkins yelled out.

The lights froze at half size. "What is it?" the Speaker asked.

"What happened to the marines who went through the Ayers Rock portal?"

"They are secure. We will let you see them and allow them to return to their start point."

"What about Don Batson?"

"What about Don Batson?" the voice replied.

"Where is he? He came through Ayers Rock with

us but disappeared when we linked up with Colonel Tuskin."

"Batson's present location is unknown. We will scan for him."

"Are there are any other portals that we can return through on Earth besides the one at Ayers Rock?"

"The Tunguska relay is only temporarily closed. We can reopen it."

Hawkins looked at Tuskin, who shook his head. "It's well guarded. We'd never make it out."

"Well, we can't go back through Ayers Rock either." Hawkins shifted his attention back to the light. "Is there any other way we can get back to Earth besides going through Ayers Rock or Tunguska?"

"Why can you not return through Ayers Rock or Tunguska?"

"Because we came here without permission of our governments," Hawkins said. "We told you that."

"If you are not working in concert with your governments, how will you find the missing nuclear weapon?"

"We will go after the people who might know where it is," Hawkins said.

"Where are these people?" the Speaker asked.

"The first one we have to find is in the southwestern part of Russia," Tuskin answered.

"We need your help," Pencak said. "We are willing to do all we can, but if you could help us, it would make the odds of our success much greater."

The red point of light flared up, immediately followed by the other two. Hawkins watched, fascinated by the play of the colors. This went on for half a minute, then the flank colors subsided. "The Defender does not believe this is worth our time. The Mediator believes you should be given a chance—you have the will but not the means to accomplish the task you have set up for yourselves.

"I had the deciding opinion. We will give you some aid. The skimmer outside will take you through the Tunguska portal. The portal will be programmed to allow only the skimmer through. Once through, you may direct the skimmer to take you to any location you desire. The skimmer has"—the Speaker paused briefly, then resumed—"for your purposes on your planet's surface, virtually unlimited range at high speed. It avoids your people's detection systems by flying low, using physical features of the terrain to reduce both the visual and electronic signatures."

A small door on the side of the room slid open, the noise catching Hawkins's attention. Two large black cases lay just inside.

"Inside those are personal weapons systems used by humanoid members of the Coalition Space Force. We will lend you two to help in your attempt. The weapons are plasma projectors. They will destroy anything the beam touches; the pressure on the trigger determines the strength of the beam. The body armor will defeat most individual weapons common on your planet and aid in your camouflage. Your military men will understand how to use them. If some of you are staying here while the others search, this room and the others in this complex will be left available."

The colors disappeared and the room was black for a second, then the elevator door slid open, bathing the room with its light. Another door, previously unseen, opened to the right of the elevator and a corridor beckoned.

"We're going to get a hot reception if we go through Tunguska," Tuskin commented.

"We don't have any choice," Hawkins said.

"I think that skimmer might be more than a match for whatever your people have around the portal," Pencak pointed out.

"They seem pretty confident we'll know how to control it," Fran said. "I don't like the fact that they say they don't know where Don is. They've managed to know every time people came through the portal and where they were."

"Yes, but that might be because the portals were activated," Levy said.

Fran shook her head. "There's something more going on here than we can see. I think Don saw or knew something that he wasn't supposed to."

"What?" Hawkins asked.

Fran shrugged, unable to shake her uneasiness. "What's the plan now?"

Tuskin flipped open the lid on one of the black cases. "Look at this!"

Hawkins opened the other case and they considered what was inside. The weapon was surprisingly short—a blunt-barreled gray pistol. Hawkins lifted it,

searching for a safety. There appeared to be none—
just a trigger on the rear grip. The armor was a silvery
body suit that seemed much too thin to do what the
Speaker had said it could. Hawkins pulled his on, the
large size flopping over, causing him to tuck in the
sleeves and ankles. Apparently humanoid soldiers of
the Coalition were larger than he. When he looked
over at Tuskin, who had done the same thing, he was
surprised to see that Tuskin's suit had changed from
silver to almost white, matching the walls behind.

"The suit changes to fit the background," Fran
noted. "Like a chameleon."

"We're a lot better off than we were," Hawkins
said. "We might even have a chance now."

"Why are they helping us so much?" Fran asked.

"They aren't helping us very much at all," Hawkins argued. "Loaning us the ship and these two
weapons systems isn't much skin off their nose—that
is, if they have noses. If they really wanted to help us,
they'd come through the portals and present themselves."

"It's a test," Levy said. "If we can't accomplish
this, then we aren't worth their messing with. If they
came through the portal it would make it all too easy.
I think they are trying to see what our race is really
like and what we are capable of."

"You think all of this is just a test?" Hawkins
asked. "A setup?"

"Yes, but I also think they want us to succeed,"
Levy answered.

"That's not what they say," Hawkins retorted.

"But their actions point that way," Levy said.

"They could be doing quite a bit more in the way of help than they are," Tuskin noted.

"Something's not right here," Hawkins said, letting the plasma projector dangle. In some ways it was all too easy, but in others, all too confusing. "I think Debra's got a point—this is not what it appears to be. I'm not sure I even believe their story about the Swarm. Maybe that was just a cover for something else."

"Let's take a look at the skimmer," Pencak said, ending the speculation. "Whether real or not, we still have to get that bomb." They crowded aboard the elevator and rode to the surface in silence.

After riding the elevator up, they walked out into the cavern and up the ramp into the craft. The door to the front part of the craft was now open. The front cabin held two seats, oriented forward. Hawkins sat in one of the seats while Tuskin took the other. The rest of the party gathered behind them. There were two large video displays in front of the seats showing the view directly in front with smaller blocked areas along the side of the screens displaying the view below and to the sides and rear.

The control panel was a model of simplicity. Between the two seats was a video screen that showed what must be the map for the immediate vicinity of the planet's surface.

"That must be the Tunguska portal," Hawkins said, pointing at a dot that was flashing on the screen. His finger slid across the screen to a small rectangle highlighted in red, enclosed by a larger black square. "This red must be the skimmer and the black the building or whatever it is we're in."

"Why no writing?" Fran wondered.

"They must have so many different languages in the Coalition that they've simplified all their control systems to accommodate logical symbolic reasoning," Levy answered.

"I think we can handle this," Hawkins said. He turned in his seat to the other members of the team. "Colonel Tuskin knows where the Russian general who sold the two bombs is being held. We plan to go there, snatch him, and then make him talk. We don't know what the Russian interrogaters have gotten out of him, but whatever it is, they haven't been willing to share it."

"I do not think we need everyone to do this," Tuskin said. "I think a small element would be much more efficient than a large one."

"We have only the two suits," Hawkins added. "We'll do this. You all try to find out all you can here. We'll be back as soon as possible."

"First, you need to take care of the marines," Pencak noted.

Hawkins nodded. "I'll do that." He hopped out the door. Ten minutes went by before he returned. "They've gone back," he assured them.

After a last farewell Pencak, Fran, and Debra trooped off the skimmer. In the cockpit Hawkins looked at Tuskin, who nodded. He leaned forward and poised his finger above a glowing green button that had an arrow pointing up. "It could be the ejection-seat button, you know," Hawkins remarked.

Tuskin shrugged. "We all have to go sometimes."

"Typical Russian attitude," Hawkins remarked, and then pressed the up arrow. The skimmer lifted and, when he let go, held its altitude. He pushed the forward button and they were on their way toward the opening hangar doors. On the screen in front the entrance to the hangar flashed by and they were over a desert heading toward the black sheen that was the portal leading to Tunguska.

THE PRESIDENT

Ayers Rock, Australia
23 DECEMBER 1995, 1430 LOCAL
23 DECEMBER 1995, 0500 ZULU

"SIR, WE'VE GOT AN INCIDENT AT TUNGUSKA!"

Lamb looked up as the intelligence analyst dashed into his tent, satellite photos fresh off the fax gripped in his hand.

"What kind of incident?"

"We're not sure, sir," the agent said as he slid the first photo onto the desktop. "We've been taking shots of the site with a thirty-second lapse between frames. This is two minutes ago." The image was no different from what they'd been seeing for the past two days.

"This is a minute and thirty seconds ago." The photo showed the tarp that had covered the pit in Tunguska torn asunder. There were several black spots that looked like ink smudges in the air along with a long streak of red coming out of an armored vehicle parked a hundred meters from the pit.

"What happened?"

The agent shook his head. "I'm not sure, sir."

"Can you at least tell me what the black spots and this red line are?" Lamb asked, exasperated.

"The black spots are antiaircraft fire—old stuff, thirty-seven-millimeter cannon, airburst. We spotted several of that type of weapon dug in around the site after the Orion team was compromised. The red line is tracers coming from a ZSU 23-4. It fires almost a thousand rounds a minute, so the tracers appear as a continuous line."

"Are they being attacked?"

The analyst slapped down another photo. "This is one minute ago." The tarp was still torn, but the guns were silent. "Whatever happened, happened fast and is over now."

"Were they attacked?" Lamb repeated his question. "Was the pit bombed and that's why the tarps are torn?"

The analyst considered his reply for a long second. "No, sir, I don't think so. Looking at the way the cloth is torn and the way that fire is distributed, I think something came out from under the tarps and went up into the air."

"What!" Lamb exclaimed. He looked at the photos and then at his agent. "What do you mean, something came out of the pit?"

"That's the only thing that fits the facts, sir. And it was something the Russians didn't expect. Their guns were oriented against an outside attack. I think this caught them by surprise."

"What came out? How come we don't have a shot of it?"

The analyst spread several other photos on the desktop. "I had the focal radius reduced to increase our coverage of the area, but we have nothing. Whatever came out was damn fast and is long gone from the area."

"Something came out of their Wall," Lamb said aloud, his mind trying to grasp the implications, "something they didn't know about, and they shot at it." He looked at his analyst. "They probably think we sent something through."

The analyst was about to answer when the FM radio speaker on Lamb's desk came alive with the excited voice of Captain Tomkins. "Mr. Lamb! The marines are back! They're back, sir!"

Lamb slammed his hand down on the send button. "You hold them right there in the chamber. I'll be down immediately. I want you to be careful—something else might come out of the Wall."

Lamb leapt to his feet and was out of the tent in three quick strides. The ride down the hole was a long one for him as he tried assimilating this latest piece of news. When he emerged in the chamber he could see nine of the ten marines standing there with dazed looks on their face. The tenth was lying down, a white bandage conspicuous on his leg.

"What happened?" Lamb demanded, facing Lieutenant King.

In response the lieutenant simply shook his head, his eyes unfocused. Lamb shifted his gaze to the senior NCO.

Sergeant Johnson met the look evenly. "Private Pritchett needs medical attention, sir."

Lamb waved curtly at Tomkins. "Send the wounded man up."

Johnson relaxed slightly into a position of parade rest. "We went through and stepped into a room. It was all white, no windows, and what had looked like a door at the far end, except there was no handle on it. I don't know what the walls were made of, but it was some sort of metal—something I've never seen before. The LT tried shooting through the door and the rounds just bounced off. Pritchett got hit by a ricochet." Johnson backtracked slightly. "The Wall we had come through had disappeared just after the last man was in. So we couldn't send anybody back to report as ordered and we couldn't go anywhere.

"We stayed in there until all of a sudden the door just swished open and that Army major—Hawkins— he came in. Except he was all geared up in this high-speed stuff." Johnson shook his head at the memory. "I've never seen nothing like it, sir. He had some sort of body suit on that shimmered like that Wall." He jerked at thumb at the other end of the chamber. "And he had this weapon like nothing that I've ever heard of or seen."

"What did Hawkins say?" Lamb asked.

"He said we were going home. He said that all we had to do was go through the Wall, and even as he said it, the far end of the room turned back into the black Wall."

"Is that all he said?" Lamb asked impatiently.

"No, sir, it's not. He also said that we was to tell you that the Russians aren't behind this. He showed me and the LT his weapon and it sure isn't anything we could have made. He fired with it and took out half the wall. Scared the shit out of some of the boys. Then he asked the LT to shoot him with his pistol. The LT didn't want to do it so the major, he just grabbed the LT's pistol and turned it against his chest and pulled the trigger and nothing happened—I mean the pistol fired but the major, he just stood there.

"Then he looked at me and told me to shoot him in the chest and I did. I put a three-round burst into him, sir, and it didn't even faze him. I've never seen body armor like that. He said that should help convince you that what he told you was true." Johnson took a breath. "And then he said one last thing, sir. He said that he and someone named Colonel Tuskin were going after the other bomb. And he said they had some help from the others—the people who built this chamber and the Wall. He said the weapon and his suit were part of that help. I didn't know what all that meant, but the major said to make sure I told you that."

"How come Hawkins didn't come back himself?" Lamb asked. "He could have showed me this equipment to prove his point."

"He said you'd ask that," Johnson replied, speaking in the rote monotone subordinates often use when delivering bad news to their bosses. "He said that there were two reasons he wasn't gonna come through. First was, there wasn't enough time. He said they had to get the bomb real soon. The second was that he said he didn't trust you enough to bring that gun and that suit back here and put them in your hands."

Lamb closed his eyes briefly and tried to bring his emotions under control. It was time for clear thinking. "All right, Sergeant. After I go up, take your men to the surface and see that your lieutenant gets some treatment. He looks like he's in shock."

"Yes, sir."

Lamb clambered back into the basket and gave the signal for Tomkins to start the motor. As he rode to the surface he considered what he was to tell the President. Things had changed and Lamb knew he had to do a quick reevaluation of the whole situation.

By the time he got to his office and raised the President on the radio, Lamb had made his decision.

"What is it, Steve? My secretary said this was priority one." The President looked haggard and worn.

"The marines came back through, sir."

"You pull me out of a cabinet meeting to tell me that? What—"

"Excuse me, sir, but there's more." As succinctly as possible Lamb outlined what they had gleaned from the imagery at Tunguska and the message that Hawkins had sent with the team.

"What does it all mean?" the President asked when he was done.

"I think that whatever came out of the Tunguska Wall had Hawkins in it, sir. I think that Hawkins is on the trail of the last bomb."

"But you said that Hawkins told the marines one of the Russians was with him. This Colonel Tuskin."

"Yes, sir." Lamb looked at the computer printout his intelligence analyst had just slid across his desk. "Tuskin is a Spetsnatz officer. One of their best. I think he may well be with Hawkins."

"Then it is a Russian setup," the President said, confusion plain on his face.

"No, sir, I don't believe so. I don't think the Russians would have shot at whatever it is that came through their Wall just ten minutes ago if they were behind this and knew what was going on. And why would they have isolated the marines and then sent them back? I think they're as confused as we are, if not more. As a matter of fact, sir, I think they are confused enough to launch an assault—or at least a reconnaissance in force—on our position here. I believe the Russians think *we're* behind everything that's happening."

The President stared at the camera for a long time, his face tired, the eyes the only sign of life. Finally he sighed. "All right. So you're saying they're going to up the stakes because they think we're screwing with them?"

"Yes, sir."

"And what should I do?"

Lamb paused and rubbed the indentation on his cheek, then spoke. "Call Pamarov, sir. Offer to let them send inspectors here to look at the Rock and the chamber inside. Tell him everything we know."

The President blinked. "That's quite a change, Steve. A couple of hours ago you were sure that the Russians were behind this. I can see where you've un-covered new information leading you to change that position, but let me ask you one thing. What if the Russians *are* behind this?"

"I've thought hard about this, sir. If they are, I don't think we have anything to lose by opening up to them. If they're behind it they know everything that's happened and is happening. But if they're not—and I think the evidence strongly points that way—then we lose a lot by not going to them and laying our cards on the table. My intelligence indicates they're getting ready to launch a Spetsnatz mission off their carrier task force. We can handle it and stop it, but it'll be bloody as hell. And who knows what that will escalate into? The Australians certainly won't be happy. They may even insist we shut down here."

"What about the Orion team that was at Tun-guska?" the President asked. "*We've* already done what you want to stop the Russians from doing."

"You admit it, sir. I think that will really make Pamarov believe you." Lamb leaned forward, sweat pouring off his forehead. He threw aside the cloak of formality and addressed his old friend. "Hell, Pete, they already know those guys were ours. They just can't prove it. And we know some things about them, too, that we've never gone public with. You've seen Volkers's printouts. This world's getting ready to go down the tubes. This may be a last chance to do something right for once."

The President rested his eyes on Lamb for a long time as he slumped back in his chair, deep in thought. Then slowly he straighened and Lamb saw a look come into his friend's eyes that he hadn't seen in a long time. "All right, Steve. You're right. We've got nothing to lose. And maybe we can do something right for once. I'll call Pamarov. You be prepared there to talk to whoever's in charge of their fleet and arrange for an inspection team."

The screen went dead and Lamb sat back in his chair, his stomach churning. He wasn't sure if he'd just damned his country or saved it or if anything he did mattered.

THE COMPLEX

The Other Side

FRAN, DEBRA, AND PENCAK WANDERED ALONG THE CORRI-
dor, poking their heads in as the doors swished open,
revealing the rooms beyond. Most contained machinery, on a smaller scale than that above, the purpose of
which was unknown—although a few reminded Fran
of repair facilities, perhaps for the skimmers. Some
rooms were totally empty; others contained rows of
waist-high platforms that might have been beds. One
appeared to be a dining area.

The total absence of any life was very disturbing.
The entire facility appeared to have been built with
the idea of supporting a large number of personnel—
personnel that from the artifacts they could see, were
approximately human sized—yet they met nothing
and no one.

Pencak stepped up to another door and it slid

open. She looked inside and then back over her shoulder, her one eye gleaming. "This looks interesting."

Fran peered in. It was a large room, the true extent of which she could not see, due to dividers coming up from the floor. Directly in front of them was a bank of what appeared to be computer terminals with benches in front. Levy pushed past and ran up to one of the machines and sat down before it.

"Do you think it works?" Fran asked as she walked up.

The screen was totally gray and it was hard to tell if the computer was on or off. There was no keyboard, simply ten holes about an inch in diameter, evenly spaced, directly below the screen—a smaller version of the wrist holes in the Speaker's room.

Levy simply sat and stared, not replying. Fran looked about. "What's that?" she asked, pointing at a corridor off to the left where a red light glowed.

Pencak shrugged. "I don't know."

As Fran moved toward the light, Levy extended both hands and slipped her fingers into the slots. The screen cleared of gray and symbols appeared. Levy's normally expressionless face softened as a large smile crossed it and her pupils narrowed into tiny balls intent upon the small screen.

Fran stepped into the corridor and paused for a second, letting her eyes adjust to the red light. She moved down and the light coming out of recesses in the ceiling started shifting in the color spectrum, going from red to blue. The farther she went, the lighter it grew until suddenly she realized she was bathed in

light just as she would have been on a bright summer
day back on Earth. The corridor turned right and she
went around the corner. A glass-enclosed hexagonal
platform stood there, the door wide open.

Fran started as a hand dropped heavily on her
shoulder. She swung her head around and saw Pencak
looking at her.

"What do you think that is?" Fran asked.

"Let's see," Pencak replied. She led the way over
and stepped in the door. A small control console was
in one corner. There were three buttons: one with an
arrow pointing up, one down, and one with a horizontal line on it. Pencak and Fran looked up. Through
the glass ceiling they could see a red-lit tunnel beck-
oning straight up.

Pencak hovered her good hand over the button
with the up arrow. "Shall we?"

"Do you think we should?" Fran asked.

"We'll never know unless we try." Pencak pressed
down on the button and the elevator smoothly lifted
and accelerated. Fran's knees briefly buckled, then
the speed settled out. Red panels flashed by, marking
stops, but Pencak kept her hand pressed on the up
button.

After thirty seconds the elevator gradually began
to slow. The red panels flashed by more slowly, then
suddenly the machine halted. On the outside of the
glass there was now slate-gray metal on all sides, including the top.

"What do you think?" Fran asked Pencak.

The old woman was standing stock-still, peering

ahead as if she could see through the metal. Her hand lifted off the up button and touched the horizontal one. With a hiss of hydraulics, the roof flipped over, revealing a dark and sullen gray sky above with several odd-looking streaks of dull red in it.

The metal panels on the side began unfolding with heavy thuds, indicating their protective thickness. As the world around began to appear, Fran gasped and staggered back, holding on to the console for support. She turned to Pencak, speechless.

The older woman's face crinkled in a weary smile. "Amazing, isn't it?"

Fran looked back out, her gaze riveted on the object blocking out the entire horizon to the one side. "You knew?"

Pencak's voice was barely audible. "I knew. And it was time for you to know."

Fran looked up at the scarred and shattered object that faced her. It had been battered and smashed by some powerful force, but it still maintained enough of the original form to leave no doubt in her mind that she was staring at Ayers Rock—or what remained of it.

Hundreds of feet below, Debra Levy sat staring at the computer screen, tears pouring unnoticed down her face. "No," she murmured to herself. "No, it can't be." She pulled her fingers out of the holes and pressed them to the side of her head as uncontrollable sobs racked her body.

THE SOURCE

Proletesk, Ukraine
23 DECEMBER 1995, 1100 LOCAL
23 DECEMBER 1995, 0800 ZULU

HAWKINS LOOKED THROUGH HIS BINOCULARS AT THE SMALL dacha one last time and then handed them to Tuskin. "You know this place?"

Tuskin spit into the snow. His coverall was now white, speckled with green dots and stripes, matching perfectly with the snow and low-lying pine trees. "Yes. I know it. It is one of many places the SVR—you knew them as the KGB, but now they have a new name—takes those who will never be seen again. The guards live in comfort, the prisoners in pain. The contrast is deliberate—calculated to help in the process of breaking the prisoner. They have had many years to perfect their techniques. Too many."

"What about security?" Hawkins asked.

Tuskin gave a smile that chilled. "Who would dare attack? You would be crazy to attack the SVR."

Hawkins stood. "Well, that I am."

Tuskin stood and slapped him on the back. "We should never have been enemies."

Hawkins pointed at the dacha. "How do you want to take it down?"

"The general will be in the cellar. The guards are probably drunk. The SVR are all scum who live off of others' misery." He looked at Hawkins, as if trying to gauge his reaction. "We kill all and take the general out. How does that sound for a plan, my friend?"

Hawkins hefted the plasma projector. "Sounds good to me. Let's do it."

They moved through the woods, down the slope to the small house perched on the edge of the ice-covered lake. They'd landed in the skimmer over two hours earlier on the other side of the large ridge they were now descending. As soon as they'd stepped out of the door, it had immediately sealed itself back up, but Hawkins had no doubt that it would open again when they came back.

The ride from Tunguska had been wild. It had reminded Hawkins of nap-of-the-earth (NOE) flying in a helicopter with an expert and somewhat crazy pilot at the controls. Right after they'd punched through the Wall, the autopilot had kicked in, taking them from Tunguska to the location Hawkins had indicated on the video screen. They'd skimmed along, the bottom of the craft barely inches above the trees, always staying in the lowest ground available. Their speed had been incredible for that low an altitude—Hawkins estimated they'd flown at almost five hundred miles an hour.

Hawkins shifted his focus to the present as he reached the edge of the wood line surrounding the house. There were forty feet of open space. Two black sedans with chains on the tires sat in front. There was no sign of a guard on the outside. His heart was pounding in his ears, his senses reaching out and picking up things that would have normally escaped unnoticed. Time was slowing as he slid into combat readiness. Tuskin pointed and twitched his head—gestures most would have not understood. Hawkins felt an affinity for his blood brother in killing. He understood perfectly. He moved across the open snow in smooth steps, his entire body tuned in to the building ahead, awaiting any reaction.

Tuskin moved in his peripheral vision, heading toward the back of the building. Hawkins reached the side of the dacha and took a quick glance around the corner. A porch stretched ahead, leading to the front door in the center. He looked over his shoulder and Tuskin's eyes were on him, waiting. Hawkins nodded and moved around the corner, stooping low so he wouldn't be seen through the first window he passed. As he straightened, the front door opened and a man stepped out, still speaking in Russian over his shoulder.

The plasma projector seared the man in half, and in less than half a second Hawkins was in the doorway, spraying down the room. Men died even before their conscious minds understood what was happening. Hawkins let up on the trigger only when the far wall blew apart from the ray. A stairwell beckoned to his right. The golden ray of another projector sliced across his left front, catching two SVR men coming out of the other room on the main floor. Tuskin stepped into the room, his eyes taking in the smoldering remains of the bodies.

Together the two hit the stairs going down. A voice —disturbed by the strange sound of the wall getting blown out—called out in Russian, asking Ivan what was happening. A sustained burst blew in the heavy steel door at the bottom of the stairs and Hawkins stepped inside. The torturer was so surprised, his first round was wide, splashing against the concrete above Hawkins's head. There was no second shot as Hawkins obliterated the man. He lowered the muzzle of the projector and looked at the only man left alive in the building.

The general was naked and tied to a wooden X bolted to the wall. The car battery and alligator clamps laid out on a cart were enough to indicate the crude methods the SVR had been using to dredge information. The general's eyes widened as Tuskin walked into the room.

"Pyotr! You have come to help me!"

Tuskin didn't say a word as they cut the general free and dragged him up the stairs and through the carnage they'd caused, pausing only to grab an overcoat for the man to wear. The older man collapsed as they left the building, and Tuskin threw him over his shoulder. They made it to the skimmer in five minutes and the door slid down to admit them.

Tuskin unceremoniously threw the general down onto the metal floor. As the old man gasped for breath, Tuskin knelt over him, his words a low hiss of Russian. "Who did you sell the bombs to?"

The general looked up and smiled painfully. "Ah, Pyotr. They have asked that for a week. You did not have to kill all those guards to play this game. I will never speak. Who put you up to this? Kolgorov? Roskin? What do they care?"

Tuskin pulled his knife out. "No game, Comrade General. I am not with anyone. I am for me. Who did you sell the bombs to?"

The general shook his head. "I fought in the Great War. I served for forty-eight years after. And what did I get? Nothing. So I made my own way as the rest of the country did. Isn't that what capitalism is supposed to be? Looking out for yourself? That I failed and was caught is my mistake. I will die with that."

Tuskin put the knife against the general's throat. "Who did you sell the bombs to?"

The general didn't flinch. "The SVR did all they could for a week. You can't do more. I am a dead man."

"Not yet," Tuskin muttered as he slid the knife down the man's body and pressed it in. "You don't know what pain is yet. The SVR were amateurs. I am not."

Hawkins stared unemotionally as the screams echoed against the metal skin of the skimmer. Tuskin used the knife skillfully, choosing maximum pain with minimal actual physical damage. The colonel's voice was ice cold as his hands worked. "I am not SVR. I am not Spetsnatz anymore. I answer to no one. There are worse things than death, Comrade General. You will experience them all. If you tell me who, I will make it short and easy. Until you do, it will never end. We can keep you alive. The SVR really didn't care who you sold the bombs to, because they thought the buyers were out of the country and it wasn't their problem anymore. You were an embarrassment and there wasn't much they could do about you or the bombs."

The knife twitched and the general screamed again, curling up in the fetal position, trying to escape. "Not like the electricity, is it, Comrade General?" Tuskin asked. "You knew after the shock that your body and mind were still there. But now, now, you don't know what will be left after the blade is done, do you?"

"Why, Pyotr?" The general sobbed. "Why are you doing this to me? The country betrayed us! You owe them nothing."

"I owe the people something," Tuskin said.

Hawkins grabbed his comrade's hand, preventing the fatal twist, and shook his head. "We need him," he mouthed to Tuskin.

"The people," Tuskin repeated. "All those who have lived their lives, simply trusting that those who held the power would at the very least not destroy them." The knife moved to a less lethal position and slid in.

The general screamed and vomited, the meager remains of his last prison meal spewing onto the floor. "Please, Pyotr! Please!"

"Who, General? Who?" Tuskin turned to Hawkins. "Hold his head still."

Hawkins reached down and grabbed the general's white hair, clamping his other arm around the neck, immobilizing the old man. Tuskin moved the point of the knife to just in front of the general's left eye.

"Pyotr! You wouldn't!" The eye was mesmerized by the bloody tip, centimeters away.

"Who? You have five seconds or I take out that eye. Then the other. I'll stop the bleeding, so you will survive. Then I will castrate you. Then your hands. And we will keep you alive. We will cauterize the amputations as we go so you don't bleed to death." Tuskin's voice was totally devoid of emotion.

"Five. Four. Three. Who, General?" Tuskin paused for a few seconds. "Two. One." The knife darted forward, piercing the eye. It took all of Hawkins's strength to keep his grip as the body spasmed wildly from pain. Tuskin levered down on the knife and the ruined eye popped out, dangling by the occipital cord. Tuskin neatly severed the cord and the eye fell to the floor.

"Stop screaming, General. That won't save your other eye." Tuskin reached down and picked up the eyeball, holding it directly in front of its partner. "You have five seconds or you never see again." Blood oozed from the hole in the general's skull.

"I don't know who he was." The words spilled out like the vomit that had preceded them.

"You lie," Tuskin replied. He dropped the eyeball and stomped his boot on it, the noise causing Hawkins to flinch.

"No! I don't know. We never met face-to-face. There was a dead drop. He contacted me there and he left the gold there. After I had the gold, I put the two bombs in place for pickup."

"Gold? He paid for both in gold?"

"Yes!"

"The same person bought both?

"Yes!"

"An African?"

There was a brief pause, and Tuskin moved the knife closer to the general's eye.

"I don't know!" The general shook his head. "He wasn't African."

"But the Africans exploded one of the bombs under Vredefort Dome," Tuskin said. "Was this man a front for them?"

"I don't know."

"You are wasting my time, old man. What *do* you know?"

"The Africans may have gotten one of the bombs —maybe both. But the man I sold them to—he was Russian. And he was military too."

Tuskin exchanged a look with Hawkins. "How do you know that?"

"He knew too much. He played me well. He knew exactly what he wanted and he knew that I would do it. It is someone who knew me but who never let me know who he was."

Tuskin frowned, lowering the knife slightly. "How did he do that?"

The general had his chance. Pulling out of Hawkins's relaxed grip, he impaled his throat on the knife. Tuskin cursed in Russian as he tried to stop the flow of arterial blood.

"He's gone," Hawkins said, grabbing the other man. Reluctantly, Tuskin pulled his hands away as the general's life ebbed out onto the floor.

"We have nothing," Tuskin said bitterly.

"We have it that the buyer was a Russian. And that he was military. That's a start," Hawkins said.

Tuskin stood. "What now?"

"We go to South Africa," Hawkins said.

"South Africa?" Tuskin asked.

"We talk to the ones who bought the Vredefort bomb from the Russian. Maybe they know who he is."

"You think this Russian still has the other bomb?"

"Yes."

"Do you know where these Africans are who bought the bomb?"

"Yes. I did some checking before I came through. The South African police have picked them up. A man and a woman. The man's name is Nabaktu. He was part of a radical splinter group of the Xantha party. He was assisted by a woman named Lona. They sent one of their members into the mine on a suicide mission with the bomb."

"There was no intelligence on that from my people," Tuskin commented.

"The South African authorities are keeping it quiet. They want to interrogate and then terminate them. They certainly don't want to have a trial. They have enough bad publicity as it is. The CIA picked up this info from a source they have in-country."

Tuskin could understand that reasoning. "You know where they are being held?"

"Brandvlei."

Tuskin whistled. "That's the home of their Para Commandos!"

"Yep," Hawkins commented as he rolled the general's body out the ramp door.

"They won't be as easy to take down as these slobs were." Tuskin led the way to the pilot's compartment.

"No, they won't," Hawkins agreed as he leaned over the control panel and worked with the controls.

ANSWERS

The Other Side

"WHAT'S GOING ON?" FRAN ASKED, HER EYES MESMERIZED by the massive image of Ayers Rock in front of her.

Pencak grabbed her arm. "There's not much time. We need to go back down." She pressed the horizontal button and the armor plating resealed around the glass capsule. She punched the down button and they began their descent. The elevator came to a halt at a different level from the one they had gotten on at.

Fran tried to clear her head. "What about Debra?"

"Debra will find out on her own," Pencak replied succinctly, "if she hasn't already."

"And Don?"

"We're going to him now," Pencak impatiently answered. "There's not the time to explain things twice."

She nudged Fran forward and they stepped into

329

the corridor. A door at the end slid open into a brightly lit chamber with white walls. Don Batson was seated on a bench and leapt to his feet as the two appeared. "I wondered when I would see you again," he said as he stepped forward to Fran. He turned his gaze to Pencak. "So what now? Have you let her in on your secret?"

"I saw Ayers Rock, Don," Fran said, the shock evident in her voice. "It's above us. But it's not the same."

Don shook his head. "I know. The only mistake I made was telling the wrong person that I knew," he said, again staring hard at Pencak. "You're one of them, aren't you?"

Pencak nodded impatiently, as if that was not a serious matter. "I apologize for locking you up, but we couldn't allow you to tell the others. We didn't take into account your background when we brought you through."

"Tell the others what?" Whatever patience Fran had had was long gone now.

Don was still staring at Pencak. "It shouldn't surprise you that a geologist would recognize his own planet. When I saw the wall of the cavern below us, I knew exactly where we were—after we'd been cutting through the same sandstone feldspar for the past several days."

Fran blinked. "But I don't understand. How can we be back at the Rock? Where are all the people that we left? And the sky—it was . . ." She paused and then plaintively asked, "Where are we?"

Pencak sighed. "Not where, my dear. *When* is the key question." Pencak grabbed her shoulder. "There isn't time right now to answer all your questions. Things are happening and we're losing control—not that we had that much to start with."

The old woman suddenly staggered and Fran and Don watched in amazement as she seemed to fade slightly and then come back into focus. Pencak gripped her cane fiercely and regained her balance. "We have to get you two back to the right time while we still can."

"But I don't—"

"Trust me." Pencak cut off Don's question. "I'll explain all shortly."

A door on the side of the room slid open and three robed figures strode in. As they stepped forward, they pulled their hoods down, revealing faces as disfigured as Pencak's. The first one had no eyes at all; a thin metal plate was wrapped around his forehead with wires leading out of it directly into the back of the skull. The second's head was completely smooth—no ears or nose protruding. The eyes were recessed farther than normal and glinted with a strange color Fran had never seen before. The third held his—her?—head at a cocked angle, a twisted cord of distended muscle bulging out on the right side and disappearing into the robe.

The little glimpse that Fran had of their hands showed deformities such as missing fingers and melted skin. The lead figure's scarred face twisted in a sad smile as he wrapped his arms around Pencak. "Good-bye for the second and final time, Lois."

Fran watched as they hugged the old woman, paying no attention to either Don or herself. Done with their parting words, the three stepped back and another door opened to the side. Inside it gleamed the black Wall of a portal.

"Let's go," Pencak insisted, grabbing Fran by the arm again. As she stepped forward with Don toward the shimmering black, Fran was surprised to see tears flowing out of the old woman's one good eye.

SOUTH AFRICA

Brandvlei, South Africa
23 DECEMBER 1995, 1200 LOCAL
23 DECEMBER 1995, 1000 ZULU

"DO YOU HAVE A PLAN?" TUSKIN ASKED AS THE PLAINS OF southwest Africa flitted below.

"We land right on top of where the prisoners are being held and grab them."

"Great detail," Tuskin muttered as a walled compound appeared in the distance ahead, rapidly growing closer. "Did you spend a lot of time coming up with that?"

"As much as you did with your plan back at the dacha," Hawkins replied.

The Russian grabbed his plasma projector as the skimmer lifted slightly and cleared the outer wall. Surprised guards in desert camouflage fired a few scattered shots at the strange vehicle as it settled into a small parade field in front of the garrison headquarters.

Hawkins led the way out the door and down the ramp. "The building on the left," he called out to Tuskin. Immediately he felt the slam of bullets into his chest as a South African paratrooper fired his R4 assault rifle at the two strange figures. Hawkins cleared the way to the prison using the projector, sweeping away the opposition with blasts of energy. He felt detached from emotion as the soldiers died under his merciless barrage.

The door melted under Tuskin's fire and they made their way to the basement cells where the intelligence Hawkins had stolen out of Lamb's files indicated that Lona and Nabaktu were being held. The last guard disposed of, Hawkins blew off the lock and entered the cell. The two prisoners were gaunt and barely conscious, lying on bunks against the wall of a small, dingy room.

Hawkins threw the woman over his shoulder while Tuskin gathered in the man. Staggering under their loads, they made their way back up the stairs and onto the parade field. The opposition was still disorganized as they headed toward the skimmer. A machine gun suddenly roared out of a window in the headquarters building and tore a row of puckered dirt toward Tuskin, the rounds rising and hitting the Russian on his left side, knocking him over onto the ground. He rolled to his feet and reached down to pick up Nabaktu and then halted. The African's head was a mass of blood and brain where one of the rounds had

torn through it. Tuskin turned and fired in short arcs
at the large building, blowing walls in, silencing the
machine gun as Hawkins made it into the skimmer.
The Russian turned and followed, the ramp sliding in
and the door shutting.

The ping of rounds off the side sounded dimly
within as Tuskin ran to the cockpit and activated the
controls, getting the aircraft out of the compound and
a safe distance away. By the time he was done and
had rejoined Hawkins in the cargo bay, the American
had the young black girl conscious and was examining
her wounds.

"How is she?"

Hawkins pointed out the various injuries as he
continued to work. "They used electricity on her nip-
ples and vagina. The soles of her feet have been
beaten. Three broken fingers on the right hand. I
think she has a couple of cracked ribs. I don't think
the lung was punctured. Some burn marks."

Tuskin nodded—the usual crude methods used by
police states to gain information or simply to punish
with the goal of supporting a regime of fear.

"I thought new people were in power," he commented.

"New people, same old shit," Hawkins replied.
"Intertribal fighting is just as fierce as interracial."

"Who are you?" The words from Lona's swollen
lips were barely audible. Her eyes were straining, trying to make sense of what she could see. "Where is
Nabaktu?"

Tuskin was regarding her impassively, his hand already straying to the knife at his belt. "I don't think you'll need that," Hawkins said quietly. "I think she's already broken." He looked at her. "We need to know about the bomb."

"The bomb," Lona repeated numbly. "I told you about the bomb. I told you it was the only one. There are no more."

"There is one more," Hawkins said.

"No more," Lona repeated. "We only had the one."

"I know you only bought one. But the man you bought it from acquired two using your gold. We need to know who he is."

"I told you—he was a Russian."

"Tell us everything about him. Did you actually see him?"

Lona slowly nodded. "We met him once. In Angola. When we paid. He promised us the bomb later and he delivered. I did not want to trust him, but Nabaktu said we had no choice." She raised her head painfully, looking around the stark interior of the skimmer. "Where is Nabaktu? Where am I?".

"What did the Russian look like?" Tuskin asked, leaning over her.

"He scared me. His eyes were dead. I've seen those eyes before—the workers in the mines look like that after six months under the earth. But his were worse. He would as easily have killed us as talked to us. I don't know why he delivered the bomb—he had our gold. Nabaktu said it was because he was a professional. A man who kept his word."

"What did he look like?" Tuskin repeated, his hand caressing the handle of his knife.

Hawkins gave her a sip of water and she closed her eyes in concentration. "Tall. As tall as you. White haired. Thin. Very thin. His face was leathery—a man who spent much time in the outdoors." Her eyes opened as she suddenly remembered. "He had a large ring on his right hand. A black stone with some symbol etched into it."

Tuskin knelt down next to her, his eyes alert. "What kind of symbol?"

"It looked like a bird of some sort."

"A hawk with talons outstretched?" Tuskin asked. "Done in red on the black stone?" He held out his own hand and pointed. "Like this?"

The girl nodded. "That's it."

"*Shit,*" Tuskin muttered, and then looked at Hawkins. "I know who it is." He held up the ring. "This ring is worn only by men who have been in Spetsnatz more than twenty years and served honorably. There is only one man who wears that ring and fits that description. And he is the one man who could have done what he did."

"Who?" Hawkins asked.

"Colonel Ivan Sergot. He was my Spetsnatz commander when we went into Kabul. An old friend and comrade."

"Why does your old friend and comrade want a nuclear bomb?" Hawkins asked.

Tuskin was nodding as he thought about it. "It all makes sense now. It's about his son."

"His son?" Hawkins asked, confused.

"His son was a helicopter pilot in the army. He died of radiation poisoning from flying missions over the power plant at Chernobyl, pouring concrete on the main reactor. They buried him right there. Just dumped a load of concrete on the bodies of the helicopter crews because they were too hot to put anywhere else."

"Jesus Christ," Hawkins muttered.

"Ivan went crazy for a while. He was removed from command and then retired a year ago. Last I heard he was living down near the Black Sea."

"You sure it's him?" Hawkins wanted to know.

Tuskin stood, ignoring the girl at his feet. "There's one way to find out." He moved to the front of the skimmer. "Let's land and get her out and then head north. If my guess is right, I think I know where he might have gone."

COOPERATION

Ayers Rock, Australia
23 DECEMBER 1995, 2030 LOCAL
23 DECEMBER 1995, 1100 ZULU

THE RUSSIAN ADMIRAL STARED AT THE BLACK WALL FOR A long time before turning back to Lamb. "It is the same as the photos my people sent of what they uncovered at Tunguska. The story your Major Hawkins told you is the same one our Colonel Tuskin told. He is reported to be a very reliable man."

Lamb's gut was still tied in knots. The K-25 helicopter bringing the ranking officer of the Russian fleet off the southern coast of Australia had landed a half hour earlier and he'd spent that time fully briefing a man whom he had worked hard the last several days trying to keep from knowing what was going on. It was a odd change for Lamb and he was having trouble adjusting to it.

The admiral turned to Lamb. "So what now? I

have seen all this and can report to my superiors, but what does it all mean?"

Lamb shrugged. "I don't know. I think that is for your President and mine to decide between them." He looked the Russian in the eyes. "For me it means that we stop playing games—at least for now—and cooperate."

THE CRATER

Meteor Crater, Arizona
23 DECEMBER 1995, 0400 LOCAL
23 DECEMBER 1995, 1100 ZULU

FRAN STEPPED OUT INTO DARKNESS, STAGGERING SLIGHTLY as she felt dirt under her feet. As her eyes adjusted, she could see stars faintly glinting overhead, but all around she was surrounded by darkness. It was as if she was at the bottom of large bowl, with the sky circling overhead. "Where are we?" she asked.

It was Don who answered her. "We're in Arizona. I've been here before. We're at the bottom of Meteor Crater. Of course, I don't know *when* we are," he added.

"The location is correct," Pencak confirmed. "The when is your present."

"Then you don't need fixed sites like Tunguska and Ayers Rock to travel in time?" Fran asked.

"No," Pencak answered. "And traveling is not the

341

right word for it. We bend space and time from our master control room in the future. We can travel to any time and any place on the planet. Debra Levy was very correct in her assumptions about wormholes, but she underestimated the scale to which it could be developed—which is very interesting, considering that, in our history, she was one of the key members of the team that developed time travel."

"Then why the whole setup at Ayers Rock if it wasn't necessary?" Don asked.

"Ah, but it was very necessary," Pencak replied. She lifted up her cane and squinted at the handle in the dark. "We only have an hour. I will try to do my best to explain what is happening in that time. It is most likely that you two will be the only ones who will know what has really occurred—what is still occurring. And that is how it must be—you must safeguard that knowledge. Many people have dedicated their lives to making what is happening occur. And we will not know for another hour if we have even begun to succeed. If we have, I, and the others like me, we will cease to exist."

Chernobyl, Ukraine
23 DECEMBER 1995, 1410 LOCAL
23 DECEMBER 1995, 1110 ZULU

THE MASSIVE MOUNTAIN OF CONCRETE THAT HAD ONCE been the Chernobyl nuclear power plant loomed on the horizon as Tuskin brought the skimmer to a landing next to a two-lane tar road covered with wisps of snow.

"You think he came here?" Hawkins asked as the craft settled with a slight bump.

"I'm sure he did," Tuskin answered. "The question is, is he still in the area?"

Hawkins looked around as the door opened and they stepped out. "How hot is it out here?"

"We have a half hour with no ill effects. Longer than that"—Tuskin shrugged—"longer than that you might as well stay." He squinted into the wind blowing across the road and pointed. "There. That's the grave site. I had to do a recon of this area three years ago with Sergot. We flew in low and fast on board helicopters, taking pictures for the scientists to look at. We all received a good dose of radiation then, but the government certainly didn't care. Sergot pointed out the grave to me. He is a very bitter man," he added unnecessarily. Hawkins understood bitterness quite well.

Hawkins leaned over and looked at the ground. "I think someone's been here in a truck." He reached down and cleared some freshly fallen snow away with his bare hand. "There are tire tracks frozen into the dirt on the side of the road here."

Tuskin examined the marks. "A four-by-four military vehicle. It had to be Sergot."

Hawkins looked around. "Where did he go? The old reactor?"

Tuskin shook his head. "He could have headed

anywhere. Those tracks are several days old. He could be on the outskirts of Moscow or he could be sitting by the reactor building with the bomb armed, just waiting for the right moment to push the button. One thing's for sure—if he drove here, he's received a fatal exposure, so he has nothing to lose."

Tuskin rubbed his chin. "Let's check out the reactor building. Maybe we'll spot him there. If not, then there are many targets within a few days' ride of here that he could head for to take out his revenge. We will have to make an educated guess."

They tromped up the ramp into the skimmer and halted in amazement at the black-robed figure seated inside. The figure rose and gestured for them to come on board. "The trail is cold here and there's not much time." It was the same metallic voice the Speaker had used.

"Do you know where the other bomb is?" Tuskin asked.

"He is headed for Kapustin Yar."

"Shit!" Tuskin exploded. "We must stop him!"

"What's at Kapustin Yar?" Hawkins asked as the door slid up behind them.

Tuskin staggered over to the bench and sat down, ignoring the black-robed figure. "I should have guessed. Sergot would not waste his life in a futile gesture. He would go for the one target that would have the greatest effect."

"What's at Kapustin Yar?" Hawkins repeated, disturbed by how upset Tuskin was.

"It's a storage facility for weapons. Nuclear weapons. It's also where the SS-27's are stored."

Hawkins frowned. "SS-27's? I thought your latest version of the strategic missile was the 24."

Tuskin nodded weakly. "That's what almost everyone thinks. The 27 is not just a missile, though—it's what you would call a doomsday weapon. The final threat. I was involved in the security testing of the storage facility for the missiles at Kapustin Yar—as was Sergot. We were briefed on what was inside and it scared even me.

"The 27's are designed to be radioactively dirty. They took old booster rockets from the space program and put a guidance system on board. Then they put a relatively small-yield nuclear explosive in the payload area and then surrounded it with nuclear waste. We have much more nuclear waste than anyone in the West even begins to fear. All those warheads we had to disarm when the Cold War ended and the West would not help us dispose of the plutonium—the waste had to go somewhere.

"When the SS-27 warhead blows, the waste is spread, along with the fallout from the bomb itself, making the long-term effects devastating. There are only twenty of the SS-27's, but that was estimated to be enough to completely blanket Europe with such a high level of radiation as to make the continent unlivable for generations."

"Jesus Christ!" Hawkins exploded. "That's just goddamn great. So we're dealing with much more than one explosion here." He turned to the Speaker.

"If you knew where the other bomb was all this time, why didn't you tell us?"

The Speaker didn't move and the mechanical voice was emotionless. "We could not interfere. You had to change things."

"Then why are you here now?" Hawkins demanded.

"Because we are running out of time. We can no longer control events as we thought we could. There are too many variables. Good luck."

"What are you talking about? Control what events? What's going on?" Hawkins asked as Tuskin made his way to the cockpit.

In reply a black portal appeared and the Speaker stepped through and disappeared, leaving Hawkins staring at empty space as the portal collapsed.

Meteor Crater, Arizona
23 DECEMBER 1995, 0420 LOCAL
23 DECEMBER 1995, 1120 ZULU

"WHO ARE YOU?" FRAN ASKED, SHIVERING IN THE COLD night air.

"My name isn't important," Pencak replied.

"But you're not Pencak?"

"For your purposes I am. I assumed her identity in 1954 when she died in a car crash. Ever since I have lived her life."

Fran asked the question that was troubling her the

most. "Why? Why are you doing all this? Why did you pretend to be aliens?"

"In a way we are aliens," Pencak said. "The future we come from is very different from what you know." She paused briefly in thought. "But there really was an overriding reason why we have acted this way, and you of all people should understand it. We have statistical projection in our time—much improved over what you use. We *reversed* the process, looking for the critical node that we could go back to.

"When we asked our computers how to accomplish our goal, the favored solution—the only feasible solution—was to present the people of the past with an external threat—something that the various countries and powers-that-be could bond together against."

"What was your goal?" Batson asked.

"To change our history," Pencak replied.

"But why us? Why now?" Batson asked.

Pencak looked at some glowing numbers on the end of her cane. "Because in my past, in thirty-two minutes, a nuclear bomb is exploded near a secret weapons facility twelve hundred miles southeast of Moscow. The fallout from that explosion blankets most of Europe and eventually makes its way around the world, drastically affecting life on the planet. Economic and political chaos follows and the world drifts into what some have called World War III but is more appropriately called the Chaos." She pointed at herself. "I am one of the relatively healthy people from my time. You saw some of the others just before we left."

"Why didn't you just stop the bomb yourself?" Fran asked. "Why did you even allow the first one at Vredefort Dome to go off if you knew about it and could go back in time and stop it?"

"If you could go back in time, what action would you take to stop World War I?" Pencak asked. "Would you go back a few minutes prior to Archduke Ferdinand's assassination and kill the assassin?" She didn't wait for an answer. "But you would not know if you were successful until the time of the assassination and if you were wrong, then what? Maybe there was a plot of several conspirators that no one knew about and if you stopped the first assassin, there was another killer waiting down the street who would step forward and do the job.

"And even then, if you had stopped the archduke from being killed, would that necessarily have stopped the war? Or just delayed it, with the potential for even more disastrous results? There were many factors that led to that war, just as with any other war. The assassination was just the spark. Stopping that spark would just have allowed another spark, a potentially more dangerous spark, to ignite the conflict. The same was true for us when we looked back.

"As far as one of us coming back and trying to tell you that we came from the future—would you have believed us any more than you believed the alien theory, even when presented with insurmountable evidence? And even if you believed, would you have changed? You know as well as I do that people change only when they are forced to. We had to force you, and even now we are not sure how well we have succeeded. That is why you two must be the only ones who know the truth. The governments must still believe in the alien threat."

Pencak leaned on her cane. "We had several goals, all of which we needed to accomplish concurrently. We needed to allow the first bomb to go off to focus attention on the problem. You can recover from that explosion. In fact, it should be the spur for greater controls on nuclear weapons.

"Stopping the second bomb is just one of several actions that are taking place to change the course of our history. Even as we speak, there are unprecedented conversations going on between world leaders, focused on what they think—and we want them to think—they have found in Ayers Rock and at Tunguska. That cooperation is essential if the future is to turn out differently and mankind is to survive as a race. And that if there *is* some form of Coalition out there—and our computers indicate there most likely is—we will be accepted as a fit race for a civilized culture."

Pencak stopped suddenly and looked surprised for a second, and even in the dim light Fran could tell that the other woman was fading and then she was back again, as solid as ever.

"What's happening to you?" Fran asked.

"History is already slightly different than in my past," Pencak said. "Not so much yet that things might not turn out the same, but different nonetheless. We cannot control time—we can only travel in it. We have interfered with what happened in our past, and once our actions cause an irreversible change, we will no longer exist."

She smiled grimly. "Or at least that is what the computer says. No one knows for sure because no one has ever done this before. In my future we invented time travel only months prior to implementing our plan. I have lived an entire adult life here in the past, yet for my comrades in the future, only a few weeks have passed since I left. My fading is the effect of the ripples from the changes already made. The fact that I am still here, though, says none of the changes that have occurred so far are significant enough to have truly altered my past and your future.

"You spoke of history as a river whose course is very hard to change. So far we have only thrown stones in it. But when it does change, it will be a momentous thing for those of us in the future. Our channel of time will dry up and be gone."

"How did you destroy *Voyager*?" Batson asked suddenly.

"I planted a time-delay bomb in it while it was still being assembled in 1972. We knew the exact moment we wanted it destroyed, so it flew for all those years out of the solar system with that bomb waiting to go off."

"What about the messages for Levy?"

"My comrades sent those. I was surprised how quickly she determined how they were being sent. You

were only supposed to pick up the part aimed for you
—the two message with Levy's name. The part that
disappeared was my communication with my comrades." Pencak held up her strange cane. "The receiver is in the handle. I had to keep in contact."

"And this crater?" he asked. "It really was formed
by meteors?"

Pencak gave her lopsided shrug. "I don't know. I
have studied the crater and I do believe it was most
likely formed by a nuclear explosion, but I have no
idea how that could have happened. We took as many
possible existing geological features that we could use
and linked them together in a plausible story along
with other factors we could manipulate to try and convince your world leaders that there was an alien
threat. It remains to be seen how well we have succeeded. You do have to admit we presented a very
realistic and believable scenario."

"Why us?" Fran went back to her original question. "Why Don and me?"

"Because of your son."

"Our son?" Batson said. "We hardly even know
each other. Why would we have had a son in your
past?"

"Because you are part of the Hermes Project.
When the Chaos came, the government evacuated
those in the Hermes Project. At first to West Virginia.
Then, after a nuclear exchange between China and
the United States left most of North America uninhabitable, the survivors were moved to Australia. You
lived in a sealed underground complex under Ayers

Rock for years, working on ways to try and reclaim a planet that was unreclaimable. Your son was the leader who kept us going for all those years when our projections showed nothing but slow and horrible death. He kept us going until we achieved time travel and then he led the staff that planned this entire mission."

There was a long silence, and the howl of a coyote sounded out over the rim of the crater.

"Do you really think things will change for the better if Hawkins and Tuskin stop the other bomb from going off?"

"Things have already changed," Pencak said. "It cannot be much worse than the present I knew. The human race was dying as a species, with the entire planet not far behind. Our best-case projection gave us only another twelve point three years before humanity was extinct. We in the future have nothing to lose except a few more miserable years of life."

"What about Debra?" Fran suddenly asked. "How come she didn't come back with us?"

Pencak sighed and leaned on her cane. "The bomb going off in Russia was only the beginning of the end. Even then mankind didn't learn. The Russians suspected the Americans of causing the explosion. The Americans suspected the Russians of trying to destroy Europe. The Europeans were too busy dying to suspect anyone. The southern hemisphere spiraled into economic and ecological disaster with the loss of the industrialized nations in Europe and the collapse of the South African gold standard. China tried flexing

its military muscle and invaded Japan. The nuclear
exchange between the United States and China was a
result of the Americans trying to halt the takeover. Of
course, the fact that the Japanese islands were left
uninhabitable as a result of the war didn't stop anyone.

"But even then, staring extinction as a species in
the face, the governments still worked against each
other. Levy was picked up by the Hermes Project. She
joined you all in the underground bunker, but her job
was far different from yours. Hers was to work on
weapons of destruction—the American government's
last gasp at the ultimate weapon. And she did that
very well." Pencak swiveled her gaze to Fran. "You
recognized Ayers Rock when you saw it, but it was
different, wasn't it?"

"It looked torn up," Fran said.

"It had been. The war was still going on even as
we were running this mission," Pencak said. "Australia was the last habitable continent and you could see
that it was barely livable—we had to heavily filter the
air we pumped in from the surface. The remains of
the U.S. government and the Hermes Project moved
to Australia in year twenty-three of the Chaos. We
built and occupied that vast underground complex underneath the Rock.

"Levy was the key to the team that developed the
theories that allowed construction of the plasma projectors. A splinter group of survivalists used those
weapons on our support facilities outside Ayers Rock
when they discovered our plan to change the past and

destroy our present. We stopped them temporarily, but only to gain time to complete this project. You could see what their weapons did to the Rock.

"The Russians—what remained of them—also worked on their own weapons. The other three men whose names we sent to the Russians were part of that team. Their deaths portend a change of our future even if the bomb does go off, because they will not be there to complete their particle-beam weapon, perfected twenty-five years after the start of the Chaos. Whether others may step into the breach and complete it we don't know. All we do know is that in twenty-seven minutes, the first true major change may or may not occur. All the other actions are a backup to that."

Fran looked up—there was a hint of light gray on the eastern lip of the crater. She shivered in the cold and wondered where Hawkins was right now and how close he was to succeeding in his mission.

Vicinity Kapustin Yar Strategic Missile Test
Center, Russia
23 DECEMBER 1995, 1440 LOCAL
23 DECEMBER 1995, 1140 ZULU

THE RUSSIAN DROVE SITTING IN HIS OWN FECES, NO LONGER able to control his bodily functions. He didn't even notice the discomfort of it as the pain that racked his dying body overrode such trivial feelings. Only the in-

tensity of his single-mindedness allowed him to continue to control the truck along the deserted logging
road. He knew he was close because he'd passed the
first warning signs that he was entering a restricted
area fifteen minutes before. If he kept going along
this road, in three or four miles he would reach the
outer security fence. He didn't plan on having to go
that far. Just another mile or so would be close
enough for the yield of this bomb to vaporize the
greater part of the main post of the facility—particularly the mobile rocket launchers holding the SS-27's.

He reached up and slid his shaking hand along his
jacket pocket, ensuring that the remote detonator was
still there. He'd rigged the bomb yesterday, knowing
that today he would not be well enough to do the
intricate wiring work. All it would take was to flip up
the cover on the detonator and press the switch, and it
would all be over.

His eyes were so intent on the road that it took
him a moment to realize that the sun had been
blocked out and he was in a shadow that extended
only a short distance on all sides of the truck. He
slowly became conscious of a howling sound. The
wind was swirling around the vehicle, blowing snow
up into the air. He pushed the brake and rolled down
the window, leaning out and looking up.

TWENTY FEET ABOVE, TUSKIN LEANED OUT THE OPEN DOOR
of the skimmer and recognized Sergot as the older
man squinting against the downblast from the thrusters. Tuskin considered vaporizing the cab of the vehi-

cle with the plasma projector, but quickly vetoed that idea. For all he knew, Sergot might have rigged a dead man's switch, in which case the bomb would go off. Or the bomb itself might be up in the cab, in the passenger seat, and he was unsure what effect the projector would have on it.

Hawkins appeared at his side, having set the controls to hold the skimmer in position. "The nearest place to land is about two hundred meters ahead!" Hawkins screamed into his ear.

"He's there!" Tuskin yelled above the roar of the thrusters. "There's no time to land."

The door of the truck opened and Sergot stepped out. He held something in his right hand. As Hawkins swung up his weapon, Tuskin made his decision. He leapt out the open door and fell the thirty feet to the ground, landing on top of Sergot.

Tuskin heard the snap as his left leg broke and could feel several ribs on the side that had hit Sergot splinter and tear into his left lung. He ignored the pain as he reached with both hands and seized Sergot's right hand, squeezing with all his might. The older man was dazed when Tuskin landed on him and desperately tried to flip open the lid to the firing device. Tuskin kneed him with his good leg and dug his thumb into the other man's wrist, forcing the fingers open. Tuskin grabbed the device as he heard the roar of a pistol and felt the thud of a large-caliber bullet slamming into his gut. As Sergot fired again with his left hand, Tuskin threw the firing device clear of the two of them and turned his head up at Hawkins, hovering in the doorway of the skimmer overhead.

"Shoot!" Tuskin screamed, but his words were blown away by the roar of the engines.

Sergot shifted and again fired into Tuskin at point-blank range. Tuskin felt his hold on the other man slip away as a darkness came over his eyes. With all his might he gripped the other man one last time to keep him from crawling after the detonator. He smiled for the briefest of moments as he heard the crackle of the plasma projector come from above. Then the smile was obliterated along with the rest of his body and Sergot.

HAWKINS GENTLY LOWERED THE SKIMMER INTO A FIELD A short distance away and then walked back to the truck. He stepped, with hardly a glance, around the black charred spot that had been two men, and pulled aside the tarp that covered the back. The bomb sat there all alone in the rear. Hawkins got into the cab of the truck and drove it to the skimmer and trundled the bomb on board.

He went up to the cockpit and set the controls for Tunguska.

TIME

Meteor Crater
23 DECEMBER 1995, 0455 LOCAL
23 DECEMBER 1995, 1155 ZULU

"FIVE MINUTES," BATSON MUTTERED, LOOKING AT THE glowing face of his watch. The gray in the eastern horizon was now an ever-brightening reddish tinge, heralding the coming of the sun. Fran could now make out the outline of the eastern rim of the crater hundreds of feet above her head.

"Why were you sent back so many years before now?" Fran asked.

Pencak had been fading and coming back into focus every thirty seconds or so, for the past ten minutes. The old woman wearily looked at the younger one. "I was the one who had to help set up the whole scenario here in the United States."

"That's why you wrote all those articles about nuclear explosions forming the craters," Don observed. "And why you made your living here."

Pencak nodded. "But I had much more to do than that." She paused, faded, and then came back. Her voice was shaky as she tried to explain. "I had to monitor events and people. I have watched all of you at various times, as did my comrades. We had the facts laid out in our books and computers, but we wanted to know about the people themselves—would they be up to the tasks set before them."

"Were you the only one?" Don asked.

Pencak sighed. "No. My husband went back when I did. Except he went to Russia and he went earlier—1943."

"Felix Zigorski!" Fran exclaimed.

"Yes. We got to see each other only every few years and then he died in 1990. But he had done his job well enough by then that the plan could go forward without him."

"You've sacrificed much to change things," Fran said.

Pencak looked at the younger woman for a long moment. "Our sacrifices will be for nothing if you do not make your own from here on out."

Tunguska
23 DECEMBER 1995, 1757 LOCAL
23 DECEMBER 1995, 1157 ZULU

THE ANTIAIRCRAFT SYSTEMS SURROUNDING TUNGUSKA
didn't even have a chance to fire as the skimmer hit
the portal at over two hundred miles an hour. Hawkins flinched in the front seat as the front display
showed nothing but trees just below until, at the last
second, the craft skipped over the lip of the excava-
tion and dived straight into the black Wall.

He was out on the other side before he had a
chance to fully comprehend what had happened. By
itself the skimmer threaded its way through the underground complex to the elevator door. The door
slid open and Hawkins landed the skimmer. He rolled
the bomb down the ramp and settled it on its side. He
glanced up as three figures dressed in robes appeared
and seemed to glide forward toward him.

Hawkins ignored them for the moment. He leaned
both Tuskin's and his plasma projectors against the
bomb casing, then straightened and stared at the figures. "I've recovered the second bomb. Colonel Tuskin died getting it."

"Yes, we can see that you have the bomb, Major
Hawkins." The sound seemed to come from the center figure. "There are only a few minutes remaining."
The Speaker slid his hood down, revealing his mis-
shapen features. "My name is Raynor. I am human
like you and come from your future."

Hawkins didn't even blink. During the ride back to

the portal he'd put many of the pieces together. He stared at Raynor. "You're trying to change history."

"We *have* changed history, now that we have that bomb here. It was scheduled to go off in two minutes and twenty-three seconds. When it doesn't, this complex and my comrades and I will no longer exist. This future will no longer exist."

Hawkins shrugged wearily. "It doesn't look like a future I would want."

"It isn't." Raynor stepped forward. "You don't care about your own future, do you?"

Hawkins shook his head. "No. Here's as good a place as any to die."

"But it's not your time," Raynor replied. "It's our time." A black portal appeared on the side wall. "You must go back."

"What about the others?" Hawkins asked.

"Fran Volkers and Don Batson have already gone back. Debra is staying here."

"Is that her choice?" Hawkins asked.

"Yes. It is her choice." The three figures faded to the point of almost disappearing, then reappeared. "We may not be able to keep the portal open much longer. Go!"

Hawkins unfastened the protective suit and threw it on top of the bomb. He walked to the portal and stepped through without a backward glance. The portal flashed and he was gone.

Meteor Crater
23 DECEMBER 1995, 0459 LOCAL
23 DECEMBER 1995, 1159 ZULU

"ONE MINUTE," BATSON ANNOUNCED.

"What will happen now?" Fran suddenly asked. "What did your projections show as the most probable course of events if the bomb is stopped and the governments cooperate?"

Pencak smiled. "That, my dear, is for you to live." The old woman's smile dissolved and faded, along with the rest of her, and Fran and Don were left alone at the bottom of the crater.

"It worked," Don whispered.

Fran looked up where the first rays of the sun were lancing over the rim of the crater and tickling the far side with their warmth. "It worked so far. But now it's up to us to make sure things stay on track." She reached out and took Don's hand. "It's a long walk to the top. I think we ought to get going." Together they walked across the crater bottom toward the closest side, where a winding trail led to the rim.

Ayers Rock
23 DECEMBER 1995, 2130 LOCAL
23 DECEMBER 1995, 1200 ZULU

THE WALL DISAPPEARED, LEAVING BARE ROCK IN ITS PLACE.
The Russian general turned and looked at Lamb.
"The twenty-four hours are up."

Lamb nodded. "They've closed it off."

"They've been doing that at Tunguska on and off
over the past day," the general commented. He
reached a hand up and pressed an earplug tighter in
as he strained to listen. "Tunguska has closed again.
My men also report that the strange craft went back
through just three minutes ago." The general pulled
the earplug out and regarded Lamb solemnly. "What
do you think the Coalition's decision was?"

Lamb felt something give way inside himself and
suddenly he felt lighter and freer than he had in years.
He put an arm on the Russian's shoulder. "We may
never know. We can only hope it was to extend the
perimeter. If not—well, either way we must join together and prepare either for eventual acceptance
into the Coalition or to fight the Swarm. But we no
longer have to wonder what path to choose—it's been
chosen for us."

Epilogue

Leesburg, Virginia
12 SEPTEMBER 1991, 1400 LOCAL
12 SEPTEMBER 1991, 1900 ZULU

HAWKINS FELT TERRIBLY DISORIENTED FOR A FEW SECONDS. His hands twitched on the steering wheel and the pickup almost swerved off the road.

"Watch it, hon!" Mary exclaimed, her hand squeezing his arm.

Hawkins slammed on the brakes and pulled off the road onto the shoulder.

"What's wrong?" Mary asked, looking at him with concern.

Hawkins steadied himself against the back of the seat as he looked at his wife, alive and vibrant in the bright sunshine streaming through the windshield.

"Are you all right?"

Hawkins nodded. "I'm fine. Just fine." He fought

back the confusion and forced a smile. "What's to-day's date?"

"Twenty-second June."

"What year?"

Mary playfully punched her husband on the shoulder. "Oh, come on, now. What are you trying to pull?"

"Please, Mary, just tell me the year?"

The smile faded from Mary's lips as she saw tears forming in her husband's eyes. "Nineteen ninety-one."

He turned off the engine and grabbed her with both arms, squeezing her tight to him. "Tell you what. Why don't we just sit here?" He wrapped her up tightly and waited, letting the minutes tick by until he knew it was safe and that the future was now much different.

Ayers Rock, Australia
6 JULY 2018, 0430 LOCAL
6 JULY 2018, 1900 ZULU

THE WORLD DISSOLVED AROUND DEBRA, AS IF EVERYTHING were going through a portal and she were the lone point of stability. There was a flash of white and then, in a dizzying array of colors, everything came back into focus—except it wasn't what had been.

Ayers Rock loomed in the near distance, intact and spectacular in the early afternoon sun. The desert that had surrounded the monolith in her time was replaced by rolling green plains.

She was standing in the center of a large circle, carpeted in some sort of soft red fabric. A waist-high railing surrounded the circle and there were people gathered all around. As soon as they saw her, a tall, strong-looking man strode forward, his arms outstretched. "Welcome, Debra. I am Raynor Batson-Volkers and I welcome you to your time." He pointed at a skimmer, parked at the side of the circle. "My parents are waiting to talk to you."